RESISTANCE
RISING

RESISTANCE RISING

A Genre Wars Novel

WRITTEN BY ROBIN C. FARRELL

Story by Justin Moe and Robin C. Farrell
Inspired by the *Genre Wars* project, created by Ron Newcomb

:

ISBN: 1544288948
ISBN 13: 9781544288949

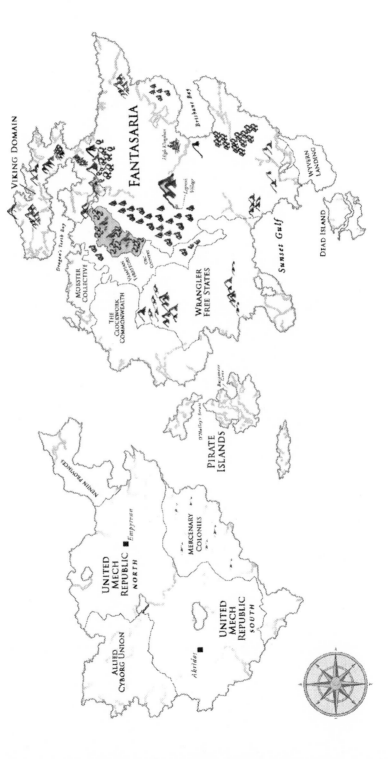

KABATHAN

PROLOGUE

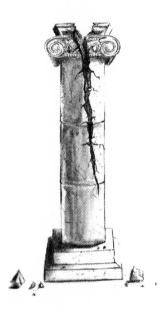

Light seeped through every crack in the worn and weathered door. The hinges creaked as Mr. X pushed against the flat wood, springy under his fingers from the recent rain and many years passed. The room beyond was quiet, but warm and inviting; a proper Fantasarian shrine. Ornate torches stuck out of each wall and candles, ceremonial and decorative, were scattered throughout the room, all of them lit. Mr. X slid through the doorway and the flames flicked away from him. Two guards stood in opposite corners and glanced, fleetingly, in Mr. X's direction as he crossed over the threshold, but their eyes did not stay on him long after he stepped forward and let the door fall back behind him. It clicked shut and the night's chill was cut off entirely. The flames calmed.

How safe they think they are here.

Mr. X slid back the heavy hood of his traveling cloak. He looked at the center of the room where a single, glowing orb, roughly six inches in diameter, hovered in midair above a pillar of white marble streaked with dark grey.

"The Oniyum," he whispered to himself. He had never looked upon it in person before. In his lifetime, his people had never been its Caretaker, never ruled the Tribal Council, and never been gifted by its Light. He had steeled himself against its beauty. That was the most common thread in all the history he had studied. By scholars and the masses, it was universally accepted as a magnanimous prize, which bestowed gifts, truths, and betterment to anyone who stood in its Light; be it individual or an entire clan. Mr. X had always believed the rumors — the Oniyum was the center of Kabathan's world order and had sourced the evolution of the planet's many, disparate cultures — but now he knew for sure that it wasn't just smoke and mirrors or some obscure subset of *Magic* that he had been unable to tap. A question drove him to the shrine, though, one that made him cross land and sea, leave behind friends and loved ones; a question that burned in his gut. Why had no one ever tried to claim ownership of the Oniyum by other means? The Tribal Council had begun to complain when this tribe or that got another turn at serving as its Caretaker, and certain other tribes would gripe about how they had not been blessed to serve in nearly a century, but still, it was never challenged. The Oniyum would darken every half-century and select who would rule next by the virtue of its Light. No one had ever tried to take it whether the Light had dimmed or not.

The more he studied, the more that curiosity grew into obsession. *What would happen if one were to just walk up and snatch it?* No one would think to stop him. No one would even know who he was.

He had travelled the world, studied with the Necromancers and all other dark *Magic* users he could find, covering his tracks at every turn. He even shadowed a couple of Jallorian Knights for a short time before they tired of him. They knew he'd been there all along, of course; they were the chosen Agents of the Oniyum, blessed with a small portion of its power. They were foot soldiers though, placed about the world. Had they been there, in the Fantasarian shrine that night, Mr. X would not have come. The guards actually present were merely coiffed puppets of the Fantasarian Court.

Standing there, bathed in that legendary Light, he realized he was rooted to the spot; in an incoherent daze of wonder. It was like taking a first, deep breath, not having realized he had been holding it in the first place. Unlike other artifacts in museums and royal galleries, the Oniyum was not protected behind a glass case, leaving it vulnerable to anyone who stood before it. As the oldest artifact in recorded history, he had expected it to look worn and tarnished like the door protecting it — not much, given that it had, in fact, lasted nearly 200,000 years — but he could see no wear at all; in fact, it was perfect, gleaming and majestic.

He shook his head and shut his eyes, breathing deeply. *Is this how it works?* he thought at it. *How you get the tribes of Kabathan to do your bidding? You twist our very thoughts?* Fantasarians responded to the cryptic and *Magical* above all else, so, here in the heart of their High Kingdom, the Oniyum had morphed from its natural form into the shape of a floating crystal ball, small enough to carry in one hand. It had no face, no hard edges, only the eerie, churning Light, but was very much alive. Once upon a time, Mr. X would have laughed at such a notion, but standing before it, he could not ignore the sheer otherness it was giving off.

The Oniyum's brightness increased, as though waking from a doze to give him its full attention. He heard a melody coming from it; like a breeze in the air. It was comforting and pleasant, but it sent a chill through him, despite the warmth of the room.

Mr. X rolled his shoulders back. He raised his hands and he took a well-rehearsed stance. His fingers twisted as he pulled them taut. The Oniyum shuddered.

"Hey, what are you doing?" one of the guards called out. Mr. X didn't take his eyes off the Oniyum and began chanting the dark invocation, committed to memory. The Oniyum's melody grew stronger, but Mr. X remained focused on the words.

"Step back," said the other guard, more forcefully. Mr. X ignored them. He flexed his hands more aggressively and chanted louder, over the song, which, like the Light, grew stronger.

The guards rushed him. Mr. X threw his arms wide and both men hurled backwards and collided with the walls. They fell and did not rise. The Oniyum's Light shifted suddenly from bright blue to deep indigo and the melody stopped altogether before the sphere emitted a sharp, high-pitched screech, terrible and nearly crippling. Mr. X tried to move closer, but met a physical force now emanating from the Oniyum. It was fighting back. When he'd first imagined this moment, he'd thought it might just go dark; roll down onto the floor and play possum, but the Oniyum was challenging him. He grinned. *Give me your best shot.*

The Oniyum's force slackened. Mr. X lunged forward, right arm outstretched and as his finger brushed the surface of the orb, it convulsed, as though struck.

With a deafening CRACK, it transformed. Back in its natural state as an enormous crystal, it was far larger, all rough surface and jagged edges. Midreach, the floor trembled beneath his feet. A matching a pulse rolled beneath his fingertip and inside his chest. The Light shifted again, plunging the room into a deep scarlet. The screech returned, and with a lurch of horror, Mr. X saw a crack appear in the crystal. Then another, and another. *Self destruction.* In a last, desperate reach, his fingers closed around one of those jagged edges.

The room exploded.

Mr. X soared backwards like the guards, but stayed pinned to the wall. He struggled pointlessly, noise roaring in his ears. Something pierced his eye with blinding pain and he collapsed, terror-stricken, disoriented, clutching at his face. There was no blood, but the skin of his face burned, white-hot, while a cold sweat broke out over the rest of him.

He could no longer see the room or feel the floor beneath him and he wept. Images spiraled behind his eyes. Was his life flashing before him? No, the visions were not his own. They pitched at him in a stream of blurred imagery, but as they slowed, they took focus at random. Awful things, beautiful things, the expanse of centuries compressed into a heartbeat and single moments stretched into a lifetime. Events throughout all of history swept in and out of his mind's eye, each with a different mental lash. He was all of them; every victim, every victor, and he knew all of their stories. He couldn't stand the enormity of it, feeling everything at once. Was he descending into Hell? Scenes from his own life flicked into the mix, joining the company of strangers' faces, world leaders, prophets both false and legitimate. And there were events, yet to happen, in some uncertain future.

His left eye, apparently undamaged, flew open. The room was still there, silent and dark. He couldn't see much from his unobscured left eye or from where he lay on the floor. The light drifted in, grey and dim, through the cracks of the door and window panes. The first mist of dawn. *How long have I been lying here?* His bones creaked as he pushed himself up. The pain in his right eye miraculously dulled, though the pressure had not ebbed much and he could barely see out of it. In fact, a tinge of red lay over everything. He gingerly touched his face again. His skin no longer burned, nor did it hurt. His fingers met no dried blood or open wound. It was the softest his skin had ever felt. Unnaturally so. He inhaled quickly and pulled his fingers back. He looked around again. The two guards still lay on either side of him, staring out of intact, but glassy eyes. Mr. X crawled nearer to the one on his left and in the half-reflective surface of silver armor, an unfamiliar reflection stared back at him. His face should have been a charred mess of burns or cuts, but instead he looked downright Elven. His skin had known harsh weather and ample amounts of sunlight, but no trace of it showed. Every blemish was gone; every birthmark removed. In addition to all of this, his right eye shone red. It made him look like a Cyborg or Android.

Mr. X leaned closer to the metal, his breath fogging the surface. The rest of his face was briefly clouded, but the harsh red light remained visible. He tilted his chin up, down, back and forth. The light, the reflection, all moved with him. He dabbed his face again, still smooth and eerie to the touch.

"What have you *done* to me?!" he yelled at the Oniyum, turning back towards the center of the room.

Except the Oniyum wasn't there, not even in a thousand broken pieces on the floor. *Where is it?* The room may have exploded, but the Oniyum had been in his grasp, cracking. Mr. X looked down at his hands, flat against the floor. He searched the area around him. Nothing.

A dull pulse emanated from his socket, but it didn't match the frantic hammering in his chest. *No…it can't be…*

The pillar, now only a dull chunk of ugly stone, it supported nothing. The Oniyum was gone.

Mr. X scrambled up and staggered, half-falling, onto the pillar. A single dark crevice now split the marble surface, deep into the rock.

The Oniyum is gone. He swallowed. *Someone will come. The Jallorian Knights will know, they'll come and they'll fix this and they'll heal me—*

His right eye stung then, sharp, but fleeting. The light grew brighter, too; the room glowed redder. Something pulsed harder behind his eye; shivered in the manner of a frightened, cornered animal. And he knew with sudden, instinctive certainty that it was not a busted blood vessel or damaged organ, but something entirely separate from him. Something conscious.

He raised a hand to his face, lightly touching the top of his cheekbone.

"*Shh,*" he whispered. The shuddering stopped. The light decreased, but still shone.

Fighting back premature delight, Mr. X reconsidered the fractured pillar. Because of its proximity to the Oniyum, it had been pristine and gorgeous when he'd first entered the room. Now, the Oniyum was gone and the pillar was dirty and broken along with everything else. Except Mr. X himself. He stood, transformed, unnaturally beautiful and in possession of some unknown power. In his wildest imagination, he could not have planned such an outcome, but he could work with it. So long as he survived.

Outside the shrine, the courtyard was empty. Mr. X hesitated at the door, wondering how no one had heard all the racket. No *Magic* or living souls were in his vicinity. He knew that, felt it, like the weight of his clothes hanging off of him.

Perhaps the most momentous event in history had just taken place, but the world slept on, unaware. He dismissed this and strode forward, glancing up. The sky, still grey and cloudy, was also dappled with red. A sailor's sunrise. The crystal hummed in his eye, almost pleasant again. His hands tingled. He had fought the Oniyum and won.

An old phrase from long ago sprung to mind and he spoke aloud, to no one and to the whole world, because he could.

"Take warning."

PART ONE
PRISONERS OF WAR

ONE

REMAN

"Falcon to ICORE Base," Reman chanted into the mech's empty cockpit. "Dropship is nearing the target area."

"Copy Falcon. You're coming in nice and clear," replied the calm, disembodied voice of Ensign Sterling. "Retrieve anything you can regarding the whereabouts of the Oniyum. You are to report anything you find."

"Copy that. Preparing to dispatch."

"The last known coordinates are in that western mountain range; you're to concentrate your search on the valley."

"The blast site. Got it." Reman reached past the words of *International Corps of Regulated Enforcement* embedded in the dash to adjust the holographic screens and signaled the docking bay doors to open below.

"Detaching," the mech's A.I. cooed.

The pod trembled as the massive metal clamps beneath clanged and disengaged. Sunlight flooded the pod bay as the doors swung open below. Reman maneuvered the pod up, hovering just slightly, then forward, through the bay, and out, into the sky.

A shocking amount of green spread out below. How so many civilizations thrived on this side of the world, he still didn't comprehend, given how wild so much of it still was. He drifted along the valley, following it around the corner of the biggest mountain and descending further into the valley.

The mech maneuvered like a dream. Reman knew he shouldn't feel special, but he'd expected to wait years before getting his own vessel, let alone the very latest in the SENTRI Air-Walked hybrid line. Barely five hours ago, he'd been out on the barrack's training grounds for his usual morning run before assembling for duty with the rest of his squad. And now, he soared over rural Fantasaria.

His first solo mission.

He'd been rounding his sixth lap when Ensign Sterling had flagged him down and shoved a battle report at him.

Southwest Fantasaria. Fourteen Mercs confirmed dead. No survivors.

"Whole thing ended with the detonation of a Brimstone missile," Sterling had said.

"What brought them to *that?*" Reman had asked.

"That's what they're sending you to find out."

"But…why me?"

She'd shrugged. "Above my pay grade." Like him, she'd advanced quickly through the ranks, given the state of global war, growing only more dense and costly with each passing year. The Mech Republic was managing to hold their land, thanks to ICORE, but the Oniyum was still missing, the Fantasarians still refused to stand down — along with every other tribe on Kabathan — and, above all, casualty rates rose daily with no end in sight.

As the mech drifted above the valley, waves of anxiety sloshed in Reman's stomach. The battle had already happened, so the conditions were low-risk. He probably wouldn't have to do any close combat — let alone kill anyone — but he'd never participated in a battle beyond the hull of a heavily armored vehicle. What if he had to engage with Fantasarians…up close?

The mech's computer stuttered out a fresh sequence of beeps.

"Detecting traces of sulfur and *Magic* use," the A.I. recited.

"This is definitely the place," Reman muttered to the Ensign, shaking away his nerves. Readings collected on the dash, specifying an area ten miles due west.

He checked the coordinates. It was off his main course; straight up the mountain, almost at its peak, not remotely matching the specs from the blast site.

He maintained course and dipped the mech further into the valley, searching for a proper place to land. "Analyzing battle data."

The screens blinked as the pod's computer provided him with detailed close-range specs of the previous day's explosion.

"Battle results indicate two tribes were involved; Mercs and Fantasarians," Reman read off the monitors.

"Proceed carefully; there may be more still lurking around," Sterling warned him.

Reman shook his head, even though Sterling couldn't see him. "No one could have survived that blast. It wiped out the entire area. Looks like whatever this battle was for, neither side got what they wanted."

He gritted his teeth. *Another battle, another dozen lives…obliterated.*

"On my way here, the computer detected a hotspot. I'm gonna go check it out."

"Copy that."

Abandoning the search for a landing spot, he altered the mech's trajectory and ascended the nearest mountain. Climbing into the upper altitude, the surrounding landscape abruptly shifted. The grass dissipated under fast-expanding blankets of snow, while the trees grew bare, bent, and spindly, also splattered with snow and ice.

"Whoa…"

Over the mountain's peak, snow lay even thicker and the A.I. confirmed icy temperature readings outside the hull. Reman spied a break between the clusters of thin trees and lowered the mech to the ground with a distinct *crunch* of metal on snow.

"ICORE, you seeing this?" Reman asked as he activated the walking controls. The vehicle rose up on its legs and marched forward, through what should have been underbrush.

"Affirmative," Sterling said.

A high-pitched beeping sequence erupted from the dash. Then another. Reman scanned the landscape. No life forms had appeared, not even regional wildlife, and no other activity had changed. What was tripping the sensors? There couldn't be a glitch in a ship this new, right?

Movement caught Reman's eye on one of the smaller scanners — a quick blip on the dash, once, twice, then nothing. Something was kicking up dust. Or, rather, snow.

"I'm getting strange readings from a clearing up ahead," he informed Sterling, "but only in fragments. Probably interference from all the *Magic* in the area."

He altered course again and, as he moved forward, the readings continued to flicker sporadically, the screens lodged with assaults of visual static. He squinted through the windshield, but couldn't see anything except a barren wilderness.

Peculiar or not, though, he had a job to do.

"ICORE, I'm leaving the mech to proceed on foot for further investigation. I will report my findings at 0800 hours." He slowed the mech to a halt and switched off the walking controls. The mech's legs compressed, lowering the pod to the ground. "Switching to mobile link."

"Copy that. Mobile link established and locked," Sterling replied as he slipped on the ear comm.

"System powering down," the computer informed him.

"Be careful, Reman."

Reman stopped. To use real names broke protocol. Such human moments, expressions of friendship, had become so rare. Not even his own sister had said as much in the past year.

Had ICORE even informed her of his mission here?

Would she even care?

He shoved those thoughts away. "I will."

The buzz of connection dissipated in his ear. Reman took a deep breath, picked up his rifle, and opened the hatch.

The wide, stark landscape rolled out before him. Icy air pinched his lungs as he stepped out of the pod. His boots crunched into hard-packed snow and his steps echoed through the empty clearing. Nothing else moved. No wind shook the bare branches. No forest animals scurried through the frozen vegetation.

Silence.

The air seemed to tighten around Reman, making him reluctant to breathe. This kind of silence may have been common in Fantasaria, but no matter how far one traveled from a central metropolis, noise permeated every moment of every day. Ships overhead, transit vehicles, radios, phone signals, and public alerts…all gone. Without them, Reman felt physically incomplete. Perhaps such stillness was what was causing the faulty alarms?

Somehow, Reman didn't think he would be that lucky.

He clutched the rifle tighter. His leather gloves creaked against the grip. He'd wanted to avoid close combat — wanted to avoid Fantasarians altogether — but standing in the hushed clearing, however, those concerns vanished.

Be careful what you wish for.

Even so, the stillness itself felt like some other, sentient presence, watching him.

Gritting his teeth, Reman punched the activation code into the portable scanner on his wrist without looking at it. No alarm. He was still alone.

He adjusted the laser settings on the rifle and started forward at a cautious, but steady pace.

In ten steps, his toes were frozen. His teeth rattled and he itched for his snow boots, stashed safely under his bunk, back at Base.

After he'd received his mission, he'd shuffled off the track and ran from one place to another in preparation. He'd received a hasty haircut and a brand-new grey Aviator uniform, battle armor and premium grade weapons, including the laser-powered rifle and pistol. His mech pod, per standard, stored a mandatory medical kit, emergency food packs, a second jumpsuit, backup sensors, and batteries…but no fleece-lined jacket. His new attire might have looked official, but they lacked warmth.

He caught a glimpse of the other mountains in the distance. They too, were capped with ice and shone, silver-white, in the fading light. The sun drooped towards the horizon, sending streaks of orange across the sky. Reman wished he could see it fully, without all the trees blocking his view. Politics and warfare aside, he had to admit it was beautiful here.

Since joining ICORE, Reman and his squad had accepted missions almost everywhere on Kabathan. Though Reman had never set foot on foreign territory, the landscapes he'd witnessed from the air would haunt him forever. Leveled fields, destroyed homes and dust as far as the eye could see. For that, Reman despised the wars. He despised the Fantasarians for causing them in the first place and despised himself for partaking.

And yet, he could not bring himself to return to civilian life. To withdraw was to do nothing and he wanted to see the wars end. As many of ICORE's recruitment ads declared: *Protect, search and defend. The people, the land, the Oniyum. Whatever the cost.*

What possessed the Fantasarians to take it, though? Had they expected the other tribes to wipe each other out in the quest to retrieve it, leaving almighty Fantasaria in charge? Reman snorted. Every gun on the planet — real and figurative — had been aimed at the Fantasarians for five, long years. They'd taken major hits, but Reman couldn't feel sorry for them. They'd maintained their defenses and the Oniyum's absence endured. Soldiers in Reman's squad believed that there was no rhyme or reason to any of it; a mindset shared by ICORE itself, apparently, based on their battle strategies. *Recover the Oniyum first and we'll sort the mess out afterwards.*

After what Reman experienced and lost in those five years, he didn't believe in coincidence anymore, especially when it came to the Oniyum's disappearance. But he'd kept that to himself. He just wanted the wars to cease, whether through his normal day-to-day orders with the rest of his squad, or successfully fulfilling a solo mission. The fighting would end. Everything would go back to normal. Nothing could revive those already lost and he could only guess how it would affect his sister, Jenda — would she leave ICORE? Doubtful — but everything would be set right. That would be enough.

A twig snapped behind him.

He spun, crouched, and raised the rifle.

Nothing.

After a few long, tense seconds, a bird took flight some feet away. Reman lowered the gun and straightened back to his full height, trying to view the animal properly, but it was already out of sight and he was alone again.

Except…if a bird had been out there this whole time, other things could be hiding too, watching him. He pivoted on the spot and scanned the area one more time — and spotted movement to his left. His stomach clenched. Two tall, slender figures wove through the trees. Pale and graceful, wrapped in silver cloaks and furs, their long, pointed ears arched sharply through their golden hair.

Elves.

Reman fought an instinctive rush of awe as well as panic and stayed put. He watched them glide over the icy ground, longbows and fully loaded quivers perched on their shoulders, sheathed knives fastened to their belts. They had not raised these weapons, though. In fact, they weren't even looking in his direction. Somehow, *they had not seen him.*

A crooked, rotting tree trunk sat a few feet to his right.

The Elves continued to weave gracefully through the trees, still ignorant of his presence. Regardless, if his tech was inoperable, he would have to abort the mission or call for backup. In two, nearly-silent steps, he crouched by the stump and pressed a finger to his ear comm, leaning around the bark to make sure they hadn't changed direction or disappeared.

"Falcon to ICORE Base."

The line was fuzzy with static — and nothing else. He bit back a string of curses.

"Falcon to ICORE," he said again. "Come in."

The Elves stopped moving.

"ICORE, Sterling, do you copy?"

Still nothing. The Elves turned their heads in perfect sync and their gazes met his. He was compromised. His hand whipped away from his ear and back to the rifle. He clutched the trigger and raised the barrel, ready to fire, when a streak of silver winked in the corner of his eye. He hesitated just as the curved edge of steel eased into the space just below his jaw, the flat of a knife blade held cold and persuasive against his throat.

"For all that armor, you're still terribly vulnerable."

Her voice was stoic, but had the slightest mocking emphasis. He couldn't really see this new, third party; just her shape crouched next to him. Reman tried to lift the gun but she gripped the shoulder of his armor and pressed the blade harder against his throat.

"Don't be stupid." There was no amusement in her voice that time. He eased his head sideways to get a better look at her. She allowed it. She didn't attempt to stop him, anyway.

Small and slender, she peered at him through bright, green eyes and a tan, round face. Her dark hair, tied partially back, exposed semi-pointed ears. So, she was an Elf, too, but some obscure lineage he couldn't identify. She wasn't exuding the acrid stench most *Magic*-wielding Fantasarians carried around. Even after just a few whiffs of the scent off of returning soldiers who had engaged in firefights with the 'Sarians, Reman could never forget it; a potent, vile odor like sewage and burnt coffee. He was sure it served as a defense mechanism just by wafting in their enemies' directions. This girl didn't have it, but a sense of power still radiated off of her, despite her size.

Reman tightened his jaw and averted his eyes, glancing around. They still appeared to be alone, but he remembered Sterling's warning, along with a catchphrase from back home: *you can never trust what you see in Fantasarian country.*

The Elf girl confiscated his rifle, snatched the comm from his ear and ordered him to remove the pistol from his leg holster, which she then took along with the knives from his belt. While she struggled to figure out how, exactly, to hold the rifle, he slid his fingers over his wrist and pressed against his sleeve, which had, miraculously, fallen over his wristband. He attempted to activate the pod's remote unit, pressing a few buttons blindly and hoped that, back in the clearing, the pod would boot up. The girl shoved the barrel of his own gun against his back and hissed, "let's go." They marched forward. Reman thought hard, picturing the process, willing his commands to have been accurate; the dark screens suddenly flickering on, the radar map popping up and scanning the area, finding him —

The missile exploded ten feet away, throwing them both sideways, off their feet. Reman recovered quickly enough to scramble up, a bit lightheaded but unharmed. He spotted his rifle, fallen just out of the girl's grasp. As he lunged for it, stepping past her, the girl's hands sprung forward and seized his ankles. He slammed back onto the ground next to his gun. The world spun, and then spun again, but he managed to orient himself enough to flip over and tug back his sleeve. He aimed his device's exposed sensor at the girl, who still clutched his boots. He activated the device and a blinding flash flew out at her. Blinded, her grip loosened and his foot slid free. She reached for him again, but he kicked, landing a blow against her face and she lurched backwards. He scrambled up, grabbed his gun, and ran for the clearing. He pressed his scanner again, mid-run, and glanced briefly over his shoulder in time to see the girl twist up into a crouch. She glowered straight at him, her face completely undamaged.

He ran faster.

When he skidded into the clearing, within eyesight of his mech, he scanned the surroundings. He found no sign of the girl or anyone else following him, but his mind still reeled. He'd have to remember this moment the next time he was on the barracks track: the speed of his pulse and the numbness in his fingers. After all, he wasn't likely to be sent on another away mission anytime soon —

An arrow soared past his shoulder, barely missing him. He whipped around. On the far side of the clearing, just beyond the mech's direct reach, the other two Elves reloaded their longbows around trees. As arrow points swung up in his direction, Reman pelted forward again and slid behind another tree for cover as more arrows whipped past him. He turned the rifle's power up to its highest setting and waited until the volley of arrows stopped, but still didn't move. Could he wait them out? Probably not. They were Elves, so he might not hear them...and they likely had more patience.

Reman jumped up, swung around the tree and fired. His shot missed both Elves, but before he could fire a second blast, a streak of flaming light shot towards him. Before he could move, blinding, pain blasted into his right shoulder where the arrow made vicious contact, compounded with a staggering, unnatural force that sent him straight back off his feet. His head collided with the icy ground and he knew no more.

TWO

REMAN

He smelled wood smoke. A dull ache throbbed in his right shoulder, upper arm and neck, but his body ached all over. Coarse straw lay under his hands, resting at his sides. Voices hummed nearby, but Reman couldn't make out the words over the popping of flames.

He creaked his eyes open.

Above him, the ceiling was light-toned wood with a hole cut out some distance to the left. Smoke disappeared through it in thick tendrils. Reman couldn't lift his head to get a proper look around. Though awake, all of his adrenaline had waned and left him weak. He could only make out small portions of the room from where he lay. The flames sprouted from a fire pit, situated a few feet to Reman's left. Candles and torches illuminated the space, incense burned on a shelf a little ways above him and stacks of supplies were scattered everywhere; hay, logs, great sacks with labels he couldn't read, and dozens of wooden crates.

He lifted his left hand, which took considerable effort, to touch his right shoulder. His fingers met rough cloth wrapped tightly around his shoulder and neck. And he remembered: a flaming arrow. Had it been on fire, though? Beneath the fabric, his muscles felt tense, sore, but not burned. The unmistakable odor of *Magic* hung in the air, but not on his person. If his altered state was the result of some intense *Magic*, he would have been gagging from the intensity of the smell. It probably would have been what woke him.

"...and the soldiers all seem to be in high spirits?"

"They're complaining about not having enough ale, but other than that..."

Laughter.

Reman craned his head to the side. Roughly seven feet away on the opposite side of the fire pit, two men hovered beside a rickety table, chatting softly with their backs to Reman. One barely moved, draped in a sleek, black cloak, the hood drawn low over his face. The other, bald and brawny, swayed back and forth as he talked and laughed. Viking runes glinted along the edges of his leather armor and off the blades of two giant axes strapped to his back.

Beside them, a girl relaxed against the wall with a steaming ceramic mug clutched in her hands. A feathery shawl lay over her shoulders and a curved dagger hung in a sheath at her waist. With a jolt, Reman recognized the shape; it matched the blade had been held to his neck. He looked back up at her face. Only now did he notice her semi-pointed ears.

"When do you move out?" she asked the Viking.

"Dawn, day after tomorrow. The fleet should reach the eastern shores in three days' time."

She nodded and raised the mug to her lips. Her gaze drifted lazily over to Reman. When she caught him looking at her, she froze, her ears pulling back. He held his breath, certain she was about to attack, but instead, she lowered the mug again, smirking.

"Legren." She turned to the hooded man. "The Mech is awake."

Both men twisted around and Reman glimpsed the tabletop between them. Several scrolls were spread out, held down by bags of coins and tiny bottles filled with dark liquid.

"I'll just be off, then," the Viking said, gathering up a scroll.

"Thank you, Bosa," said the hooded man. The Viking, Bosa, passed the girl and headed for the doorway — an open frame with a single drape hanging over it — but halted on the threshold. He turned, grinning, to survey Reman one final time. Reman held absolutely still, trying everything to keep his face blank.

"Relax kid. You're only a prisoner of war." Bosa laughed boisterously and disappeared through the drape. The Elf girl grinned openly now, too.

Reman cursed himself. *How scared do I look?* He'd always been a terrible liar.

Reman forced himself to sit up and pain roared through his shoulder. He slumped against the wall, breathing hard.

"Easy, Falcon," said the hooded man — Legren, the girl said? — and Reman went stock-still.

"What did you call me?"

"That is your name, isn't it?" She drew Reman's earpiece from the folds of her shawl. "It's what your friends keep calling you."

The silver edge glinted smartly in the firelight, woefully out of place amongst the red and brown hues of the room. Reman fought a reckless urge to dive for it.

"Falcon, please respond," she mimicked in a robotic monotone. "Calling Falcon, come in…"

"Though I also heard someone more confidentially refer to you as… Reman?" Legren added. Before he could stop himself, Reman turned his head sharply toward Legren.

"That must be it." The Elf girl smiled, tucking the device back under her shawl. Reman took a deep breath and sank back against the coarse hay bales.

"What do you want?" he groaned.

"I beg your pardon?" Legren asked.

"You attack me and have the perfect chance to kill me, yet I wake up here, bandaged." He gestured to his shoulder and arm, finally looking down at it. The bandages were hand-woven fabric, covered in crisscrossing lines of calligraphy, also hand-stitched. "With all this…Elven gibberish scrawled all over me."

"They're healing runes," the Elf girl corrected him.

"Whatever."

Someone cleared their throat outside the doorway. The girl crossed the room and pulled the cloth slightly back to peer out before swiping it aside completely for another new face. A man wrapped in a traveling coat — thicker and far more ragged than Legren's — strode through the doorway. A long-neck clay pipe stuck out of his mouth, probably bought off a Clockwork peddler.

"Sethera," he muttered, nodding at the girl as he passed her. His face was weatherworn and heavily scarred. While the girl, Sethera, slid the curtain shut again, he approached Legren and planted a small satchel on the table. Legren seized it and withdrew several sheets of parchment, the edges frayed and crumpled. Sethera read over his shoulder, eyes moving side to side. Though Reman couldn't see Legren's face, Sethera's eyes widened. She leaned forward and her jaw dropped open.

"Vampians," Legren muttered.

"And *Mobsters?*" she added, looking up too. The newcomer glanced at Reman and cocked an uncertain eyebrow. Legren nodded and the man shrugged.

"Another tribe was involved," his voice rumbled. "We can't yet tell which one. Brock stayed behind to gather more information, but, in the meantime…"

"The other camps must be warned," Sethera said, gripping Legren's shoulder.

"Mmm," Legren agreed. "Please inform Xettar."

Some warlock or sorcerer, no doubt, Reman suspected. The man bowed, retreated back to the doorway and disappeared, without any last word of cryptic warning. While Legren continued to read the parchment, Sethera set her mug down on the table and put her hands on her hips; uncomfortably close to her dagger. When she glanced back at Reman and found him staring at her weapon, she pivoted and gripped the handle, pretending to dive for it. His arm sprung toward his belt, where his pistol should have been, but of course, the holster was empty.

Sethera flashed a mocking grin at him, before looking sidelong at Legren, who's hood had swung around towards her.

"Sorry, couldn't resist," she said.

Legren remained silent and moved closer to the fire, still scanning the papers from the satchel.

"Nothing personal," Sethera continued, easing back against the wall. "I've held a grudge against all the other tribes for a very long time."

Good cop, bad cop, Reman thought. *How original.* He tried to shift his position to claw at the bandages. Legren's hood lifted.

"You don't want to—"

"I don't want your pity," Reman interrupted. "You're probably going to kill me, anyway."

"Do you especially want to die?" Sethera asked, undoubtedly willing to oblige. Reman suspected this was just one of a million questions they would throw at him. He wanted desperately to deliver a clever comeback, to get early control of the conversation, but as he strained his memories of ICORE training, his mind blanked. *What would Jenda say?* How would his tough-as-nails sister combat an interrogation?

He stuck out his chin. "If it means you giving back the Oniyum, yes."

Sethera closed her eyes and shook her head in a weary sort of disbelief.

Legren shook his head, too. "Because we stole it, right?"

"It was last seen in your territory."

"So?" Legren asked, in the patronizing manner of a teacher shepherding a student.

"I may not like your kind, but I am well aware of the strength of your military force and I know you're not stupid. Even with the threat of the entire planet's forces bearing down on them, Fantasarians have maintained their defenses. Not even sheer dumb luck can accomplish that."

Legren's hood swiveled back towards Sethera, who shrugged.

"Get on with it," she said, waving a hand at him.

Setting the papers down on the table, Legren leaned back against it to peer at Reman squarely over the dancing flames.

"For the record: we don't have the Oniyum, and as such, we don't understand it any more than you do."

Reman snorted.

"You're a soldier, yes?" Legren asked. "You eat, sleep and fight when commanded. Direct orders are the law. Those orders define the truths by which you are to live; force you to base your entire view of a person or a whole group based solely on information you've been fed. So, ask yourself: how do we gain?" He smacked a hand against his chest. "How does our perpetually lying to you — and everyone else — benefit us? It's made us a mutual target for the rest of the world and yet I've seen no good come of that. Have you?"

The poignance of the question — and the lack of an answer — sent another chill through Reman.

"The Council had even come to that conclusion, before—"

"The Council?" Reman interjected with another derisive laugh. "Representatives from every tribe trying discuss peace? Yeah. That's going really well."

"It could work, if only given a real chance—"

"We're at war. Tensions are only growing and hostilities will eventually rise, even among them. No treaty can prevent that forever and they know it."

"There have always been hostilities." He paused. The hood tipped down and when he continued, his voice was quieter, more delicate. "Take Sethera's parents for example."

Behind him, Sethera went rigid and her gaze flicked to the back of Lauren's head.

"What are you doing?" she said.

Legren ignored her. "They were advocating for peace within the Council long before the Wars and no one was interested. No one wanted peace."

Lobbyists, Reman thought. *Great.*

"Once the Oniyum disappeared, they became exhaustively devoted to finding peace again, but no one listened—"

Sethera grabbed his shoulder and spun him around to face her. "*No.*"

The amused glint in her eye had vanished, replaced by the intensity Reman glimpsed back in the woods, down the edge of her knife blade.

"Trust me," Legren implored softly.

"I do, but don't drag my family into this." Silence lingered, broken only by the popping of embers. "Not yet," she finally finished, through gritted teeth.

"Fair enough." He backed away from her, circled the fire and crouched down before Reman's hay bale bed, but even on an equal plane, his face was still almost entirely obscured by the hood.

"The battle that brought you to the valley," Legren said. "I presume you've analyzed the details of the blast?"

Reman thought of the mission folder, full of vague statistics about the incident. He tried to remember the details the mech's computer showed him oh-so-many hours ago.

"More or less."

"No survivors."

"Well, obviously—"

"Except me."

The data had been obscure, but all three of his sources — Sterling, the ICORE data and the mech's computer — had confirmed the same thing: a Brimstone had made impact.

"A blast like that would have been impossible to survive," Reman insisted. "I've studied those missiles extensively."

"Normally, I'd submit to your expertise, but it's true."

"You don't reek of *Magic* and neither does she." Reman lifted his chin towards Sethera, who hadn't moved, shifting focus between himself and Legren. "So why should I believe you?"

"Well, I think the reason I'm alive is because the Oniyum itself interfered."

He reached up and threw back his hood, revealing a perfectly normal face — young, bearded, thin — except for the left eye, which was additionally covered by a green and gold handkerchief. A long, ugly scar ran from a few inches above his eyebrow, under the kerchief, down the far side of his cheekbone. Smaller, jagged scars splintered out from around the socket like shattered glass. It didn't look like the haphazard result of a stray talon or claw, but no weapon Reman knew of could leave a mark like that. He had seen soldiers back home with far worse, just as bizarrely shaped wounds and not all of them *Magical.* Legren removed the kerchief and despite the terrible scarring around the eye, Legren's eyeball was whole, unscathed, and *glowing.* Bright blue streaked the damaged tissue and the iris matched. The light sparkled under the skin like phosphorescent strips of energy, like live circuitry, but not like cyborgs.

Reman blinked, trying to clear his vision, but nothing changed. Goosebumps marched down his arms. At a loss for words, he looked between Sethera and Legren, trying to decipher a meaning. They both just stared back, waiting.

Typical Fantasarians. All cryptic drama rather than straight answers. He couldn't trust this display, could he? With no trace of *Magic* at play — only a soft hum in the air, not unlike a static charge — how could he not accept what was before him? If this was really an act of the Oniyum, then he could still fulfill his mission. He held very still. Even with a new lead, he still had to get out of this alive and make it back to base.

"So...you *do* have it, then."

THREE

REMAN

Sethera smacked Legren's shoulder. "See? A lot of good that did."
She stormed out of the room without another word. Legren took a deep
breath and rubbed his eyes, the unearthly glowing diminishing. Reman
scrutinized the scars and cuts, which were unlikely to fade anytime soon,
emitting a mystical light or not. Opening his eyes again, Legren withdrew
the green and gold handkerchief from inside his cloak and wrapped it back
around his head.

"So…" Reman prompted, curiosity outweighing caution. "You don't
have the Oniyum but it mysteriously reappeared for a few seconds to save
your life?"

He attempted to sit up again but though he barely moved, pain seared
down his arm and back. He gnashed his teeth and waited for it to pass.

"What did you people *do* to me?"

"You took an arrow to the shoulder."

"Besides that. Was it laced with *Magic* or something?"

"I doubt it. That's not really Tali's style. You feel like this because of the
arrow. Elven steel."

"And that means what, exactly?"

"It is a sort of *Magic*, though not in the typical sense. Not being Fantasarian, you had a rather…severe reaction." He paused before adding, in a quieter tone, "I *am* sorry about that."

"What, am I dying?" Reman asked, only half-serious.

Legren chuckled. "Not quite. The fog will clear soon, once you rest properly."

"And, what, you're going to provide me with deluxe accommodations? The best medical care this side of the Central Sea?" Reman knew how foreign detainment worked. He would either be confined to this room or escorted to an enclosed dungeon.

"Yes," Legren answered. "Room and board, at least, for however long you need to recover."

Reman's head tilted in disbelief. No way was he going to buy this hospitality act. They would probably lull him into a false sense of security, then murder him once his guard was down. But then, why the charade to begin with?

"You know I'm nobody, right? Just an average pilot, not some bureaucrat, emissary or even the son of a senior officer, so if you were hoping to hold me for ransom—"

"Ransom," Legren laughed, shaking his head. "This may be more difficult than I thought."

"What—"

"The Oniyum is not in our possession and so we've turned our attention to more pressing matters, like keeping our people out of the line of fire and the only way to do that, I believe, is…" He shut his eyes — or, at least the one that was visible. "Tomorrow. I will explain all of it tomorrow."

"If I'm still here."

Legren opened his eyes. "Do you plan to leave?"

"You'd let me?"

"Certainly, but I rather doubt you would get far in your injured state."

"I'm fine."

"Are you? Can you even stand?"

Reman knew he shouldn't try it, but couldn't quite resist the challenge. He pushed himself forward, trying, this time, to ignore the pain jumping in his shoulder, but his vision blurred and he slumped back on the hay bale.

Legren didn't say anything, but crossed the room and pulled back the drape slightly, speaking to someone outside in a hushed tone. A shadow moved on the other side and, moments later, the second familiar face of the night entered the room; one of the long-eared Elves. She was not the archer who fired the infamous arrow — Legren referred to that one as Tali — but the one who ran beside her, armed with the spear. A slender thing and categorically fragile-looking, she strode right up to him, grasped his wrist and lifted his arm. He tensed as she touched him, but before he could resist, she was already moving him. To his extreme surprise, the ache in his shoulder dulled as she draped the length of his arm across her back. Too stunned by the lack of pain, Reman cooperated, shifting his legs off the hay bales and placing both feet on the floor. The Elf eased him up until he was standing, somehow providing all the strength needed, without any sense of strain. He found his balance, standing on both feet. He had heard of Elves' uncanny gift of strength, but he never realized how true those rumors were. She released his undamaged arm then, stepped in front of him, and started to untangle the cloth wrapped around his afflicted shoulder. He did pull away then, taking a step back. She stopped, her hands in midair.

"This is Telena," Legren supplied belatedly, having watched this exchange from beside the doorway. "It was she who dressed your wounds."

Reman kept his eyes on the Elf. He waited for her to show some sign of impatience — pursed lips or a clenched jaw — but she just peered back at him and continued to wait, hands raised. Elves were considered wholly more mysterious than regular Fantasarians, and yet, he wanted to trust her. She'd lifted him off his feet without hurting him. She could have easily killed him already or at least tortured rather than heal him. She'd held a spear in the clearing, but never thrown it. Why?

He lowered his arm. After a few seconds more, she closed the gap between her fingers and his bandage, almost as though giving him the chance to change his mind. Her hands moved in a blur, reworking the arrangement of the fabric until his arm rested in a sling. Then she turned and swept from the room as though she'd never been there.

Reman stared down at the sling and then took a step forward. No pain. "Elven runes, you said?"

"Powerful, aren't they?"

"Elves or the runes?"

Legren just smiled and Reman found he was grinning back. *Did I just share a joke with a Fantasarian?*

"If you'll follow me..." Legren pulled back the cloth in the doorway. He stepped through the opening, then paused, waiting for Reman. Frozen in place, Reman struggled to recall any training for this type of situation, but nothing came. Alone, tech-less and without orders, he didn't know what ICORE would have him do.

Gather intel. That had been the mission from the beginning, and he could pursue it even now. Depending on his location, he could be near a Mech safe-house and the Fantasarians might not even know it. He might be stripped of weapons and tools, but he could still get a look around.

Reman stepped forward, following Legren through the doorway. Almost instantly, he regretted it. First, the smell nearly knocked him over. *Magic,* layer upon layer of it, slammed into him. His eyes watered and shut them, hard, fighting the urge to gag. Nearly a full minute passed before he could breathe easily. The shock of the *Magic* stench slowly wore off and he adjusted to the biting cold. When he could finally open his eyes again to take in his surroundings, he realized that his plan was thwarted before it had begun.

He couldn't see a damn thing.

Oh, sure, there were lanterns and lit torches all around, and he could make out all the people — what few of them there were, walking from one side of the dark to the other — but the blackness of night seeped into every unlit space like spilled ink. He exhaled, but couldn't tell if his breath was visible; it was cold enough, but there wasn't enough light to reflect it. From what he could see, they stood in some kind of center square.

"This way." Legren waved his arm ahead of Reman.

They walked. Through the dark, around the dark, and back through the dark again. Reman could have been surrounded by a dozen 'Sarians and been none the wiser. What if he wasn't being led to a dungeon or cell or other such prison, but out to the darkest part of the woods for some ritualistic execution? Reman focused on his breathing to keep from such speculations. Finally, they turned into another pool of torchlight, between a cluster of small, canvas tents. They were packed together, with barely room to walk between them, but through the fabric, light shone out in flickering intervals. Reman gaped. They lit fires inside? The antiquity of Fantasarian life still baffled him. How did they not burn the place down?

Even in the darkness, Reman sensed that Legren had led them into a clearing. A shadow loomed in a straight line up to the dark sky. A few more steps revealed the shadow to be cast by a small stone building with half a tower sticking out of the roof. From what he could see, the structure fit what Reman knew of normal Fantasarian architecture, with stone-and-mortar walls and thatched roof. Legren stopped walking — Reman took a quick step back to keep from running into him — and withdrew a ring of brass keys from his cloak. He approached the door, blocking Reman's view. The sound of scraping metal gave way to a vehement creak as the bolt shifted and echoed through the dark. The door, thicker than the width of Reman's hand, swung inwards, revealing a black void beyond the now-open threshold.

Dungeon after all. "You first," Reman said. Legren shrugged and stepped inside. With his movement, the door rocked backward, but not all the way closed, behind him. Staring at the blank face of the door, it then struck Reman as a whole different kind of trap. He wished, desperately, for his gun. Still, he pushed the door forward with his fingernails, trying to touch as little of it as possible. It didn't look especially dirty, but the state of the building was old and unkempt, like it hadn't been seen-to in any recent time frame. He ducked around it and stepped into the room.

He shivered. The air was just as chilled in here as it was outside; colder, even. With a jolt, he realized that as they'd walked through the camp, there hadn't been any snow on the ground. He may not have been able to see through the dark, but his boots were dry, as were the cuffs of his pants. Still, the air was cold. In fact, the condensed space struck him as something of an ice box.

"Am I supposed to freeze to death in here?" he asked. Light sparked in his peripheral vision, coupled with the sound of ignition. Legren moved away from a small hearth that stuck out from the wall on the far side of the room, which had previously been just another collection of shadow. The room sprung up in vivid relief, painted in an orange glow. It was, indeed, a house. A spinning wheel stood next to a small table topped with a flat slab of green stone. A miniature shelf hung above the table, supporting half a dozen volumes with unreadable text along the spines. Smaller, narrower cubbies of the shelf held piles of various sized sticks, probably for kindling. Opposite these, a small circular staircase of broad, wooden beams bolted together, curved upwards to a thin square in the ceiling, which Reman presumed to be an attic door. The walls were smooth, rather than a bumpy collage of roughhewn stones as he'd seen in various maps and photographs of the larger, older Fantasarian structures, most of which were in the central city, the "High Kingdom," as they called it.

Beside the hearth where Legren stood, a bed and side table with a single drawer.

What was this place? And why was it was out here, by itself, rather than with an assortment of other housing? Was it an old lookout station of some kind?

Looking down at the ground, Reman saw not rugs, but slats of wood. He noted the scent of *Magic* in the air here, too, but fainter. Like the exterior, something about it seemed isolated, even out of use, given the thin layer of dust over most of the furniture. Yet, books lay open on the table. Tousled sheets on the cot implied someone had slept there recently, but roused late and left the bed unmade. Something about this theory caught Reman off-guard; imagining a Fantasarian practicing the same daily motions as himself —

"I think you'll find this will keep you sufficiently warm." Legren gestured to the hearth, his hands empty of flint or matches. A few posts stuck out of the smooth walls, but they held no torches. Legren must practice *Magic* after all. *Except he doesn't stink of the stuff.*

"A lot nicer than some dungeon cell," Reman muttered.

"You're not a criminal, as far as I'm aware, so you should not be treated like one," Legren said with a slight bow.

Reman raised an eyebrow. "So what was with Bosa calling me a prisoner of war?"

Legren smiled. "Viking humor. Occasionally...sarcastic." He sidled towards the door. "I can give you a proper tour of the village, come morning. If that's of interest to you?"

Reman shook his head. "Why all the theatrics? Why play me? It'd just be more productive for everybody if you just name your terms, straight out."

Legren shook his head. "There is no game, no manipulation. I have..." he glanced upward for a moment, then back at Reman, "an idea. If I have any kind of...*scheme*...it's that I will insist on sharing this idea with you. Tomorrow."

Without another pause, he left. Once the door shut, Reman heard no subsequent scraping of metal on wood, so he presumed he was not locked in. Should he try the door to be certain? No, he decided, because, really, what difference did it make?

He scanned the room for some possible way to bar the entrance. He lifted his heel and pushed against the bedside table, testing its weight. With minor pressure, it moved, so, he pushed harder and slid it across the room until it smacked against the door. Low-tech, but better than nothing.

Feeling slightly more secure, Reman sank onto the edge the cot, trying not to jostle the sling. Steady crackling from the hearth harmonized with the sound of the wind outside and firelight danced over the walls. Deep shadows drew Reman's attention to a painting that hung above the spinning wheel; three men circled around an enormous, glowing crystal. Each stared, wide-eyed, but one leaned closer to the stone with outstretched arms. Reman knew this scene all too well, of course. Everyone did; the Brothers Brisbane first discovering the Oniyum. Countless history and political compendiums chronicled this event. Further down the wall, another painting depicted a similar scene; a Council ceremony. One member from every tribe clustered around the Oniyum, each face rendered in open awe. Whenever the

Oniyum's light dimmed, tradition and global law dictated that it be brought before the Council to establish its next caretaker. This usually occurred every few decades, so the Oniyum routinely passed from tribe to tribe, though in no particular order, and perpetuated each society's disparate advancement.

In this painting, however, no individual stood apart. The figures formed a perfect, even circle.

Frenetic beeping interrupted the stillness. Reman's mobile scanner, still strapped to his injured arm, announced that sync to his mech pod had been lost and power was low. Grimacing, Reman loosened the clasp with his free hand and shut off the alarm. He shuffled to the bedside table, where he opened the drawer and froze.

His pistol lay inside.

FOUR

"They're lunatics," Reman whispered. They'd give him back his weapon? Gamble that recklessly on Reman's morality?

Of course, one gun, low on ammo, wouldn't do much in any case. Without knowing the full security detail of this place — whatever he was — Reman would risk being way outnumbered. Worse, he'd probably have to fire on innocent people. He couldn't imagine that, not even on Fantasarians. Still, he took comfort in knowing that now he wasn't completely vulnerable.

He wasn't going anywhere for some time. Being offered information willingly would have been enough to keep him there. *This "idea" of Legren's must have to do with the Oniyum...* He would hunker down here and, despite what he'd said, play along as best he could. He considered sneaking back out for a look around on his own, but with his shoulder so fragile... Besides, there was bound to be some sort of Night Watch. Reman would just have to follow Legren's lead. *Even if he is a Grade-A nutcase.*

He checked the safety, then lay down in the cot and shoved the gun under the pillow. Not ideal, but close enough for a quick-grab. He settled his head on top of it and slowly relaxed, surprised that the bed itself was actually comfortable. Within moments, he was asleep.

A sharp, steady, knocking broke through the blackout. Reman's eyes flew open, but he held still, assessing the noise. The surrounding room was quiet and still. A distant bird chirped somewhere outside, accompanied by the bleat of livestock. Something clanged, metal — hammer on an anvil? — but it wasn't the same sound that woke him.

The noise came again; a swift *bang* against the door. Someone was knocking, and not with their fist, judging by the way the door shuddered against the hinges. The side table even wobbled forward on impact.

Reman sat up, fast, sending his head spinning. The air shifted around him, cold, and his limbs creaked from tension and chill. In fact, he was shivering, vaguely feverish.

Waiting for the vertigo to pass, Reman blinked the room into dull focus. The flames had completely extinguished in the hearth, but a lone trail of smoke drifted out of the ashes. He shifted on the cot, realizing that he had not moved at all from the position in which he initially laid down.

Another knock.

Reman dragged the gun from under his pillow and pushed himself up, off of the cot. He staggered across the room, barely maintaining balance, and tucked the gun in his waistband. He shoved the table aside, but did not open the door.

"Yeah?" he called through a coarse throat.

"Ah! He lives!" cried an unfamiliar, though delighted voice from the other side. "We were starting to worry. The midday meal is on, my friend, and we—"

"*Midday?*" Reman reached for the door handle and heaved it open.

Through the narrow opening, a new face popped into view; a black man with soft umber complexion draped in a long, emerald green cloak with the hood drawn up over his head. As Reman leaned forward, however, the man immediately pushed back the hood, revealing ears pierced with tiny, silver hoops, and hair cropped so close it could have passed for a new ICORE recruit. His deep-set brown eyes twinkled as he flashed Reman a wide, toothy grin. "Not usually a late sleeper, eh?"

29

Reman pressed his eyes shut, tight, trying desperately to think straight. "No, not usually…"

"You're still recovering. Telena will take a look at your wound a little later." He smiled and extended his right hand. "I'm Xettar."

The familiar gesture made Reman's brain stutter, but, instinctively, he accepted the offered handshake. "Reman."

Xettar inclined his head slightly. "Nice to meet you. Hungry?"

Nausea still droned in Reman's gut. "Well…"

"Join me anyway," Xettar said, waving Reman forward. "I'll wager you're just dying to get a good look around, right? Take a walk with me and let me show you that we're a quiet, little hamlet on the west 'Sarian border just trying to get by. And, maybe, make things a little better."

Had Xettar honestly just used the slang for Fantasarians? Legren hadn't. Reman rubbed his eyes, attempting to recall the previous night's conversation.

"And how does Legren's 'idea' fit into all that?" Reman asked.

Xettar's head wobbled back and forth. "It's not really his idea, per *se*, but that's for him to explain later. It's a good thing. Not some evil plan he's hatched to take over the world."

He extended his other arm out, towards the village beyond. In the daylight, it had taken shape; clumps of houses and misshapen structures. Funnels of smoke drifted up from every direction and now Reman could hear distant chatter of human voices and laughter. *Just a harmless village.* A field off to the far left was lined with identical squat, canvas tents. *Wait…tents? Is this a military outpost?*

Xettar grinned again. He'd been right; curiosity prickled in Reman's brain, waking him up more fully than anything else.

"Shall we?"

Reman needed answers, of course — that hadn't changed — but something about Xettar's earnest disposition caused Reman to wonder for the first time, if, as both Legren and Xettar had said, maybe this was not a trick. After all, he had nothing to offer them and they knew that —

Or is that what they want? For me to let my guard down and start to trust them? These were Fantasarians. They took the Oniyum. Maybe not these individuals, but their people, with whom there could be no trust.

Right?

Xettar sauntered into the village, allowing ample time for Reman's head to swivel in every direction. He marveled at the creaky water pumps, stables, wells made of crumbling cobblestone and ivy-wrapped lampposts, the small barns and especially the houses; hand-crafted stacks of wood and stone that must have been built several generations back. Childlike interest pulled at Reman when they passed the blacksmith's forge and butcher's stall and he fought the impulse to run up for a closer look. He needed to focus on more important things; like getaway points and the overall size of the town.

So far, Reman theorized that the town couldn't be more than 10 kilometers wide at most. Did the Mech Republic even have residential communities that small? Intermittent sections of wood fencing marked the outmost perimeter, but did not completely enclose the border. Xettar led Reman past a few open fields beside the barns and stables, but they were void of livestock.

Just beyond, jutted up against the trimmed grass, the rows of canvas tents began. And it clicked. If the fields weren't for livestock, then they had to be training grounds, like the ones back at his own ICORE Base…except much, *much* smaller.

"How many troops do you have stationed here?" he called out to Xettar.

"None. Why?" Xettar stopped walking and turned to face Reman. "You think this is a military outpost?"

Reman swung his uninjured arm at the tents.

Xettar chuckled. "Those belong to Fantasarian refugees."

"They what?"

"It's wartime, but that doesn't just mean outright death, does it? A lot of folks are being turned out of house and home. Livelihoods lost, families torn apart…so, by royal decree, a few towns have been expanded into refugee settlements."

Reman's eyebrows lifted in surprise.

"But these locations needed to be safe and secure, so the Royals drafted a few retired knights and soldiers, but also took volunteers. Legren was the first. Of course, they weren't thrilled about that, as he was far from retired and a favorite in the King's personal guard," Xettar continued. "But Legren insisted. And, with him, came a few of us, his likewise capable associates."

He grinned — the same, infectious grin Reman had seen earlier.

"So no," Xettar concluded, "there's no military intel for you to gain here. We're exactly what I said: a harmless community in rural Fantasaria with no ties to the bigger goings-on in the war."

Reman shifted uncomfortably. Was he that predictable? Just because he was a Mech?

Of course, it could have been a lie, just like the rest of it.

"We get attacked now and then," Xettar added, "but that's usually by roving bandits or wayward platoons. You couldn't be further from the action here — and we'd like to keep it that way, if it's all the same to you?"

"Sure, but tell me this." Reman pointed at himself. "Why is that room I slept in empty if you have all these people here? Why do I get special treatment, with the roof and solid walls?"

"Because that's Marcus' house."

"And, what, he's away this week?"

"He died in the explosion that brought you here."

Reman's stomach heaved. He'd slept in the home of a deceased person?

Xettar's head wobbled again. "We could give you a tent, but — shot in the dark — I'm guessing you're not used to rustic living?"

Reman searched for some trace of malice or hidden ill will in Xettar's face, but his eyes only twinkled in good-willed mirth, inviting Reman to join in the humor of the joke, not the morbidity of someone's death.

When Reman didn't answer, Xettar resumed his trek forward.

They squeezed between a more confined cluster of houses, almost city like with the buildings rising up on either side, and when they emerged, Reman nearly knocked someone over. They'd stepped into the village's main square, filled with people, the scent of *Magic,* and less disgusting aromas.

Chatter swarmed around Reman and Xettar from the horde of townsfolk seated, milling about, and encircling an enormous fire pit at the center of the square. Above the flames, two wooden spits held up a large, round cauldron and what looked like a boar, roasting on a rotisserie. Two barrels sat beside the fire. One practically overflowed with apples and people approached in a steady stream to pluck up an apple or reach inside the other barrel for a chunk of bread.

Xettar hung by the edges of the crowd, but shook hands and exchanged greetings with almost everyone. In turn, Reman received dark, narrow-eyed scowls or he was ignored altogether.

"Are all your lunches like this?" he asked Xettar.

"Like what?"

"Communal?" Not even in the ICORE Mess Hall had he seen this sort of camaraderie at a meal.

Xettar shook his head. "We usually just hold community feasts for festivals and celebrations, but Legren established a monthly practice. Today happened to be that day. Lucky you."

Reman surveyed the crowd, searching knights or soldiers, but all he saw were civilians. Most of them looked happy and healthy enough, but distinct groups bore scars, burns, their clothes hung loose and drab off of their bodies and a high percentage were elderly.

Refugees…innocent bystanders, caught under the lash of war…

Xettar must have been telling the truth.

Reman jumped as a hand touched his shoulder. Legren had approached and offered Reman a plate piled with food; a slab of meat, a cheese wedge, and brown bread. While it looked edible and smelled fresh, even appealing, Reman's stomach convulsed with a fresh wave of nausea. He bit down and shook his head.

"Perhaps some broth would be more favorable?" Legren suggested and handed the plate to Xettar.

Reman grimaced and gingerly shifted his shoulder. "How long is this going to last?"

"Another day or two at most," Xettar said through a mouthful of bread.

Reman scowled. On the opposite edge of the square, Sethera perched on an oversized rock, deep in conversation with the same stony-faced messenger from the previous night.

Reman sneered, reassured only by the weight of the pistol tucked in his waistband.

He turned back to Legren. "So. You have an idea?"

Xettar clapped Legren on the shoulder and muttered, "good luck," before walking away.

"You said the Oniyum 'interfered,' to save your life," Reman said, undeterred. "How could it do that if you don't have it?"

"I don't really know," Legren admitted. He traced the scars etched in his face. "It's difficult to explain. More like an instinct, a gut feeling…" He dropped his hand abruptly. "But I believed I was spared for a reason; to form a Resistance."

"Aren't you already doing that? Isn't everyone?"

"Not a Resistance to any specific nation," Legren explained, "but against the Wars themselves. I intend to rally together a group of multiple tribes. Like the Council, but start fresh, with people who haven't been corrupted by power and politics. People who have seen the cost of the wars up close. As many tribes represented as possible by anyone who is willing to listen."

"And you propose to do this…how?" Reman said.

"Once there are enough volunteers, we'll hold an Assembly for everyone to gather under the cover of *Magic*, preventing weapons from being used. Firearms, swords, harmful spells and everything in between…they will not function."

Reman's mouth went dry. Such a thing would be impossible, requiring an unfathomable amount of power. But if Legren had access to that kind of power, he was far more dangerous than Reman had remotely considered. Even with the most honorable intentions, to introduce that kind of force into the world now…if it got into the wrong hands —

Reman forced a deep breath, fighting back panic. *All he's got is words, no proof of the rest.* Such an idea might have just been one man's delusions, which would make Legren that much more insane. Still plenty dangerous, though.

"How many have you got so far?" Reman finally asked, rubbing his coarse chin. He needed a shave.

Legren, however, did not answer, but smiled feebly and arched his brows at Reman.

"You've got to be kidding me."

Legren shrugged. "I must start somewhere."

"I'm a Mech!" Reman howled, incredulous.

"Yes, everyone seems rather focused on that."

"Look, you keep trying to convince me that you didn't steal the Oniyum, which, honestly, I was starting to believe. But if you're telling me that pulling off a spell like that is possible, then it would have been all too easy to take it—"

"We did not create this problem. But I believe we might be able to solve it." Legren shifted his shoulders back and stood more upright. "Say the Oniyum reappeared tomorrow. What would happen?"

"Things would return to normal," Reman said automatically.

"Would they, though? With all the accusations, all the fighting, all the bloodshed and mistrust that's spread across Kabathan, how could we possibly return to life as it was?"

The notion had flitted around the edges of Reman's mind, but he'd never properly asked himself the question outright. *What would happen after they found the Oniyum?* He'd taken it for granted that the wars would just stop, but...

"Too much has changed," Legren said, practically reading Reman's mind. "The Oniyum would serve as a bandage over a wound never to fully heal."

Panic stirred in Reman's stomach again. He suddenly feared a global catastrophe worse than what they had already seen.

"If we returned to the old way of governing," Legren continued, "passing the Oniyum from one tribe to another, letting its Light determine who would possess it until it went dark again...I do not believe it would work. Or, at least, not for long. The whole process would be laced with mistrust and underlying, stifled resentment."

"A ticking bomb," Reman interjected. A chill spread over him, though the air was pleasant and warm. "And you think you can prevent that by talking? Having one conversation with a collection of gullible misfits?"

Legren closed his eyes in a slow blink. "How else does one begin?"

"Go to your High Kingdom or the Council itself. You argued last night that it's not a lost cause."

"I argued that there have always been hostilities. But the Council became misguided and power-hungry even before the wars. Now, they're riddled with hate and fear. The Fantasarian Royalty won't take us seriously; Sethera's parents tried already, years ago. They would not hear it then and they won't hear it now. Reaching out to them is futile."

"Then what about other tribes?"

"Ah, yes, because just convincing you has been *so* easy." Legren steepled his fingers. "It comes down to getting attention from the right people and demonstrating that peace is possible, without the Oniyum. We have become dependent on it and I am tired."

"Of what, the Oniyum?"

"Its absence and aftermath thereof. Of the death and unnecessary misery. Warriors and soldiers on all sides sacrificing their lives when they need not. We are all people of Kabathan, and not once since the Brothers Brisbane discovered the Oniyum have we reconsidered that. Do you disagree?"

Reman heaved a sigh. He did agree, but how was any of this possible? The weight of the planet loomed over him — the magnitude of trying to reach every person in every tribe.

Legren straightened his posture again. "So, the first step, as I see it, is to lay down arms. To stop fighting and resist the wars themselves, by whatever means necessary. I'm open to suggestion and discussion, but this is the plan I have come up with and one idea is better than none."

"Okay, but the problem is," Reman countered, "even if you *do* get some people's attention, the wars aren't just going to stop. If anything, you may attract too much notice." He suppressed a shudder, thinking of the Vampians, Orcs, Gargoyles. And Pirates.

Legren nodded. "Indeed, some tribes thrive on war. But I refuse to let that prevent me from trying. So, what do you say? Will you join us?"

It was as though they were alone in the square, for how focused their conversation had become. Reman looked away from Legren. Much of the square had emptied, but some of the refugees remained by the central fire; clusters of faces that resembled one another. A knot in the back of Reman's neck loosened a little. At least one family was still together, though the children milled about, voices muted, heads down, not looking at one another.

He could see the Elf sisters, Tali and Telena. Sethera and Xettar stood together, talking, but each threw furtive glances in his and Legren's direction.

The knot tightened in his neck again. "And if I refuse?"

"Nothing has changed since last night. You are not a prisoner here and you may leave whenever you like. So long as you do not cause harm to us in return, or actively interfere with the Resistance. Take time to consider. If you take nothing else away from what I've said, remember this: we all share the same ancestors, but the Brothers Brisbane were not the first people of Kabathan. The world existed before the Oniyum. It can exist without it, as well."

"Peacefully?" Reman challenged.

Legren pointed a finger at Reman. "That is precisely the point."

"And if you fail?"

"Then I fail. But I'm willing to take the chance and find out. I'm willing to risk all that I have in order to bring the world back out of the dark. To find a new source of Light. The question is," he said, and tilting his head slightly to the side, "are you?"

FIVE

REMAN

In the two weeks following Legren's "pitch," Reman tried to stay in his appointed room as much as possible while his shoulder healed. The sling came off in three days, and the pain and nausea receded with it. The dank *Magic* smell slowly diminished in his room and it seemed as convenient place to take cover while he remained there. In spite of all the kindness he had been shown from Legren and Xettar, Reman still felt it prudent to gather as much intel as possible.

At first, he refused, point-blank, to wear any of the Fantasarian garb provided. He had his uniform, after all…but that was it. After a few days, when the gray jumpsuit began to turn tan from layers of dust and dirt, he relented. While his washed uniform hung on a line to dry, he dressed like the rest of them; in a brown cotton tunic, drawstring pants, and crude leather boots. He looked ridiculous. The townspeople stared openly while he walked back and forth through the town.

Most of Reman's gear still grappled with interference — *Magical* or otherwise — but he tinkered with his resources until he managed to construct a lock for his door. Half-electrical, it operated by key-code. Working with the equipment provided a welcome distraction from having to consider the Resistance. Reman flopped back and forth between replaying Legren's speech on a loop in his head and doing anything he could *not* to focus on their exchange.

Perhaps inspired by the success of the lock, Legren sent some men out to the snow-covered clearing to drag the abandoned mech pod back to the village. Reman's elation at seeing it was short-lived, however, as the engine refused to boot up. So, he extracted the medical kit, emergency rations, and second jumpsuit from the storage compartments, as well as the box of repair tools, backup sensors, batteries, and spare wiring. Most of it struggled to function, too, but some, miraculously, performed better than ever before.

"Would be possible to set up some kind of security system with these devices?" Legren asked one afternoon, visiting Reman's room, which was turning slowly into a workshop.

Reman laughed. "Doubtful. I'd need a sustainable power source and I can't link up to any satellites, let alone undetected…"

Legren hummed and smiled at the activated gear on Reman's desk.

Reman dropped the pliers he was holding to cross his arms. "It won't work."

"Prove it, then," Legren said, his eyes twinkling.

The symbolism was obvious. *Is the impossible task actually possible?* A dull ache started in Reman's forehead. He squeezed his eyes shut and pinched the bridge of his nose.

Should he succeed, he might be able to send out a secret homing beacon to ICORE, but he wouldn't. He wasn't in any imminent danger and his gathered intel wasn't valuable enough to report. Not yet.

Reman lowered his hand. "Fine, I'll try. But don't hold your breath."

So, Reman spent that afternoon wandering about the village. Legren indicated where they had been the most vulnerable to infiltration and Reman digitized the map into the memory of his scanner. He didn't actually start planting sensors until the sun nudged the horizon. Once finished, he trudged back to his room, making final connections.

Rather than just watch the progress bar crawl forward, he scanned the bookshelves spread around the room. Apparently, this Marcus had been quite the scholar. Dusty tomes were wedged into every available space on the shelves.

Some of the spines looked as though they had been around since Brisbane the Eldest. Several additional volumes spread across every other spare surface.

Reman flipped through one book, which read like a historical account of local Fantasarian lore. A lot of it was gibberish and Reman questioned heavily the truth of what he did understand but, still, it fascinated him. In an abstract, objective sense, anyway.

The scanner beeped on the tabletop. *Low storage space.* Reman shoved the book back onto the shelf. He was also likely to run out of battery life within the next day or so and he'd have to switch to one of the spares.

The device beeped again and a new messaged blinked on the screen: "SYNC COMPLETE." Reman stared at it in disbelief. A miniature map popped up, indicating benign heat signatures scattered about the town square, Assembly Hall, stables and so on. *It worked.*

A knock thudded on the unlocked door.

"Come in," Reman called without looking up.

The door creaked open and shut behind him.

"Going well?" Xettar's voice asked.

Reman's head swung up, having expected Legren. "Just finished the sync."

"Excellent," Xettar said, drifting over to the table. "It would appear that science and sorcery can, in fact, work together."

Reman consulted the screen again. No interference. Sync Complete.

"Who'd have thought?" he said aloud.

"Legren, apparently," Xettar mused.

Reman cast a sidelong glance at the Mage.

"He wishes to speak with you," Xettar added. "But not just about this, I'd wager."

Reman heaved a sigh and tugged his sleeve back down, over his wrist. "Yep. I'll bet he does."

At almost full dark, hardly any civilians were still out and about, and a chill tightened around Reman as he moved through the night air. Those few folks he passed watched him warily, except for two women talking and giggling by a horse paddock. One of them had a splash of red hair, which seemed to glow in the twilight. A man in a long traveling cloak and sturdy, scuffed boots crept towards them, grinning. When he tapped the shoulder of the woman with her back to him, she turned and gasped. Her face split into an astonished smile before she threw her arms around his neck. He picked her up to spin her around and when he set her back down, they kissed and embraced. Reman thought he overheard he heard her say, "welcome home!"

Reman stopped walking, entranced by the scene. He'd witnessed these kinds of moments dozens of times between soldiers and their spouses back home. To actually see it here, before him, was surprisingly unnerving. The man looked past his wife and spotted Reman. All joy drained from his face, replaced by disgust. When the woman saw Reman in turn, she didn't glower. She backed away and pulled on the man's arm as he stepped in Reman's direction. Reman could have claimed he meant no harm, but it probably *had* looked suspicious; his standing there, watching them. How would he react in a reversed situation?

A Fantasarian warrior roaming around a Mech neighborhood.

In spite of his present circumstance, the notion made Reman's skin crawl. He raised his hands in mock surrender and kept walking.

As he reached the stone stairway leading to Legren's study, a shadow fell across his path. Sethera descended the stairs above him, her gaze fixed over his shoulder. Reman hesitated. They were hardly friends, but he opened his mouth to offer some sort of greeting. Before he could make a sound, she shoved past him, knocking his arm out of her way. He spread his hands after her, but she didn't turn around. She stalked past the nearest building, headed towards the edge of the village. Why, he couldn't begin to guess.

He grimaced and resumed his ascent.

As Reman approached Legren's study, he heard rustling papers and muffled voices from within. He knocked on the wooden frame, reached for the black hanging cloth in the doorway, and stepped into the room.

Dozens of candles flickered in earthenware jars. Small trinkets of gargoyles, thick rugs, and hand-woven tapestries draped everywhere. Seated at the square table in the center of the room, Legren sifted through sheets of paper, feather quills, and unfamiliar-looking tools. His scarred eye was covered by his green and gold bandanna. Beside him sat Brock, an Elf that Reman had not yet officially met, who pored over a large map.

They both looked up. Brock peered silently at Reman while Legren gave him a slight nod.

"Reman." Legren turned back to Brock. "It's been a long day; let's pick this up tomorrow."

So much for that introduction.

Reman crossed the room to lean against the wall as Brock stood and made for the door. Like Sethera, he didn't so much as glance in Reman's direction as he passed and disappeared through the drape.

Legren, still seated, picked up the map Brock had been holding.

"You're keeping busy," Reman observed.

"Trying. Slow down for a moment and it could all fall apart," Legren said without looking up. "What about you? How are your efforts developing?"

"It's all set. If anyone tries to intrude, I'll know." Reman braced himself for Legren's amused, upward glance…but it didn't come. He just nodded and rifled through other sheets around the map.

Unsure what else to do, Reman pushed away from the wall. "If that's everything, then—"

"Have you made a decision yet?"

Reman closed his eyes and sighed. When he didn't answer, Legren's head finally swung up. "Reman?"

"I'm still considering your offer."

The frown lines deepened in Legren's face, but he didn't speak. A spark of annoyance ignited inside Reman. Though no one had attacked him outright, no matter how humanely he might be treated, this was still enemy territory. He had a large target painted on his back they were choosing to ignore. Besides, the Resistance could very well be a complex psychological trap, designed to manipulate Reman. *But…*

Reman rubbed his eyes. "You're asking me to turn against everything I know. I mean, I agree with your ideals—"

"So you've said," Legren interrupted, "and I understand. But while I dislike having to rush you, our situation only worsens as you consider—"

"Go on without me then. I don't have an answer for you yet."

"We can't proceed any further unless you join us," Legren countered.

"Why not? You just need someone to join you, right? Find someone else, someone closer to home, someone less…" He searched for the word, then shot Legren a meaningful look. "Foreign."

"That is the whole point," Legren insisted. "To start strong; a Mech joining this cause alongside Fantasarians would prove that *anything* is possible."

Reman made a face. It was a strong enough theory, sure, but sounded a bit fanciful, even for Legren. He opened his mouth to ask, *but why me?* just as he posed to Sterling, two weeks ago, but Legren raced on.

"Besides, we haven't the time. Vampians have invaded the Viking Domain and Jallorian Knights are on the move."

"The Jallorian Knights?" Reman repeated.

"The Council's peacekeepers."

"I know who they are," Reman snapped, "but what do you mean, 'on the move'? They're tribe-neutral. Don't get involved with stuff like this, unless… is there some new development?"

"Hostilities have intensified — as you predicted. Disorder has permeated the Council to the point of more injuries and even more deaths, so the Knights have had no choice but to step in."

Reman snorted. "Why are council members dying at all, Legren? I said it before, and I'm saying it again: the Council is a lost cause."

"What do you propose then? Simply resign ourselves to an unending future of violence and destruction?"

"We protect our own and defend the people and the land that we can," Reman said, parroting ICORE's rhetoric. He thought saying the familiar words would be comforting — safe, even — but they tasted strange and insufficient.

Legren blinked and stared at Reman, taken aback.

"What?" Reman snapped.

"You just…sounded exactly like Sethera."

Reman's laugh caught in his throat and choked into a cough. "How ironic."

"As I said, take none of her bitterness personally," Legren said. "You have no idea what she's been through."

"No, I don't," Reman said sharply, "and I'm sorry, but so what? She doesn't know anything about me, either, so—"

Legren stood up. "I need your answer, Reman. Will you join us or not?"

The swift and not-so-subtle redirect made Reman wonder if there was some dark history between them.

Whatever. He didn't care.

The scanner on his wrist buzzed, but he ignored it. "You can't expect me to change like this at such short notice."

"Reman, try to understand. Lives are at stake."

"Oh, like I've forgotten that?"

"We have the chance to make a change. To start a real revolution."

"It's going to take a lot more than just me to get that started."

Legren must have heard it, the slight trace of wistfulness in Reman's tone, because he leaned forward and said, in an entirely different manner: "It starts with one. It starts with you. A single outsider. That is the first, crucial step—"

The device buzzed on Reman's wrist again, this time accompanied by a screeching alarm. He swung up his arm to check the device.

"What is it?"

"You have silent intruders." Reman crossed the room, threw aside the drape in the doorway and bounded outside. He heard Legren following behind him, but didn't wait. He crossed the building's threshold, looking frantically around. The night was loud with the singing of crickets and cicadas. The grounds were nearly deserted except for small figures in the distance; the Night Watch, meandering towards their posts along the perimeter.

Reman checked the scanner and its inferred projection just as Legren came up beside him.

"You should raise the alarm," Reman said, but Legren shook his head, adjusting his grip on his broadsword and stepping past Reman.

"Are you insane?" Reman grabbed Legren's elbow.

"We don't know what we're up against," Legren hissed over his shoulder.

"Two at least, who got past your guards and—"

"And, what? I should cause a potentially unnecessary panic? Or provide our assailants with open, obvious targets?" Legren shook his elbow loose. "Where are they?"

"North end of camp. Two of them. In the field by the barn, but—"

Legren didn't wait for the rest. He lurched forward, cloak fluttering and disappeared into the dark. Reman, meanwhile, ran to his room. He knelt by the bed, pulled back the mattress and withdrew his rifle. He powered it up, adjusted the settings to stun, and charged back out the door.

The signal was strongest in the field. Eyes adjusting to the darkness, Reman spotted Legren, crouched about twelve feet from the barn, waiting. According to Reman's scanner, the figures had moved. He signaled to both sides of barn. Together, he and Legren slinked towards it from opposite directions, two shifting shadows in the dusk. The signal grew stronger and, slowly, Legren disappeared from view.

Reman continued forward, confident in their advantage, when something smashed against his back.

Pitched forward, his rifle spun out of his grasp into the sea of dark grass. Reman rolled and sprung up onto his feet, trying to get his bearings. A woman dressed in all-black silk garb and sashes of blue wrapped around her waist cartwheeled towards him, but he scurried backwards, away from her and the glowing lights from his fallen gun. Undeterred, she leapt forward still, closed the distance and landed in front of him. She lodged fists and kicks at him, but he dodged them. He even threw a few good punches of his own before she cartwheeled back again and froze in a defensive position. Her wrists, encircled with ornate silver chains, glittered discernibly, even in the half-light. She raised her arms again, this time in wide, graceful circles. The tiny symbols engraved in the chains began to glow bright orange. And so did her irises.

Nenjin, he realized as flames burst from her fists. *Perfect.*

SIX

LEGREN

Beyond the barn's thick walls, startled voices bubbled up in the streets. Cries of combat rang out, followed by the clash of metal and bodies falling and the telltale *woosh!* of flames surging to life. Each strike of the main gate's heavy iron bell landed like a lash across Legren's neck. Inside the barn, panic and relief thundered through him in equal measure. He had a responsibility to defend this township. His warriors were skilled, but few, and the townsfolk and refugees would be helpless. *And these invaders aren't just passing brigands.* A dormant impulse stirred, compelling Legren to unleash the prowess of his days as *The King's Favorite* in the Royal Guard.

And yet, something held him back. Newer, keener intuition pulled him deeper in the barn. Sword drawn, Legren crossed the opposite threshold and waded into the tall grass of the meadow beyond. He made no sound, but without his armor, every inch of exposed flesh tingled.

A white blur flickered at the edge of the field.

Legren turned just as a man emerged from the shadows, bedecked in a gleaming white kimono and hakama. His hand clutched the handle of a katana hanging from his waist.

Dorojin.

An elite Nenjin assassin with whom Legren had crossed swords once before. Forced to a draw, neither had expected to be so evenly matched. Legren was a different man now, but his pride still bristled at the memory of that last match.

He stalked in Legren's direction, closing fast.

What's brought him here, though? Legren's relocation from the High Kingdom to this village was far from common knowledge. Had the Nenjin, like the Mechs, gotten word of the missile explosion? Did they know of Legren's survival?

Dorojin's gaze swept over Legren's left eye. The scar prompted the familiar puzzled stare, then the furrowed brow and barest trace of revulsion.

Over Dorojin's shoulder, a flash of orange lit up the adjacent field. A Nenjin woman hurled flaming streaks of energy at Reman. He ducked and punched back, but she was clearly winning.

Moonlight glinted off the katana as Dorojin dragged it free of the scabbard. Resigned, Legren swung up his blade and pelted forward. Steel met steel with a fierce *clang* that ricocheted through the field. They lunged and parried and though their skills still matched, the thicker, Fantasarian broadsword held advantage. In one swing, the katana soared out of Dorojin's grasp and sank into the grass. Legren hurled the broadsword down, but Dorojin flung up his scabbard. The impact forced Dorojin to his knees.

"I know what you are looking for. It is not here," Legren said and stepped back.

Dorojin hesitated before he lowered his scabbard. He smirked and stood to retrieve his fallen weapon. "You do not know much about the Oniyum, do you?" His voice was every bit as arrogant and patronizing as Legren remembered.

"We don't have the Oniyum. We never had it," Legren insisted.

"Are you sure?" Dorojin taunted. He stood up and retrieved his fallen weapon. "What about part of it?"

A wave of energy curled the air around him. *Magic* was at work, but no kind Legren had ever witnessed in person. Another force of energy and light contracted around Dorojin's hands and projected outward. Legren sailed backwards, groaning as he hit the ground.

"We have a Viking prisoner. Bosa."

Legren's head flew up.

"We *made* him talk," Dorojin sneered.

"You lie!" Legren scrambled up and lunged.

Dorojin disarmed Legren this time, but, far from satisfied with such a swift ending, he tossed the broadsword back at Legren's feet. It was not a threat, but an invitation, one Legren could not resist. He scooped up the sword, but held it at his side, point down.

"The Vikings know where the Oniyum is?"

Dorojin tilted his head again. His eyes danced, momentarily, back to Legren's scar. "Part of it."

He sprang forward. Legren lurched backwards, but not fast enough as paralyzing pain bit deep into his stomach.

The ground swayed under his feet. He couldn't see Dorojin anymore. His vision swam, blurring everything except the gold handle of Dorojin's katana protruding from between his ribs.

When the missile detonated that day in the clearing, acute awareness broke over him as explosions had burst on all aides. He'd slipped into oblivion only to be yanked back to consciousness by piercing cold at the base of the mountain. His body had been in motion, wavering forward through a blizzard. He'd collapsed, snow biting hard under his palms and knees. His limbs shook from cold and shock, but he'd known without the slightest doubt that he would survive. He was *meant* to survive.

Now, as he stared down at the sword handle, brutal pain in his core gave way to numbness. His focus shifted to the stems of grass far below as moisture seeped through his shirt and vest. Where was that certainty of survival this time?

Blackness crept into the edges of his vision. Distant voices called out to him, but he couldn't make out the words.

The ground tilted. The barn swam up sideways before him and something struck, hard, on the side of the face. Laying on his side, he could not move, even as he felt the katana withdraw from his body. Blood streamed down his front, along with his life force.

Where is the Oniyum now?

Just as in the clearing, in his last few, aching seconds, he felt not fear or anger, but regret. They would all die like this, destroying each other, rather than consider another way. He'd had so much time. Influence too, and he'd squandered both. Given a second chance, he had tried, made an attempt to fight the wars, leading him here, on the ground in a helpless heap. It had been a gamble, but he just couldn't walk away from it any more. He never would have taken up the charge if not for his walking out of the demolished clearing, from what should have been certain death. He'd survived only long enough to eventually be stabbed by an old enemy, but he had made use of that extra time, and only for that, did he succumb to the void in peace.

SEVEN

REMAN

Reman cursed ICORE again as another of the Nenjin woman's blows landed against the side of his face. The training program for hand-to-hand was useless and Reman's heart hammered against his chest. He'd fought back, but her reflexes were lightning fast. In spite of the blood rushing in his ears, he could hear his own breathing, heavy and fast, while she didn't look the least bit tired.

Without his gun, his time and stamina were running out. She'd knock him down, and then what?

So, when she flipped backwards, out of reach, presumably to lodge another round of *Magical* flame at him, he frantically searched the ground for his rifle. The grass grew high here, too, hiding everything the twilight shadows didn't. The reeds in one area to his right bent in an oblong shape. Close enough. He dove for that dark spot and his hands closed around familiar grips and levers. He popped back up, thrusting the gun towards the woman — but she wasn't looking at him. She crouched and held up her arms, pointed out towards him in a defensive position, but her head was turned to the side. Her eyes widened and her mouth fell slightly open. Reman gripped the gun tighter, then followed her gaze.

In the adjacent field, a male Nenjin towered over a figure, lying motionless in the grass. *Legren.* A dark stain spread rapidly across his tunic while the Nenjin held a curved silver blade, smeared with blood.

Reman could only stare, rooted to the spot.

Wait, no, that can't —

"You're not a Fantasarian," the woman's voice called. Reman's attention snapped away from the field, back to the threat across from him. The woman's hands still hovered, poised in midair, but no flame encircled them. Yet.

"And?" Reman said.

Her head tilted to the side. "What is a Mech doing fighting alongside a Fantasarian?"

"*Quit the chatter* and tell me why you've come here!" Reman demanded.

Her narrow-eyed scowl morphed into a crooked, devious smile that reached her eyes. They flashed, catching some nearby light.

"You know why we came," she said, her voice like velvet. "It's here in this camp."

Reman shook his head. "No, it isn't. The Oniyum—"

An arm suddenly encircled his throat and pulled him backwards, his face forced skyward. Reman fought back, his lungs already desperate for air. He raised his arm, prepared to fire, when his weapon was kicked from his grasp — the woman had raced forward. Before she could strike again, he slipped out of the choke-hold, just in time to see her fist swipe the air where his head had just been. He hurled punches and kicks at both his assailants, barely even seeing the one who'd tried to choke him, and they both toppled. Rather than scramble after his rifle, Reman ran, charging in to the denser woods beyond the village's perimeter.

Something bright and white-hot hurtled past his shoulder.

The woman was sending a volley of fire blasts after him. He dodged as best he could, sprinting further into the woods, but a flame caught his leg. He yelled and fell sideways, crawling behind a tree for cover.

She continued to throw fire at him in rapid, alternating spurts. Heat surged on all sides as blasts seared the branches above him. Bark singed and sprayed over his head. Ash flew into his eyes, stinging fiercely, though it was nothing to the pain spreading through his right leg. He knew the burn was severe and the only reason it wasn't more agonizing was due to the adrenaline surging through him.

Cowering against the tree's massive roots, Reman expected to strain against more smoke, but this was enchanted fire. Nenjin *Magic*, even more unpredictable than the regular stuff, though it didn't leave behind any sort of smell, foul or otherwise — save the sharp, earthy odor of singed wood.

Another volley of flames pounded the tree and Reman sank lower to the ground. With the force of the blasts, he wasn't sure how long he'd be protected there.

And then, without any explanation, it stopped.

The space around Reman went temporarily black with contrast from the light of the fire from only heartbeats before, surrounding him from both sides. He blinked, several times, forcing his eyes to adjust, trying to listen as the pounding in his ears subsided. Half-expecting the attack to come again, he waited, straining to hear the sound of her feet crunching towards him through the underbrush. Nothing; only a distant clattering and a few voices crying out.

Leaning around the side of the tree trunk, Reman got a clear view of the field. She stood, motionless, in the center, staring at him, while blurred figures of more Nenjin warriors sprinted past her. She held Reman's eye contact, weighing him. He didn't feel a swell of anger, but rather confusion and curiosity and even from the distance, he could tell that she regarded him in the same way. They both seemed to be thinking: why are you here?

She'd asked him outright and he might have considered mentioning the Resistance, if not for the shock of Legren's fall. Plus, despite Legren's repeated assurances that he was free to go, some part of him still felt paradoxically trapped and unwelcome there, just by his very identity.

But this attack didn't make tactical sense. There were no persons of importance here, no treasury to loot. If Legren was their target, why storm the place? Or were they on a mission to murder innocents?

The woman was too far away for her to hear him if he spoke. With all the ash in his throat, he doubted he had the capability to properly yell anyway, and, apparently, he didn't need to. She shifted her weight, turned, and ran back towards the town.

Further bewildered and slightly dizzy, Reman thought longingly of his commanding officers back home; a source of orders. All he had here was his weapon, the only trace of home, but where was it now?

Reman twisted back around against the flat, cool side of the tree and tugged his right pants leg to get a proper look at his injury. The fabric fell apart, singed, almost to the knee, smoking a little. The burn covered most of his calf, blistering, but not as bad as he'd feared. Walking would be difficult for sure. Hopefully he wouldn't need to fight any more tonight. Resigned, Reman stood, pushing against the tree for support and limped forward.

In the midst of the commotion, it dawned on him that his flight had carried him well beyond the village grounds. This solitude probably wouldn't last long, though. Someone would inevitably approach and ask him to return or flat-out usher him back.

But nothing happened. No Elves burst from hiding places in the underbrush. No daggers flew out at him.

He was out. He was free.

He imagined himself crossing back into ICORE Headquarters, rejoining his squad, reunited with comrades he hadn't seen in what seemed like months. He would regale them with the tale of all he had seen and done. Even Jenda would be impressed —

Someone screamed, echoing back and forth among the trees. Reman spun around. More sounds followed, which he somehow recognized, but had never experienced raw; a blend of disjointed babble and scattered crashing, peppered with another, occasional, scream. The aftermath of battle.

Reman turned his back on it and continued forward, focusing on how to best use his damaged leg, but he was far from distracted. The faraway racket still seeped into in his ears and he was unable to stop his mind from sketching up a mournful scene: Nenjin fleeing in blurred whisks of shadow, while townspeople tended to those who'd dared to fight back, learning, one at a time, that their leader lay in the field. Some were probably crowded around Legren's corpse in shock, horror, and shed tears.

So much for the Resistance.

Reman halted. Only then did he cease to notice the distant clamor. The ideas Legren had been trying so desperately to sell — to Reman, to Sethera, to anyone who would listen — they were dying with him. The Resistance itself and any variation thereof, would never happen. The wars would go on just as they had, without hope or end. The Nenjin woman's voice circled back to him.

What's a Mech doing fighting alongside a Fantasarian? She'd said it almost like an accusation, like the whole thing had to be a setup, a trap. It was preposterous. Hadn't Reman said almost the exact same thing to Legren only hours earlier? And now, who would contradict him?

It was more than unfair. It was wrong. Reman had spoken in earnest when he'd agreed that the wars would never end if things kept going as they were, but what could Reman's participation possibly accomplish in the course of such an immense undertaking?

It starts with one.

The shouts and wails persisted from the camp. There was no accent to them, no defining tribe or other. They were just voices. People.

Before he realized he'd made a decision, Reman had already turned, limping back the way he came.

Mayhem reigned. As Reman moved through the field towards the village, he could see slashed tents and buildings on fire, churning out thick layers of smoke. Men and women Reman didn't recognize vanished in and out of the dark, dashing to and fro. Most of their faces were damp with sweat, spattered with ash and some were even bleeding. They extinguished flames, ushered confused townsfolk towards the center of the village, wrangled escaped livestock, and helped fallen citizens to their feet. They carried the injured; those who could not walk. Somewhere a child was crying.

The meadow where Reman last saw Legren was crowded, but Legren's body had been taken away. A dark circle stained the flattened grass and the townsfolk were giving it a wide berth. Most of them didn't even notice Reman but those that did said nothing. Their startled, scared faces only gazed up at him in the dark. Unlike his first walk through with Xettar, he saw no open-faced hate, only dismay and helplessness, somehow looking the way he felt.

Reman swayed on the spot, coughing. He'd seen the aftermath of battle plenty of times, both at home and abroad, but always from the air. He'd volunteered in military hospitals and visited friends in emergency recovery wards, but he had never seen battle up close. He'd attended memorial services for fallen soldiers and even witnessed ships getting shot down, but only from behind his windshield. Being here, surrounded by the victims, however, was an entirely different experience. He caught glimpses of some of the wounds; they mirrored the inflictions he'd seen in those hospital wings, on soldiers struggling through physical therapy.

But these were not soldiers. These were innocent civilians.

In the back of Reman's mind echoed the words of the ICORE advert.

Protect, search and defend. The people, the land, the Oniyum. Whatever the cost.

Is this what they meant? Did ICORE issue acts of this nature on innocent lives? It was wartime, but…how was this protection? Defense?

A streak of green caught Reman's attention. Xettar ran, his cloak flying, towards a woman sprawled, motionless, on the ground. Reman watched the Mage check her pulse, perform CPR, then wave his hands over top of her, casting spells, but her eyes remained open, unblinking. Xettar bowed his head, then moved a hand to her face to gently close her eyes.

A swell of nausea hit Reman and he staggered. Xettar looked up and they stared at each other, sharing a sort of unprecedented solidarity. It didn't last long. Someone crouched next to Xettar and the two of them lifted the woman up to carry her away into the dark.

Off to his right, a woman tried to help a man to his feet. The side of his tunic was slashed, displaying a burn not unlike the one that Reman had acquired. Without thinking, Reman changed direction and reached for the man's other arm, the one flailing about, almost of its own volition. When he turned and realized it was Reman helping him, he recoiled. Then pain rippled across his face and he nodded, accepting the help and the three of them wobbled forward. Reman didn't know their destination, but a minute later, another woman ran up to them, not quite smiling but still looking overwhelmingly relieved. She took the man's arm from Reman and bowed her head in thanks. They teetered away, leaving him alone again. It was just as well; the added weight tormented his leg. He stood there for a few minutes, catching his breath and resting his leg, before winding his way through the houses and tents to the Assembly Hall.

Reaching the massive doors, Reman stepped inside without hesitating, unsure what to expect on the other side, or who to see, or how to explain his actions.

Telena looked up at him first. Her head tilted to the side, quizzically, before she turned away again, back to the person slumped in front of her, seated on one of the long benches against the wall.

Legren, very much alive, held still while Telena finished wrapping a heavy bandage around his torso. His clothes should have been slashed and drenched with blood, but the fabric was new without the slightest stain.

"L—Legren?" Reman said.

Legren's head swiveled towards the doorway, wearing a puzzled frown of his own. "Reman?"

The bandanna had been re-tied around Legren's face, covering his left eye, but Reman could see blue light leaking out from underneath it.

"I—didn't you—?" Legren stammered.

"Changed my mind," Reman grunted and rushed on. "Didn't *you*…?" he gestured to the bandages.

Legren looked down and shrugged.

"Your guess is as good as mine this time," he said, sounding tired and even the slightest bit frustrated. "But…you came back. Should I take this to mean you've made a decision?"

Reman stayed silent. Recalling his flight to the woods and the opportunity of escape, he felt a spasm of regret. Yes, he had decided to return at the idea of Legren's death, but Legren's life had been spared — again. Reman wasn't needed after all and he opened his mouth to say this when the Nenjin's question rang through his head again.

What is a Mech doing fighting alongside a Fantasarian?

Why had he taken up arms with Legren? He hadn't hesitated for a moment. These people weren't his responsibility and he'd never considered himself a humanitarian before. He could have just told Legren that there were intruders and watched the Fantasarian leave the room to go deal with it. It wasn't his problem. Before this night, Reman had no reason to believe that they could not effortlessly fend off any foe. Yet Reman had been the first one out the door, weapon at the ready.

It starts with one.

In the opposite corner of the room, Telena set down her bandage supplies. She and Legren waited, watching Reman, full of anticipation.

"Yes," Reman said at last. "I have."

Telena tended Reman's leg with the same ease as she had done with his shoulder. No runes appeared on his bandage this time, but the pain reduced considerably once she was done. It still ached, of course, but, he felt a vaguely familiar sensation of lethargy. When he asked Telena if this was normal, she nodded.

"The fire was *qì*," she said shortly. "And you're a Mech."

"So it's like Elven steel?"

"Precisely."

She stepped away, continuing her work just as Sethera burst into the Hall. Hair flying behind her, she made a b-line for Legren, who now sat comfortably on the far side of the room. She strode up to him, eyes ablaze, not so much as glancing at Reman. Legren just watched her approach, all composure.

"Nenjin break in," she seethed, "there's a fight, you nearly die — again — the Mech runs off, the same Nenjin vanish into thin air and nobody tells me?"

Legren smiled, but it was half-hearted. Tired.

"Hardly meant to leave you out," he said. "Next time, you'll have your pick of the goons."

"You nearly got killed and no one told me until after it was all over," she said, hunching her shoulders and speaking with an unexpected level of tenderness. "What happened to you, anyway?" she added, even more quietly.

"It's...complicated. We're waiting for—"

"Never mind. I don't care." She straightened and shook her head, adopting her matter-of-fact tone again. "Is the Mech gone?"

Legren rubbed his chin, but didn't answer. When he finally did open his mouth to speak, Sethera held up her hand.

"I won't gloat," she said, "but I am relieved that he left. He's not our problem anymore, no longer distracting you, me, and everyone else, and we can *finally*—"

Reman cleared his throat.

She whirled around and found him sitting along the far wall, just out of the firelight. He felt an odd mix of satisfaction and offense as the amusement and triumph drained from her face, replaced with outright horror. Reman could just barely make out Telena in the corner of his eye, looking back and forth between the two of them.

Sethera's jaw slid shut into a rock-solid line as she slowly faced Legren again.

"Sorry," Legren said, almost offhand. His posture straightened a little.

"*Explain,*" she hissed.

"I've joined the cause," Reman said, behind her. "Officially."

"You cannot be serious." Her voice grew quiet again, but lacked her earlier warmth.

"He came back, Sethera." Legren extended a hand out — a calming gesture. "He thought I was dead, saw a chance to get away, but chose to come back."

"And you still trust him?"

"Why shouldn't I?"

"His transmitters all work now. He probably contacted his Mech friends with inside information about us while he was out there—"

"Hey!" Reman stood, weakly, but upright. "I'm not interested in betraying your people, all right?"

She pivoted towards him, but slowly, her eyes narrowed. She wanted a fight.

"You really think I'm capable of subterfuge like that?" Reman pressed on. "Of doing something that underhanded?"

"I wouldn't put anything past a Mech."

"I'm not a good enough liar to pull that off, Sethera—"

"Oh, okay then," she said with false sweetness. "You're right. Bygones."

The patronizing smile she gave him chased away the last bit of his sluggishness, filling him with the old resentment he thought he'd grown past. Evidently not. "I'm taking a huge risk in being here, agreeing to do this, but you can't get off your high horse even for a second to acknowledge that. You'd probably still rather just kill me and be done with it."

Her smile wavered into a sneer. "At last, he gets it."

He lunged forward, impulsive and aggressive — unsure what he was going to say next — when she whipped out her knife; silver suddenly pointed at his face.

Legren jumped up and slid between them. "Enough!"

Sethera lowered the blade, refusing to meet his disappointed glare.

"There is a long way to go," he said, "but don't let it begin like this. Not like this."

"Should we perhaps come back later?"

They all turned. Xettar and Tali stood just inside the doorway.

"No, come in," Legren said, gesturing for the group to come further in. Reman lowered himself back into his previous seat while Sethera sheathed her knife and stepped away, but Legren caught her shoulder. Gently. They exchanged a few words, but Reman could not make them out, in spite of their standing so close. He watched her posture relax and her attention shifted back to Reman over Legren's shoulder. Her eyes drooped and she nodded, all complacency. Legren stepped away and once his back was turned, her expression became even more roguish as she sat down next to Xettar. She continued to watch Reman, absently toying with the green pendant hanging from her neck.

"Where is Brock?" Legren asked Tali.

"Boundary check. Though he mentioned wanting to know why you didn't sound the damn alarm at the start of this catastrophe. His words, not mine," she clarified.

"I didn't wish to cause panic," Legren said.

"We should consider it fortunate that more Nenjin didn't show up at the start," Telena observed. "You might both have been killed."

"Well...one of you," Tali finished.

There was a very awkward pause.

"We were lucky," Legren concurred, side-stepping his survival altogether. "But with Reman here, his Mech tech prohibited them from taking us completely by surprise."

"They must have been studying our practices," Xettar mused. "They got past our wards and security points effortlessly. I'll be investigating how, exactly, they did it. In the meantime, I've applied new and different spells as a precaution."

"So, are we at risk right now?" Sethera asked.

Xettar shook his head. "Just want to be thorough."

"As we all should be because we can start planning the Assembly," Legren said.

Tali and Telena exchanged raised eyebrows while Xettar smiled and Sethera kept her face blank.

"You've decided to join us?" Xettar said to Reman. Reman nodded, slowly but surely. The delight in Xettar's face was a welcome contrast to Sethera's dismay.

"You do realize it's not that simple, don't you?" Xettar added to Legren.

"There's a tremendous amount of work ahead, yes, but we can finally get started with it. How soon can you get the *Magical* side of things up and running?"

"Quickly enough, but even without all the additional complications of this little Nenjin-invasion, it won't be much by myself. I need to run a few tests and, if it's all right, I think I might invite a friend of mine here to lend a hand with some of it."

"Tilesse?" Legren said. Xettar nodded. "She's more than welcome. Now, we should discuss the preliminary necessities…"

They launched into a lengthly list of action items. Reman tried to pay attention as best he could, to follow the plans of reaching out to other tribes, the details regarding *Magic*, and combining more of his own Mech tools with their security…but his concentration slipped. Between the stinging in his leg and all of the night's images fluttering around in his head.

Most distracting of all, though, was the glare Sethera gave him from across the room.

EIGHT

LEGREN

Legren was euphoric. Downright giddy. In fact, he found it difficult to focus or even remain visibly calm. The wound in his chest griped each time he so much as twitched, making the stitches shift uncomfortably, but already like the subdued groans of long-standing, mostly-healed scrapes. Somewhere in his mind, he marveled at the absurdity of it all, but no amount of wonder or pain would distract him from the incomprehensible joy welling up inside him. He was just grateful that the bleeding — and the glowing — had ceased.

It hadn't taken much to get the conversation rolling. Even Sethera was contributing and Reman spoke nearly as much as Legren was, offering information, perspective and suggestions that Legren never would have anticipated.

By the time Brock appeared in the doorway, they were halfway through concocting a plan.

"It won't work," Reman was saying. "Start with someone else, somewhere else—"

"We already are," Xettar replied, with significantly more patience. "A lot is going on concurrently."

"And it's not enough, whatever you're doing?"

Legren held up his hand at that point to halt the debate and acknowledge Brock.

"All clear," the Elf announced. He looked at Telena. "Three dead. Few more injured."

She turned to Legren, who nodded. Telena stood and slipped past Brock, out of the room. Brock, meanwhile, did a slight double take at the sight of Reman, sitting amiably among the rest.

"They've been studying our practices," Legren said. "They got past our wards and security points effortlessly, but with Reman here, his tech prohibited them from taking us completely by surprise."

"And the wards are back up?" Brock asked Xettar.

"To the best of my ability," the Mage replied.

"There's rebuilding that will need to be done from the fire damage, but it's not as bad as it could have been. All the structures are still standing in some part or other. Shoddy work, really," Brock noted offhand, more to himself than to the group.

"Good news indeed. Join us, though." Legren gestured to Telena's empty seat. "We're discussing the Assembly."

"And you want my input?" Brock asked. "Why?"

"Just sit down," Xettar said, "we need another opinion."

"Do we, though?" Sethera muttered.

"Yes. A clear, level-headed perspective. Please, Brock."

Brock sat, looking more curious than anything else. "I take it someone's put forth an idea?"

"The same idea — recruitment — but with a new twist," Xettar said.

"Trying to reach Reman's associates," Legren said.

"It won't work," Reman reiterated.

"Why are you so sure—" Xettar started.

"Because Jenda doesn't think like that," Reman hissed.

"Jenda?" Brock repeated.

"My sister," Reman said dismissively. "She'll report it to ICORE. Immediately. For all I know, they could just hit me over the head and drag me away without letting me get so much as a word in."

"How many Mechs are we talking about?" Brock interjected.

"Four, counting him," Sethera answered. "And all ICORE soldiers."

Reman exhaled heavily. "The policy for search parties is three to four, depending on how many officers that can be spared. I'm not a significant loss to the Corps and I'm not from an important family, so there probably isn't a lot of effort being put into a search for me. My money's on a team of three. Two of my close friends and...probably my sister," Reman finished, with an uncertain, borderline bitter emphasis on the 'probably.'

"On bad terms, are you?" Xettar asked.

"No, it's just..." He stopped again, reconsidered his words and sat up straight before he continued. "I've been gone past the time allotted for a search of a second-class pilot — especially one who went MIA in Fantasaria. I've likely been declared dead."

"Oh, well, we could validate that, if you like," Sethera offered pleasantly.

"Oh, and prove them right?" Reman retorted, but calmly. Brock smirked, clearly impressed with the kid's grit. Sethera shrugged.

"Friends and family will be predisposed to listen to you," Xettar said, looking back to the rest of the group and diffusing the tension yet again. "Certainly more than strangers who wear your same uniform. If you seek them out and then bring them here, they will be naturally inclined to..."

Reman was shaking his head again.

"They'll think I've been brainwashed. The second they know this location, they'll report back to ICORE and try to bomb this place."

"Bomb it?" Xettar repeated. "A civilian settlement?"

"Or, as an alternative," Brock suggested, "you could just initially leave out the exact coordinates of our village."

"Well...they'd report it no matter what specific intel they get. And then..." Reman looked at Legren. "Then they'd just follow their orders."

After a very palpable pause, Sethera cleared her throat. "And what if you were still inside with the rest of us?"

Everyone turned to her, all of them uncertain if they'd heard her right.

"Send someone else to get them," Brock interpreted. "Draw them in."

She nodded slowly, clearly glad someone had kept up with her.

"Are you volunteering?" Legren asked, smiling.

"No," she said pointedly. "But if those are my *orders*" — she looked at Reman — "I will follow them."

"You'd have to be really convincing," Reman said.

"I could help with that," Xettar said. "Some kind of persuasion charm or other."

"Or physical evidence," Tali suggested. "Do you have any sort of keepsake your sister would recognize?"

He glanced down at his wrist and held it up, indicating the black scanning device he had strapped around it.

"Don't you all wear those?" Sethera asked.

"Yes, but each one has a serial number."

"Good to know," she muttered.

He rolled his eyes. "They'd just think you'd taken it off my corpse after killing me."

"Quite the savages, aren't we?" Brock noted sarcastically to Xettar, who nodded with a bit of an eye-roll of his own.

"Since when do Fantasarians take trophies from our kills?" Tali asked, sounding thoroughly disgusted by the idea.

Reman shrugged. "That's what they'll think."

"So, use it," Sethera said. "Offer yourself as bait."

Reman didn't respond for several long seconds, until, begrudgingly, he nodded.

"We have a plan then," Legren said with a swift look around at them all. As if on cue, a rooster crowed in the distance.

"Which we can finalize in a few hours," Xettar decided and stood up. Legren nodded and also stood. Tiredness seemed to finally settle in over all of them. They all made their way towards the door, but Legren caught Brock while everyone else filed out of the room.

"Contrary to our earlier conversation, the Vikings are not quite as ahead of themselves as it would seem."

"Meaning?" Brock asked.

"They lost to the Nenjin after all. At least, they managed to take prisoners."

"Bosa?"

Legren couldn't bring himself to say it aloud. He nodded.

"How do you know?"

"In my duel, the rōnin said…"

"It doesn't matter." Brock waved a hand. "Even if he was telling the truth, there was something else going on with that invasion. He was a diversion. All of it was. I'm convinced. Nenjin never do anything so arbitrary or chaotic."

"Maybe not," Legren conceded, "but I think it would do well for you to go north."

There was a slight twinkle in Brock's eye as Legren gave him the order and it rekindled his own euphoria.

"But take a few men with you this time," Legren amended. Brock bowed and disappeared, leaving Legren alone in the room. He would follow shortly, but turned to survey the room. This was where it began, where realizing the Resistance would grow into reality. His chest contracted with emotion, making his stitches ripple with pain. It reminded him that he was fragile, and so was the cause.

Outside, cicadas still buzzed loudly. No light yet softened the horizon. Apparently dawn was not as imminent as they thought. Reman had been first out the door, but he had lingered. He leaned against the porch rail, head bent and shoulders hunched.

Legren approached slowly. "Having second thoughts?"

"Would it make a difference if I was?"

"Certainly."

Reman scoffed.

"I said it before, and I'm saying it again," Legren said. Reman turned towards him, clearly catching the irony of hearing his own words from only a few hours prior. "We can't proceed with this plan without you."

"Maybe with certain things," Reman started, "but not with—"

"With all of it."

Reman pulled a face, disagreeing, and Legren stifled a wince of his own. If Reman still didn't accept that his participation was the most important aspect of all of this, where would that leave them?

And then another emotion flickered across Reman's face. The muscles tightened around his eyes and his brows knitted together. Legren had felt worry like that many times over. Concern for the safety of another.

"You are not chained to this decision to join us, or to the knowledge you have provided, but I think you have done right; and that it is in everyone's best interest."

"Everyone's?"

"Everyone's."

Reman chuckled and pushed against the railing to stand up straight. "If you say so."

Legren watched him turn and walk away, hoping that this wasn't the early sign of a mind about to change.

"You two are thick as thieves." Sethera materialized out of the shadows around the Assembly Hall doors. "Are we going to have a new second-in-command soon?"

She sauntered up next to him and slouched against the opposite porch post. It was as if all of her resentment had dissipated.

He didn't believe it. Not for a second.

"You didn't say much about this new plan; even regarding your role in it." That wasn't entirely true, but he hoped this might prompt a more honest reaction from her; an argument to say the least.

"So?"

Apparently not.

Legren sighed. "Is this how it's going to be? You just stew in silence? Carry out orders simply because you feel obligated? Then pick fights with Reman at every turn?"

"I noticed you didn't give him this same lecture," she observed.

"He's not the one I'm worried about."

"Just me, then?" She shrugged. "Suppose I should be used to that by now."

She has a point. She may have been referring to his lack of self-concern and inexplicable escape from death. Somehow they had avoided the topic during the meeting, apart from her initial deriding him when she arrived in the Hall.

Her turmoil had been so clear in her voice — even Reman must have noticed it — and now, this laid-back demeanor made him yearn to ask her directly. Could he do that? Breach the question that had been eating away at him for so many months? With this new plan in motion, was there finally room for a real, open conversation between them?

"Sethera…" He stepped closer to her, and she tensed. Her her jaw clenched and leaned away from him. As she moved, the shadows deepened on her face, cast by the flickering torches.

He was probably just imagining it.

"You seem…troubled," he finished lamely. She didn't say anything, nor did she move anymore and they stood there, silently gazing at one another.

"If you are really with us, if you really believe in the Resistance, then *be with us*. So much is at stake."

"And by that, you mean…?"

"Reman won't be the only new addition to our group. I don't believe he's going anywhere and we need to treat him — and any that come after him — not as some sort of *other*, but as equals. That's the whole point to this."

"And if I'm right?"

"And if you're wrong?"

Her eyes widened. His reply caught her off guard. She stiffened and pursed her lips.

"Just because I'm on board doesn't mean I have to especially *like* every-one," she said. "You can't order me to do that."

Legren opened his mouth, but Sethera spoke again.

"I won't kill him. I promise. You don't need to worry about me."

He would anyway, of course. In spite of everything that had passed be-tween them, as far as he was concerned, they were still family. Even in her sharp expression, he could see the creases of well-rehearsed lies. The distress, the anger, was still there, just out of sight. Her grip on it was tight, but some-day it would slip. The fear that gripped him was that, since she was pushing him and everyone else away, no one would be there when she did. All he could do was try to stay near her; in hopes that she would not abandon them all.

She should go on the mission.

The idea should have make him balk, but maybe distance from them all — including him — was well-timed, especially for a mission that would bring her face-to-face with three other Mechs who had personal ties to Reman. Yet the thought of sending her away scared him, even on a task that he knew she would see through.

"You'll do your part? Pull your weight?" he asked, unable to stop himself, in an attempt to hide his own uncertainty about it all.

She smiled, not unlike the way she had done at Reman. "Don't I always?"

He didn't return the smile as she slid away from the post and glided up next to him.

"Relax," she said, just above a whisper.

Legren didn't need to watch her as she slipped past him, but he did anyway. The darkness enveloped her and she was gone; her footsteps silent and untraceable.

The candles burned low by the time Legren returned to his study. He could feel the beginnings of a headache and his feet were suddenly heavy. He moved around the table, glancing without much concentration at the maps and scrolls he'd abandoned so many hours earlier. Legren grimaced, thinking of the amount of work he had ahead of him. The candle flames struggled, their wicks almost gone. He felt compelled to light new ones and slump back into his chair to update his records and confirm a few of the more important details. He glanced at the makeshift bed in the corner. He had a separate bed chamber upstairs, but slept here, in his study, almost every night. The closer Legren could be to the work, the less time was wasted. Time was the highest commodity now, after all. However, he could sense that he would not be able to make any real progress, as weary as he was now. It could all wait for at least a few hours' worth of sleep.

It was just as Legren leaned towards candles to extinguish them that his eyes brushed the surface of the desk one more time, and he saw it: dark dust, scattered across one side of the nearest map. He straightened, wide awake again. No trace of *Magic* or *qì* lingered, but that didn't mean it wasn't there. He froze, breathing hard. Someone else had been there. He eased towards the paper. If there was an enchantment left behind, he didn't want to rattle it, but as he moved closer, he realized that the dust lay in the shape of a handprint. It was visible only from certain angles and barely then. How Legren had spotted it at all, he would never be sure. Not worried about a trap now, he reached out to touch the stuff, pinching it between his fingers. It was dry, ash-like, but dense, far more so than dust. It ranked somewhere between soot and soil, yet it evaporated almost instantly against his skin. Would the dust contaminate him somehow? He would ask Xettar, but from the little he knew of Nenjin *Magic*, this was some sort of absorption charm, which left behind harmless residue.

"A diversion," he whispered to himself. Unlike the mercenaries and so many other invaders, they weren't attempting any sort of misplaced Oniyum recovery. They were here to steal intelligence. And they'd gotten it.

Heat crept up his face in embarrassment and anger. He crossed the room and sat down, hard, on the edge of the bed. His chest ached, but he ignored it. Staring at the table again, he doubted that they would be able to make much sense of what they had, but it was still cause for worry. Alliances had sprung up all across Kabathan since the wars had begun; insofar as bargains struck from blackmail or resigned mutual hate towards the bigger tribes. The High Kingdom had been fending off such threats for years, but more in the recent months. Would Dorojin take this information to his master? *No. Dorojin is masterless.* So, why sneak in to steal intelligence? Would he go directly to the Fantasarian Court? He didn't know that Legren still lived, but perhaps he would wish to underscore his victory over the former "King's Favorite."

You do not know much about the Oniyum, do you?

Evidently, no.

With a deep breath, Legren flopped back onto the bed. He was grateful to be alive, certainly, but inexplicably surviving now two death sentences, was a fact he shouldn't ignore. His beliefs were unchanged: that the Oniyum somehow controlled these events, but he would have liked just a bit more insight.

He could continue with the Resistance as planned, even if the Nenjin knew what he was up to. Legren would just have to keep his ear pressed that much harder to the ground, in case they had to move quickly. Otherwise, not much else had changed —

Bosa. We made *him talk.*

Sorrow whipped at his heart as he remembered Dorojin's taunt. Though Vikings had remained allies to Fantasaria, Bosa was more than just an ally. He was a personal friend.

Dorojin's words might have been false. *Bosa could still be perfectly safe.* Tortured, possibly, but alive. Still, Legren couldn't shake the idea of Bosa dying at Dorojin's hand...and as a means of personal revenge...

But why? Was Dorojin involved with his the wars of his kin? Or was there something else at play here? Something or someone out there pulling strings other than the Oniyum?

Exhaustion pulled at Legren, making his mind stutter and his eyes itch. He would send out a scout tomorrow for information about the Vikings. No need for a honorary burial just yet. The thought didn't entirely comfort him, however, and as he drifted into an uneasy sleep, his mind lingered on that new question, stirring up fresh, further bewildering concern.

His sleep was fitful, spotted with familiar, unsettling dreams filled with battles large and small, twisted depictions of events passed, and an alluring, eerie face he didn't know, but somehow seemed to recognize. When he woke several hours later, all he could remember was that feeling of recognition, but the details of her face were lost to him, like the *qi* dust left behind on his desk, which, too, had vanished completely in the light of the new day.

What are they after?

NINE

LEGREN

As the days turned, Reman remained quiet, but he left his room more and no longer avoided the subject of the Resistance. He didn't seem in a hurry to leave anymore, either. He took seriously the added Mech security and checked the sensors multiple times a day without fail.

The biggest concern now had to do with Xettar and Sethera. The Mage was also unusually quiet for the past few days, though he was preoccupied and the pressure was heaviest upon him. And Sethera…

Legren avoided thinking about Sethera if he could manage it.

To everyone's surprise, Brock and his party returned earlier than expected.

"The entire northern border is blocked," Brock explained to Legren over mugs of mead in the Assembly Hall. "Where Mobsters and Vikings aren't openly fighting, the Nenjin are hanging around. Meanwhile, Vampians are holding their position in the west. They're not advancing, but they're not retreating, either. Sooner or later, we're going to have to deal with *them*, too."

"In that case," Legren said grimly, "I'd rather have you here, anyway."

Brock returned a wan smile and they raised their goblets in a lackluster toast.

The following day, Legren strode through the square, trying to banish his underlying apprehension. Now that the preparations had begun, actions taken, his entire focus was on the outcome. He could not allow himself to be distracted by any unfortunate consequences. It was his purpose. He *must* succeed. And if this failed…

Legren slowed his pace as he approached the Assembly Hall. He slipped in through the front entryway but passed the main room, and walked down the side corridor. He wound his way through the building until he reached the back room, the door to which was closed. He knocked once, lightly, then, carefully and quietly, pushed the door open and stepped inside.

This space was often used for storage, but Xettar preferred to perform *Magic* here because of how secluded it was. A ladder led up to a miniature loft, and, as Legren stepped inside, he saw Xettar and Tilesse up there, seated across from each other.

They were in the midst of a spell-casting. Xettar's eyes were closed and his hand was outstretched over a circular amulet, which glowed and hovered above the floor. The two of them sat on a multicolored quilt that, if he had to guess, belonged to Tilesse. Numerous other talismans lay around them, but for the moment, their entire attention was focused on the amulet. Energy poured from Xettar's fingers to the orb. She, meanwhile, stared at the amulet with open eyes and held a hand about an inch or two above his, in what Legren assumed was a sort of support or even a safety precaution. Or both. He knew a smattering of *Magic*, but he did not bother attempting to understand their advanced, intricate process.

Legren had only met Tilesse once or twice before when she had been passing through. She was a *Magic*-user, but disassociated from any particular tribe and travelled with a group that avoided others.

She peered down at Legren, who nodded in silent greeting. She blinked and placidly redirected her focus to Xettar. He opened his eyes — barely — and gave a sidelong glance down at Legren, without moving his head.

"Tilesse? Take over, won't you, dear?" he said. Still, she said nothing, but, together, their hands moved with a smooth, liquid-like motion that allowed them to shift the energy from his hand to hers. She, then, closed her eyes as muscles tightened in her forearm and her back straightened ever so slightly. Xettar half-stood and climbed down the ladder.

"Any progress?" Legren asked.

"Y…es."

"Are you sure?"

"It's slow going, but we are headed in the right direction."

Legren frowned. "That doesn't inspire much confidence. You said it could be done—"

"And it can. But I also told you it would take time."

"Will it still be ready for the Assembly?"

"I believe so."

"You *believe?*"

Xettar blinked, slowly, as Legren continued.

"Our entire plan is counting on this. Without it, everything falls apart. Our best warriors have already scattered into Wrangler and Clockwork territories, looking for more recruits, but even with them here, it would be no match for—"

"Legren. You have asked me to do something never before attempted in the entire known history of *Magic*. Alone. There is no way to know what will happen, even if we do finish."

"You didn't have to agree to this."

"And, what?" Xettar scoffed. "Allow you to proceed with your plan anyway? What, exactly, would that accomplish?"

"*Allow* me—?"

"We'd merely provide an occasion for history to repeat itself."

Legren's prepared comeback stalled. Xettar's statement could have referenced to any number of events that had happened in the recent past, but Legren was fairly certain which one he meant. Although not a direct assault on Legren's actions, Xettar offered a warning to the kind of devastation and heartache that his current actions could cause.

"What do you suggest?" Legren said after a long, charged pause.

"That you let me work as planned. Creating a *Magical* barrier of normal magnitude would be…*involved*, but adding the condition of all acts of violence is the most complex undertaking I have ever done."

"You've already told me this—"

"It is difficult, but not impossible. I do believe I will finish by the time our warriors return with new recruits but you have to trust me and give me room to breathe."

Legren nodded and looked up, back to the loft where the hovering amulet still glowed in a slow, steady rhythm.

"And besides, would you really prefer we stop now?" Xettar asked.

Legren didn't answer. They couldn't stop now, even if they wanted to.

"More *Magic* users might help move things along," Xettar pondered, tilting his head to one-side. "Strength in numbers and all that. Any chance you can summon a few?"

"I'll look into it." Legren retreated towards the entrance.

"What's the word on Sethera?"

Legren stopped. He let the silence linger for a few moments before he glanced over his shoulder in Xettar's direction without actually looking at him, though was fairly sure he could see, out of the corner of his eye, Tilesse peering down at him as well.

"Nothing," he said at last.

"At all?" Xettar said, genuinely surprised. "That'll be…what?"

"Two weeks tomorrow. And yes. It's disconcerting."

He made eye contact with Xettar, almost certain he knew what was coming.

"And the Mech?"

Legren shut his eyes, exasperation washing over him. He didn't want to have this conversation *again*. "What about him?"

"You asked after my progress; I'm inquiring after yours."

"I have no reason, as of yet, to doubt him."

"Well, then. Good news."

"I'll send word to other *Magic* users in the area."

"Much obliged."

"Keep me informed."

He nodded to Legren and was about to climb back up the ladder, when Telena careened onto the threshold of the side-door, breathing hard.

"Telena, what—" Legren started.

"*She's* here," the Elf interrupted.

Legren could feel the blood drain from his face as he exchanged a look with Xettar.

"Are you—"

She nodded.

"And—"

"She asked for you, specifically," Telena said.

"Where?"

"The stable."

Legren looked from Xettar to Telena and back again, his mind racing.

"Plan A," he said, not sure if their contingency would even work, but he saw no alternative. Telena nodded and disappeared again.

"What about…?" Xettar started.

Legren held up his hand, already discouraged about what had to be done. "I'll take care of it."

Xettar shrugged and climbed back up the ladder as Legren swept out of the room. His mind raced. In hindsight, he should have expected this twist of fate. *Why* now, *though? What brought her here so suddenly and without announcement?*

Thankfully, nothing major was happening that day. If she, their unexpected visitor, left this afternoon, then they would have nothing to worry about. If she stayed, it would throw everything off track and chances were it would change their entire plan.

Legren took a deep breath before he knocked on Reman's door.

"Come in," Reman called from inside.

Legren pushed the door open. Reman stood at his makeshift workbench, staring at something in his hand. When the door clicked shut again, the Mech's head shot up and his fist closed around whatever it was he was holding.

"Everything all right?" he asked.

"Ah, not exactly," Legren said. "Unfortunately there's been a slight hiccup in the preparations."

"Meaning what?" Reman said. Worry spread across his face and Legren suddenly knew what Reman had been looking at. "What's wrong?"

"Nothing as bad as you are probably thinking," Legren said. "Still…it makes this phase of our plan…problematic."

Legren closed his eyes and steeled himself for the task at hand. He opened his eyes again and Reman stared back, puzzled, but not the slightest bit wary. Legren wasn't sure if that made this chore easier or more difficult.

"Reman," he said, "I am very sorry about this."

Legren raised his arm, but realization only dawned on Reman's face just before Legren's fist collided with it.

She was alone. She leaned against one of the stable beams, her back to him, watching the rain fall onto the paddock. No doubt her guards were somewhere nearby, but it still took some of the pressure away, seeing her standing there, by herself. Legren strode into the covered part of the stable and approached the center stall.

Her dragon dozed, curled up in the corner, her damp, indigo scales gleaming. The beast cracked open one eye, then the other; her yellow irises bright and instantly aware. She straightened up and padded, elegantly, to the edge of the stall.

Legren reached up, extended his hand, and the dragon lowered her head so he could scratch behind her ears.

"How is she?" Legren said, casually, over his shoulder.

Sharp, sapphire eyes locked onto him in the dark. He froze, waiting, until she smiled and crossed the space to join him at the stall.

"I should have known better than to try to sneak up on you," she said.

He drew his hand back out of the stall.

"I must confess, I am surprised that you would want to. Your presence here is always welcome."

She smiled and extended her hand, which he took and kissed.

"And you would rob the villagers of their chance to honor you," he added.

"Are you reprimanding me?" she said in mock indignation.

"Never," Legren said, facing her properly, "only conveying the wish of the people, however badly."

They both laughed politely. He watched her, though, closely. Her amusement seemed genuine, her lightness sincere, but more than once he had seen her mood flit from delighted to furious in seconds. In this instance, however, her posture was relaxed, her smile soft.

"It has been too long," she said. "I have missed your sense of humor."

He bowed slightly. "And I have missed you, Your Highness."

PART TWO
DESPERATE MEASURES

TEN

JENDA

For the millionth time that day, Jenda sneezed. She didn't lose her balance, but clutched tightly to the thick rope of her harness all the same. Groaning, she shook her head turned back to the tree trunk and jammed the new mobile antenna into the bark, using more force than was necessary. The fuse on her temper had grown short over the last few hours. Fantasarian atmosphere always gave her hay fever, and she'd taken the last of the medicinal tablets long ago. The evening air sat thick with dust particles and golden rays of setting sunlight. And *Magic*. She perched in the highest branches of a massive Oak tree, several stories up. At least heights didn't bother her.

The antenna's screen flickered on and ran through its start-up cycle, emitting a small, pleasant tone. Jenda looked down at the tracker in her left hand. Adjusting the frequency settings, the device made a matching tone.

A buzz of static abruptly burst in her ear.

"Talon to Eagle, you read?" barked Mason's voice over her mobile-comm.

"Copy, Talon. Go ahead," Garen's voice responded.

"Red Kite, you with us?"

Jenda groaned at her call sign, but tapped her ear comm. "Copy, Talon," she said, addressing Mason. "What do you want?"

"Permission to speak freely, Eagle?" he said.

"Can I stop that from happening?" Garen muttered back.

"Am I missing something here? 'Cause I don't know about you two, but I still only got a whole lot of nothing."

Garen, too, sighed into his comm. "It is getting close to sundown…"

"We can't leave, not yet," Jenda insisted.

"But how long do we keep looking here?" Mason retorted. "We've been off-grid out here for four days and we still got nothing to report—"

"So go back home," Jenda snapped. "No one told you to come along. And while you're at it, tell ICORE you left me out here alone—"

"We have no reason to be here."

"*No reason?*"

"To be *here*," Mason repeated. "We should be moving on. Or do you absolutely insist that we waste our time?"

"Okay, no—"

"All right, cool it, both of you," Garen interrupted. "We're not going back to base, Mason, not just yet. But we can't stay separated after sundown. Not so close to the 'Sarian border, Jenda."

"Fine," she said.

"Let's reconvene for the night. Talon, you've got the best scanners there at the camp. Anything we should be aware of?"

Jenda consulted her own device and twisted around, to point it out, toward the green summit of treetops in the distance.

"There's some activity on the western border. Looks like Vampians," Mason informed them. Jenda, too, saw minor interference on her screen.

"Where are they headed?" Garen asked.

"Towards the outer 'Sarian camps in the southwest. It's not really a concern of ours, but still."

"Copy that," Garen said.

"Copy," Jenda echoed. She pocketed her tracking device and glanced down, past her feet, and past the thick branch on which she stood, into the thicket below. To some, it would have been a dizzying, stomach-churning sight. *Like Reman.*

Jenda quickly turned back to the mobile antenna. Still blinking in a steady rhythm, she knew she couldn't leave it there. The tiny solar panel on the top would keep it running. It wasn't the most reliable source, but it was all they had. Jenda unhitched the antenna from the bark and tucked it into one of her other numerous pockets. She tightened the rope around the trunk, held on, and jumped off the branch, soaring down and landing steadily. She must have stirred up the underbrush, however, because she had to pause for another sneezing fit before she could continue back towards their campsite.

In under seven minutes, she stood in a small, ivy-covered clearing like any other in these woods, except for the barely perceptible, distinctly out-of-place rumble. She tapped her ear comm.

"Red Kite to Talon."

He didn't respond, but after a few seconds, the center of the clearing flickered. The campsite popped into view as the CamoShield powered down, revealing their tent, stacks of mobile equipment, their ground vehicle (the "Camel"), and Mason, standing by the nearest of four posts that established the CamoShield itself. Jenda nodded to Mason and he to her as she crossed between the posts. Once inside, he adjusted the controls on the post and, from the outside, the campsite disappeared once again.

Garen joined them twenty minutes later. He threw his gear down and joined Mason in logging their newest data — which wasn't much — and prepared their evening rations. Jenda set up her personal workstation, establishing a sensor radius and timed security scans. Under normal circumstances, they would have also contacted HQ with their whereabouts, but out on their own, Jenda used her minimal hacking skills to tap into the outermost levels of the mainframe. She searched for any new reports coming in to ICORE; information that had to do with the war at large, or anything relating to their private mission.

Night fell as they ate. Afterwards, Jenda took the first watch. For the first hour, she stayed by the workstation and checked the radar repeatedly. Every time, she found nothing in their vicinity, and every time, she felt a chill of doubt. She peered over the monitors at the trees fencing in their camp. Thanks to the Shield, their lamps didn't cast light beyond their cover, so the surrounding pines stood like columns in some wild cathedral, with deep, patches of darkness draped between them. It seemed impossible that something wasn't lurking there, waiting to pounce. She kept expecting to catch the glint of an axe blade, the tip of an arrowhead, but there was nothing. Just the chanting of night critters; crickets, beetles and frogs.

Glancing skyward, she could see stars appearing around the twin moons, Kimbre and Lystra, just visible above the tree line. She found herself grinning up at them, two radiant spheres of blue-white. They were brighter here than back home, wreathed in a slight amber haze…probably due to some difference in the atmosphere. Like *Magic.* Their presence was a comfort, though, offering a familiar sight in a strange land and she'd always thought they were beautiful, especially in their duality. Never was one without the other.

Jenda consulted the radar again. All was calm, but her nerves itched. Like calm water on the ocean, it just didn't feel right. She reached for her pack and took out her personal tablet. A photo was wedged inside the front flap; a candid moment from several years ago. Jenda, Reman and their parents sat around a picnic table, dressed in bright summer clothing over sun-tanned skin. It was far from a perfect picture. The faces all glowed, slightly overexposed from the camera's flash, and she and their father weren't smiling, caught unawares. Out of frame, a band had been playing and they'd been distracted by their shared love of music. Still, the edges were sharp and the surface was glossy, void of dust, scratches, or fingerprint smears. Amazing, considering how old it felt in her hands. That was the last summer before Reman enlisted in ICORE — one of the last, happy moments of their lives, personally untouched by the wars. Only a few months after that, Reman announced that he'd joined the ranks of the Mech Infantry. She'd laughed. Her little brother? A soldier? She had thanked him for the moment of amusement, but saw with a slow rush of horror that he actually meant it. He was dead-eyed, more serious than she had ever seen. It wasn't a joke and he wasn't lying. Reman never lied.

Forgetting temporarily about the scanners and radar, Jenda eased the photo out of its place. Her chest tightened as pieces of the subsequent fight resurfaced. She preferred to keep those memories buried, but her mind wound back even further, into to the tumult of events that led to it in the first place.

The call had come in at exactly 13:27. She wasn't even entirely sure that it was recorded anywhere. Only the important, truly large-scale incidents were tracked and marked for future records. She hadn't been anywhere near the Base. But she remembered.

Two minutes, forty-two seconds.

She'd been in the mess hall, just finished from a shift in the stock yard. She had picked up a magazine and was flipping through the first few pages, absently debating whether or not she felt like going back to her quarters to change out of her uniform before meeting Garen that evening. While not overly tired, she had been feeling a bit lazy and they had, after all, agreed to keep the whole thing casual. It wasn't a *date*, after all—

The alarm's noise barely registered at first. In the moment, when the sound first broke into her mind, Jenda had treated it like any other occasion. She swung her legs back over the bench and jogged to the door. She presumed it was a breach along the border again. They'd had a number of such conflicts with the Mercs lately, but defenses had held. Mech technology was just better.

A few other members of her unit, along with several additional soldiers, crowded around a central monitor just beyond the mess hall doors. They all stared at the screen, mouths agape while the news had streamed, live, in front of them. Looking back, she couldn't recall what the screen actually said. Unlike the rest of them, she rushed to the nearest window and the sight of black smoke billowing up in the distance hit her like a physical hammer. She swayed on the spot, her vision swimming. Gripping the window edges, she forced herself to breathe. The clock on the wall read: 13:29:00.

She flew through the halls, feet pounding the metal floors, towards the docking bay. Chaos hadn't quite taken over yet, but it would, and soon. Military Housing, only miles from the base. Skirmishes at the border had leaped to a full-scale assault in their backyard.

When she arrived in the hanger, panic levels soared. Flight attendants shook, pilots slipped on the ladders into their machines. Jenda forced herself, again, to set aside her own panic as she slipped into her mech and was quickly airborne.

Two minutes, forty-two seconds.

Jenda half-jumped, half-fell out of the cockpit before it had finished the full landing sequence. Officers already on the scene shouted their disapproval, but Jenda ignored them. She couldn't see anything. Dust and ash clogged the air and coughs racked her lungs as she ran. Radio transmissions flitted through her periphery…the area was secure, but still burning, still dangerous. The few survivors had been evacuated and the perimeter was locked down; no coming in or out except the highest-ranking of ICORE.

Half blind, she pressed forward, through the smog. *This was home.* They hadn't lived there long before Jenda enlisted and moved out, but she had considered it their most significant home. Both she and Reman made most of their friends here, and the community banned together in unimaginable ways once the wars started. Everything changed when the Oniyum vanished and the war was declared officially, but their home, their town, had not been shaken. She had put so much stock in the strength ICORE and she never, ever thought this place could be touched, let alone overturned like this.

She found a line of soldiers, firearms drawn, and took her place at the back making their way into what remained of the buildings. She drew her own rifle and tried to unleash her fighter mentality; overcome her growing shock and do the job she was assigned. But as the line headed for the familiar-looking building with the green door, her surge of adrenaline cut off entirely. Hardly any trace of the structure still stood; mostly just a pile of charred rubble, falling around the façade of that cracked door. She had every intention of digging through the wreckage for final, undeniable proof, rather than just stand there, horror-struck, but her feet rooted her to the spot. She stared at the remnants of her former home until two soldiers emerged from the ruins in full combat armor, all of it covered in dust. One of them, his face hidden by the overlarge helmet and thick, dark goggles, had looked directly at her and shook his head. Her gun tumbled to the ground beside her. Breathing became suddenly difficult. Pain sliced through her head and chest and as the world spun around her, she thought she might be sick. She strained to find her balance until, a voice broke through the haze, laced with disjointed static.

"…live there…through…parents…sister, Jenda, she's ICORE…!"

She turned her head, thoughts sloshing in her mind like half-melted snow. Her eyes fell on the hip-radio of that same nearby soldier, whose name escaped her — Travers? — and who had stayed beside her, presumably guarding the house as she was unfit to do so. The soldier unlatched the radio from his belt, but another voice spoke through it.

"We've got a civilian here trying to get through the line. He's insisting Flynn is his sister."

"ID?" Travers said, his tone casual and alien.

"Not a one," the soldier in the radio replied, but before the transmission cut, Jenda caught a distant wail; a desperate cry she'd heard on only a few, dire occasions before.

"That's my brother," she confirmed quietly, her eyes focused on the radio. "Reman."

"You sure?" Travers said. "He doesn't have ID—"

"It's him."

"You want to let him in?"

She didn't answer right away, and as such, one last transmission came through.

"He's making a pretty big scene," the voice warned through the radio. "Starting to distress others." Behind him, she'd heard not just Reman's shouts, but the voices of other ICORE officers, undoubtedly trying to pull him back.

She snatched the radio from the other soldier. "This is Lt. Flynn. Let him through."

She dropped it, hanging her head from the fact that her voice broke as she finished speaking. She pressed the heels of her hands to her eyes and drew several long breaths, then placed her hands on her hips, waiting.

She heard him running just before he slammed into her, nearly knocking her sideways. Even through her armor, she had been able to feel how tightly he clung to her. The swell of his emotions washed over her, so powerfully that the ground tilted under her feet again. She pushed him away, holding him at arm's length. Tears still streamed out of his red and swollen eyes, staring at her desperately in a paradoxical mix of relief and panic and she knew why. *She* was alive, but he also clearly knew that they, their parents, were —

For the first time in a very long while, Jenda felt stripped of all agency and the enormity of the wars loomed down over her, leaving her helpless to bring solace to him, her little brother who was being swallowed whole by pain.

"What happened?" he choked. "Are they—really—?"

She nodded, once, and quickly looked away before his face crumpled. In her peripheral vision, she saw him follow her gaze, then walk past her, away from the house entirely. She thought he was leaving until his forehead collided with her shoulder blade. Her breath caught. This was an old practice between them, which they had not done in many years. When he was six, the neighbor's dog frightened him. He'd run around behind her and hidden, holding onto her for dear life, face pressed against her shoulder. It had become an unspoken symbol of their relationship; his trust in her strength and the belief in safety, as long as she was there. Standing in the colorless, filthy yard, the remnants of their home fragmented and burning before them, he rested his forehead against her, trusting her still.

"What do we do now?" he asked.

No words came and even if they had, she wasn't sure she could have spoken aloud, with her throat closed up.

"Jenda?" he whispered, asking for something, anything, a lifeline to help him out of the whirlpool of torment he was in.

She stepped forward, pulling away from him a second time.

"It's war," she said, more to herself, than to him. "We keep fighting."

There was nothing left for them here. She had to walk away and never look back. She would be better off at ICORE anyway.

Jenda turned, physically, away from the house, but made the mistake of glancing at Reman as she did so. He stared back, like he had never seen her before, with something that looked unbearably like disappointment in his eyes.

Wishing to look at anything else, she'd looked down, instead, at her watch. 13:31:42.

Two minutes, forty-two seconds.

"You'll be moved to ICORE Base, temporarily," she said, though she wasn't entirely certain of this. "I'm not sure when you'll see me next. If this was Mercs, then we'll probably be launching—"

"Jenda," Reman interrupted. She couldn't help but look up at him. He shook his head, confused. "We…Mom and Dad…what do we do?"

"I'll tell Garen I saw you; that you're okay." She strode forward, past him, unsure of anything else to say.

They didn't speak again for nearly a week. Even thinking about Reman had challenged her ability to think straight, to keep her mind focused on new missions.

"You need to take time off," Garen told her one afternoon. "Let yourself grieve—"

"Is that an order, sir?"

They stared at each other in silence for a few short moments before he said, "No." Then, added, "not yet."

He never did give the order. She'd found ways to cope. Reman, too, was mostly unchanged by the whole affair; although quieter. She couldn't be the emotional support he needed, not with the wars in hand, and he seemed to figure that out quickly. They fell into a pattern as the one they'd had before the bombing, but not before the wars altogether. She, herself, felt a gnawing sense of sorrow over that, but took comfort knowing that, when the war was over, things could go back to normal. To get there, however, they had to win. And as such, there was no room in either of their lives for crippling sentiment.

How that now applied to her crusade to find him in Fantasaria…she wasn't sure. She'd broken almost every conceivable rule in getting out there and hadn't, at any point, even remotely considered not going through with it. Nor would she abandon the quest, either. Whether that was driven from a desire to stick it to ICORE, or an outpouring of pent-up family loyalty, she'd have to figure out eventually, but not until she had an answer to her questions.

"Family portrait?"

The woodland sounds rushed back into her ears as she looked up quickly. Garen stood by the stove, a tin cup in his hand. He leaned forward to pick up the kettle from the stovetop and pour coffee into the cup. Jenda shut the tablet case and stuffed it in her pack.

"Last one ever taken of us all together." She pushed away from the work-table, headed for the tent, but as she passed in front of Garen, he reached up and placed his hand on her shoulder. She stopped mid-motion. Her muscles tensed under his palm and she could picture his gaze on her, heavy with the weight of concern and familiarity. This was not a gesture of a Captain concerned for another officer. She turned, slowly, giving him a very even stare, but then felt rather than saw him raise his arm. He offered her the small cup.

Jenda relaxed, accepted it, and changed her mind about disappearing into the tent. Instead, she sat down next to the stove while Garen poured another cup, then took the seat across from her.

"I'll take over the watch, if you—" he started, but as she shook her head, he pressed on. "You're no good to any of us half-awake. Especially Reman."

She glanced up at him, but still didn't speak. They were dancing so close to the subject, the whole reason they were there. He wanted to discuss it. She wasn't sure what she wanted.

"We'll find him, Jenda."

"Mason doesn't think so," she scoffed before taking a swig of coffee.

"Mason's not here to think."

Under different circumstances, she might have laughed; or, at least half-laughed, half-coughed into the cup. That was probably Garen's intent. It didn't amuse her, though; not enough to change her mood.

"Is he right, though?" she asked.

"I can't believe you said that."

"I'm not—" She caught herself and regained composure. "I'm not naive enough to ignore the fact that things look grim." Desperate for a distraction, she turned her frustration on ICORE. "Why did they let him go off on his own?"

"They must have thought the area was secure."

"A blast site? This deep in 'Sarian territory?"

"No survivors, remember?"

"They should have known better. He should have known better."

"Yeah, 'cause following the rules is a shared family trait." He grinned at her and she couldn't help but smile back.

The moment was punctured as an alarm erupted from the workstation. They both jumped and leapt up, toward the computer, just as Mason fumbled out of the tent.

"What's goin' on?" he squawked, still half-dazed from sleep.

Jenda pressed a few buttons and blinked, speechless, at the screen.

"What?" Garen said.

"Wranglers and Vampians."

"Where?"

She pressed another button and the full-screen radar map appeared. A horde of new signals formed directly ahead of the campsite.

"Right on top of us."

Lest they have any lingering doubts, a gunshot cracked nearby and reverberated around them, so close it practically touched them.

"How the hell'd they get here so fast?" Mason said, joining them at the screen.

"Do they know where we are?" Garen asked Jenda.

"They will. They're coming right at us."

"How long?"

"Ten minutes, give or take."

Garen considered, then turned to Mason. "Tear it down."

Mason nodded and turned to follow the order. "Except the Shield," Garen added.

"What, just leave it?" Jenda asked.

"You want to fight Vampians *and* Wranglers?"

"We can't just leave tech for them to find—"

A loud *crash!* prevented him from replying. Garen and Jenda whirled around to find Mason disjointing the stove unit to pack it up.

He gave them both a devious grin. "We won't."

ELEVEN

SETHERA

The sound of gunfire drew her attention first; powder-based pistol shots that echoed around the valley. Probably a Wrangler and Vampian brawl. As she drew near the skirmish, she donned the ring Xettar had given her. Stealth was the priority on this mission and while Sethera was more than capable of keeping herself hidden on her own, she had no backup. The ring carried a limited range of spells including invisibility. Xettar had explained it as more as "non-recognition," making her unnoticeable rather than entirely invisible. The Mage had also stored a limited number of energy blasts within her green pendant, though she trusted her dagger far more than *Magic*.

Both moons were half-crescents in the sky, and the light they provided was patchy at best through the thick, forest branches. The deep shadows provided such cover that she almost didn't need the ring.

She climbed up a pine to scout the action. She saw no vehicles of any kind, but knew there had to be at least one nearby. While Vampians could travel this far on foot, there was no way the Wranglers could, given the distance from their own border. Even when they snuck into Fantasarian Territory, they didn't do so without at least a horse or two.

She climbed higher. There were too many Wranglers to count, spread out through the trees and shooting at only seven Vampians. As the fight played out beneath her, a couple of Clockworks swooped in, lending a hand to the Wranglers. Apparently, their alliance was still going strong. A few minutes later, the Vampian Queen appeared in the distance, basking in a perfect patch of moonlight. She stood apart from the action; a regal figure, draped in an exquisite black gown, long red shawl, and silver kerchief. She kept her gaze fixed in one direction, which Sethera followed and recognized what had to be the leader of these Wranglers. Curiously, he seemed headed for the Queen. He was within ten feet, pistol drawn, before she vanished on the spot. Sethera caught the blur of movement, backwards and to the right of the Queen's former position, and the Wrangler's head whipped around, gun pointed in that direction. His pistol swept back and forth through the trees, firing at every fleeting streak of crimson. Sethera couldn't be sure who was cat and who was mouse. *But, how is he seeing her?* Sethera leaned forward on her branch, watching. He fired and missed again, but only just. The bullet ricocheted off the tree the Queen had been leering around, momentarily illuminating the area with flashing embers off the bark. They kept at it, back and forth, back and forth, until she suddenly appeared behind him, several feet away. He whirled just as another of his men spotted her and released a whip in her direction. With the trademark speed of the undead, she reached up and caught it, mid-crack. Another Wrangler ran for her, trying to catch her distracted, but she spun and slashed at him with short, bright blades fastened to the tips of her fingers, like claws. Vampians did have a more beastly form, but it didn't include talons. Not that Vampians needed weapons, what with their fangs, speed, and savage appetite. They were, after all, the only tribe that plunged into battle dressed not in armor, but ball gowns and silk cravats. Ridiculous, but perhaps it was ceremonial?

The Wrangler with the whip lunged forward, gun raised, but the Queen spun and slashed. He dropped and did not stir. The whip loosened on her arm and fell in a graceful coil as she arched over the first body. The head and shoulders had fallen just beyond the splash of moonlight. She crawled, leaning into the harsh line of shadow, bending over the dead Wrangler. She stretched her mouth wide, fangs bared.

Sethera had to look away out of disgust. Behind the Queen, the Wrangler leader somehow managed to creep up, right behind the Queen, unnoticed.

As he cocked the gun and aimed it at the back of her head, the Queen pushed up from the ground and twisted to face him, her chin smeared with red. She murmured something, then vanished again, but this time reappeared almost immediately, some five feet ahead of where she had just been, running at him. Sethera was sure the game was over for him, but he leaned back, raised his weapon and fired. Her red cloak soared up as she collapsed onto her side. She twitched and jerked, not dead, but defeated.

Sethera could hardly believe it. The other Vampians all simultaneously stopped and turned, perfectly and suddenly aware that their leader had been struck down. They shared the same, horror-struck expression. Only *Thanite* could strike down a Vampian so definitively. Had the Wranglers turned the substance into bullets? *I suppose it was just a matter of time, given how often they deal with Vampians.* Like the Elves, Wranglers had access to some of the best mining facilities on Kabathan, and *Thanite* was extraordinarily difficult to extract from the ground, let alone manipulate.

The lead Wrangler inclined his head in the Queen's direction, tipped his hat like a good Southern gentleman, and sauntered away.

Within seconds, the rest of the Vampians retreated, almost instantly gone. The Wranglers — what was left of them — gathered around their leader and walked, passing their fallen comrades without second glances back. A few cheered; attempts at recovering morale, probably. Sethera waited until they were a reasonable distance ahead of her before she began to slowly descend the tree. However, as she climbed, she stole glances at the Vampian Queen, who continued to convulse. Her shoulders shook, chest rising in an inconsistent rhythm. How long would it take her to die? *Would* she die?

Sethera felt no remorse for a defeated monster, but she couldn't help but remember that, at one time, this woman had established reconciliation, a truce, between Vampians and the rest of Kabathan. That harmony may have gone to pieces once the wars started, but the whole planet had fallen apart. Sethera shivered as she recalled the way the Wrangler had tipped his hat to her. It was unnecessary and sadistic. Sethera wondered if there was some kind of personal rivalry there, an old battle being fought — and ended — in that moment. She, Sethera, knew that, for herself, the only time she would ever be made to act like that over a kill would be if and when —

"LOOKOUT!"

Sethera's head jerked around. More shots and shouts tore the air, reverberating over the distance that now lay between Sethera and the Wranglers. They had reached what appeared to be a break in the trees, a sort of clearing nearby that she had not noticed. A last, lone Vampian dashed across the edge of the glade, but the Wranglers shot after her, until, out of nowhere, one of those bullets hit something. It made a telltale *thunk* of impact; metal on metal.

In the very center of the clearing, the serene and empty moonlight-dappled forest floor flickered, like a mirage, before it gave way entirely to a Mech land-vehicle and three Mech soldiers in front of it. They stood there in their black-and-gray uniforms, holding metallic cases and weapons, stock-still, like children caught out of their rooms past bedtime. The two men extended their arms towards the vehicle door handles, while the woman was mid-motion of slinging a bag over her shoulder.

No one moved. Sethera didn't even breathe. The shock was so complete, she wasn't even sure she was really seeing it. Could she have possibly run into them out of sheer, dumb luck? Was it, in fact, the right group? She stared at them harder. The men bore no special characteristics, but the woman...

Closer up, Sethera might have been able to discern her individual features carefully enough to make a better judgment. In any event, three Mech soldiers had appeared before her.

"Well..." said one of the Wranglers, taking a bold step forward, "look who decided to join the party."

And the shooting began.

Sethera didn't stop to watch the details of the fight. She adjusted her grip on the branches, jumped, and hit the ground hard, toppling slightly. She propelled herself forward, righting and balancing herself as she ran; a flat-out sprint, ducking around the trees, jumping over fallen branches and bodies, eventually circling around the shower of bullets and lasers. Ahead, the vehicle roared to life and Sethera willed herself to run faster. She was closing the gap with only a few moments to spare before the Mech trio would sail off. Lights flared on the vehicle's back. The woman and the smaller of the two men dove into the doors on either side. Sethera reached up, clutched her pendant, and a jet of light shot from her fingers. The blast hit the vehicle door, but not the handle, and the back hatch dropped open.

"MASON!" the woman shouted from inside the vehicle.

"Two birds…" the remaining soldier, Mason, growled from off to her left and held up a small device. Sethera looked ahead once more and scrambled up into the vessel.

"…one stone."

She rolled into the trunk space and slammed the door shut behind her as a deafening explosion detonated outside. The vessel swayed and shuddered. Once steady again, another side-door opened and closed before the vehicle rumbled and pitched forward. Moments later, Sethera's stomach lurched as the vessel must have become airborne. She lay in the back of the vehicle, catching her breath. *I did it.* The chances of crossing that distance and getting inside their land-vehicle — or was it an aircraft? — within a matter of minutes, which were slim at best, but she had done it. She had stowed away and judging by the name, Mason, these had to be the right Mechs.

I found them.

The vehicle landed with an unsettling *CRUNCH*. Sethera felt for her ring, to ensure she was still hidden — but it was gone.

Panic returned. She sent her fingers searching around her immediate area for any sort of cover. She snagged a sheet of utilitarian fabric and threw it over herself, huddling up as small as she could.

The vehicle still rumbled along. Perhaps they weren't actually stopping and had just decided to travel by land for awhile? The trunk space had no windows so she had no sense of day or night. Their pace seemed to slow, though, and it wasn't long before the vehicle came to a complete stop, then went utterly still as the power shut off.

Voices spoke in a dull rumble outside, followed by quiet footsteps and eventually the sound of a nearby door opening. She held still, hoping to wait until they were all gone, then sneak out, get her bearings, eavesdrop for a while, then make some kind of entrance and take them all by surprise —

The hatch of the trunk clicked open. She seized up as the objects around her suddenly shifted. A draft picked up and the light changed through the cover. Her shape under the fabric would surely give her away, wouldn't it?

A cramp twisted inside her left calf. She squeezed her eyes shut as it burned, screaming up her leg. Someone still stood nearby, lifting boxes and cases out of the back of the vehicle and if she moved, stretched out her leg as she so badly wanted to, she'd be discovered for sure. Sethera didn't care much for the odds in that situation. She listened hard, waiting for silence. When whoever it was *finally* turned away, Sethera didn't wait for the footsteps. She eased her leg out slightly, stretching both limb and fabric. The pain ebbed and she relaxed until, without any warning, the fabric flew back, off of her and she found herself face-to-face with the tall, bearded man. She didn't panic, exactly, but her mind flitted through the dozen or so ways she had to get out of this…none of them seemed especially good for anything but overall escape, and that was not her goal.

"Just you?" the man growled, looking almost insulted as he surveyed her. Sethera just grinned and raised her wrists.

TWELVE

JENDA

"What are you doing?"

Jenda looked up. Garen had turned away from the door, his back to the holographic keypad that hovered beside the manual metal handle. Instead, he gave the tablet in her hands a quizzical look.

"We've got data to analyze," Jenda grumbled.

"Right now?"

"Aren't you going to order us back to Base?"

"I'm not thrilled about it either, but we can't risk staying out here any longer." He was right, of course. They had avoided an outright fight, but both the Vampians and Wranglers had seen the ship. It was hard to say how fast the information would spread. Better to get ahead of it and get back to ICORE before the reports came in.

Garen punched in the code, the door chirped, and swung open. They picked up the gear at their feet and stepped inside. The door swung closed, but not locked, behind her, and they were plunged into full dark until Garen flipped switches and the lights stuttered on. He squinted up at them, probably wondering about their longevity, while Jenda walked directly to the far wall to fire up the computer panel. It, too, groaned out of a long-time sleep, but it booted up. Slowly.

"I still can't believe they snuck up on us like that," Garen muttered. "You think they knew we were there?"

Jenda chuckled. "If they did, then they got awfully distracted with fighting one another. Plus, that look of shock on their faces—"

The door crashed open. She and Garen spun around to find Mason dragging a small, Fantasarian girl inside. She struggled against his grip while he, with his patented smug look, pushed her to the center of the room. Garen and Jenda shifted focus between the girl and Mason, eyebrows raised. Mason forced her head back to reveal her face. Young, Jenda observed silently. *And a…half-Elf?*

"Sniper?" Garen asked.

Mason shook his head. "Stowaway."

"Ah." Garen considered the girl again. "Aren't you cute."

She sneered, then kicked, high, against Garen's chest. He fell backwards as her arms tore free of Mason's grip. She clenched the front of her tunic with one hand and swung up the other in a fist before Mason's face. A flash of light burst from her fingers and, disoriented, Mason stumbled. She thrust her elbow into his stomach and he went down. Jenda lunged forward, pistol raised. A moment of hesitation passed between the two women before the Fantasarian flung out her fist and another beam of light sprang forth.

"Jenda, look out!" Garen shouted, recovered. Jenda ducked, just as the spell exploded against the wall behind her. She felt more than saw Garen move next to her. The Fantasarian girl staggered backwards with the blade of Garen's knife lodged in her right shoulder. She slammed against the wall and her head lolled forward. Her dark hair slid past her shoulders, hiding her face.

All three Mechs back on their feet, they pulled together and waited for the girl slide down to the floor, unconscious…but she didn't. Her knees buckled, one heel slid slightly forward, but she stayed upright. Jenda's finger curled around the trigger of her gun. She had fought plenty of Fantasarians over her ICORE career, but usually at medium range, exchanging laser blasts for live flame, both real and *Magical*. When she had fought up close, there'd always been weapons on both sides. She disliked firing, point-blank, on a wounded opponent, even a Fantasarian, but this girl swayed with eerie, inhuman fluidity, unlike anything Jenda had ever seen.

When her voice drifted through the curtain of her sleek hair, the clarity of her words made them all jump.

"That," she crooned, "was a big mistake." She reached up and pulled the knife from her shoulder, without struggle.

Her head lifted. Gleaming, owl-like eyes leered out at them. She faked a lunge forward and they all raised their weapons —

And then she rocked back on her heels and giggled. "You Mech are just too easy to fool."

"What do you want?" Garen demanded.

"Don't call me cute, for starters."

Jenda couldn't help but chuckle drily.

"Why are you here?" Mason growled.

"To make an offer," the girl said. "How does a truce sound to you?"

"You call this a truce?" Garen said.

"I call this getting your attention."

"You've got it," Jenda interjected before Garen could respond. "What do you want?"

"To help you."

"Say what?" Mason barked.

"There's a disturbing movement taking place in my village. I've sought you out as an admittedly desperate attempt to put a stop to it."

She stopped speaking to look purposefully at Jenda, who snapped, "What?"

"Your name...is Jenda?"

Jenda held her face still, neutral, but both Mason and Garen shot quick, involuntary looks in her direction.

The girl smirked. "That answers that question."

Jenda's hand tightened on her gun. "And who's asking?"

"Me? Oh, I'm nobody important." The girl slipped Garen's knife into her own empty sheath. The Mech-style grip clashed grossly against her Fantasarian garb. "I'm just the one who captured your brother. Reman."

Jenda knew she couldn't believe this, or anything this girl said, but hearing the words, true or not, made her breath catch. No one moved in the room.

"Is it even worth asking what's happened to him?" Jenda finally asked.

The girl smiled. "He's still alive."

She was clearly enjoying this. They wouldn't kill her — not, at least, until they had every detail of information she possessed — and she knew it. Jenda was also perfectly aware that Garen was not watching the girl, but Jenda herself; her face and the pistol in her hand.

"So this is a ransom? Blackmail?" Mason snarled.

For a moment, the girl just continued to stare at Jenda with the same cool expression. Then she threw her head back and laughed. The sound tipped Jenda's relief into rash anger.

She swung up the gun and aimed directly at the Fantasarian's forehead. "Keep laughing. It'll be hilarious when I take your head off."

The girl stopped laughing, but her smile didn't falter.

Garen reached out and touched Jenda's shoulder. "She hasn't told us anything yet."

"*Speak*," Jenda demanded, ignoring him.

"You think I'm afraid of you?" the girl taunted.

Jenda cocked the gun. "I think I can shoot faster than you can cast a spell."

Garen's grip tightened on her shoulder.

"And, frankly, I think we've reached a stalemate," the girl countered, "which gives me the chance to tell you that Reman isn't just alive." She moved out of the gun's reach without any serious effort, as Jenda kept it pointed straight ahead, hanging on the girl's every word and hating herself for it. "He's *thriving*. An honorary Fantasarian. He's joined — what our noble leader is calling — the Resistance."

"Which is what?" Mason grunted. The girl took her time answering. Her gaze rolled on and off of them in a seemingly casual manner and, for a split second, something flickered beneath the girl's smug, self-assured coolness.

"Nothing short of a suicide mission." she finally answered Mason, but Jenda barely heard the words as she recognized the look in the girl's eyes.

Fear.

"The whole thing is absurd," Mason growled.

"It's the strongest lead we've had so far," Garen argued. "The *only* lead."

"Are you seriously suggesting we just take her at her word?" Mason said.

"She did call Jenda by name. How could she do that, unless—"

"They have their ways." Mason cast another dark glance over Jenda's shoulder, where the girl sat. They had searched her, cuffed her, and sat her down in the corner of the room. Surrounded by scans and blinking lights, the girl maintained a calm, cool demeanor. The flash of fear Jenda saw had not lasted, but she couldn't have imagined it, not that vividly. She was certain that the reason the girl sustained her calm because it wasn't the Mechs she was afraid of, but something else entirely.

The three of them had moved to the opposite side of the safe house and clustered together, delving deep into discussion for several long, pointless minutes. They all still held their ground on three varying opinions, Mason grumbling loudest of all. He kept throwing glances at the prisoner. Occasionally, so did Jenda and Garen. The girl stared peacefully at the floor, eyes slightly unfocused, until she looked up and caught all three pairs of eyes on her. In response, she flashed them a sweet smile.

Mason grimaced. "We should report back to Base. It's been way too long; we're gonna be court marshaled when we get back as it is."

"Not if we bring back a hostage," Garen considered.

"And what if she *is* telling the truth?" Jenda said. "What if Reman is alive and she can help us get him back?"

"It's not like they're keeping him prisoner," Mason muttered.

"That's *exactly* what they're doing," Jenda said, not bothering to watch her volume. "If she's right, then they've locked up his mind and free will."

"Fine. Let's just kill her, then, and be done with it," Mason suggested.

"No." Garen strode away from them, marched across the room to sit directly in front of their captive. "Spill it."

Jenda and Mason exchanged a surprised look.

"Specifically?" the girl said.

"Why do you need our help?" Garen clarified.

"I *told* you…" She rolled her eyes, but Jenda caught another flicker of fear peek through the lofty annoyance. Following it, she and Mason walked forward to stand some space behind Garen.

"The head of our camp — I suppose you would call him a general? — has begun forming an alliance with members of other tribes. Think the Tribal Council, but with random citizens rather than politically-appointed representatives."

"What for?" Jenda asked.

"To unify Kabathan in the Oniyum's absence."

A heavy, poignant silence followed this statement.

"That's…impossible."

The girl looked down, away from all of them. "No kidding." Just from her tone, Jenda knew that the statement was loaded.

"As I said," the girl continued, looking back up at them, confidently, "it is a pretentiously optimistic movement that is sure to get everyone involved hurt or killed. Legren, our general, has gained entirely too much of a following too quickly. He has to be stopped and I believe that the only way to do that is to ally myself temporarily with you."

"And you're so sure we'll agree?" Mason said skeptically.

"I'm sure you're determined to save your captured comrade." Her eyes flicked between them, eagerly now, waiting for their reaction, but they didn't take her meaning.

"Don't you get it?" she said. "He's actively contributing to plans to convert people from other cultures; how do you think it is I knew about you? Or where to find you?"

"You—"

"Have my ways, yes, but I am not a *Magic*-user."

"Could have fooled me," Garen argued.

"I have *Magical* weapons; it's hardly the same thing," she corrected him with an exasperated sort of look.

"How did you know then?" Jenda asked.

The girl smirked again, finding the same angle of enjoyment that she had earlier. "Reman told us about you. He predicted that you would be out here, looking for him. He wasn't certain if you'd be alone or not, but he was convinced that, should we go looking, we would find you."

Jenda refused to accept this, but the logic of it was not unsound.

What could possibly lead him to do such a thing?

"I volunteered, only because I saw an opportunity," the girl finished.

"And how is it you want us to help you?" Garen asked.

"I can get you in and out of the camp unseen so you can rescue Reman and drag him back to your own territory to undo the damage Legren is inflicting."

Mason scoffed at Garen. "I still say this could all be a well-rehearsed lie. Why should we believe her?" He spread his hands at her. "What proof do you have?"

She grinned and shrugged. "Nothing. Except the promise that if I wanted to cause you harm, I wouldn't go to such lengths. You have my word on that. And, of course, it really just comes back to whether or not you think your friend's life is worth the risk."

Jenda folded her arms across her chest. "Even if we help you, wouldn't this Legren just start his plans over again?"

"Reman was the first outsider to join the Resistance. If he disappears, so will Legren's other followers. It's a win-win. So..." The girl considered each of them again. "Does a temporary truce sound like something you can all live with?"

Silence hovered for a moment. The question was unanswerable, of course. They couldn't possibly —

"Yes," Garen said.

Jenda could only stare while Mason barked, "*What?*"

"I'm still Commanding Officer of this team," Garen raised his voice. "And I say we do it. Save Reman, if we can."

"If she's lying and we walk into a trap—" Mason began, but cut himself off as Garen stood up again. Jenda, meanwhile, held her breath as Garen closed the short distance between them, and delivered his decision.

"We have a chance to bring back one of our own and to possibly soak up valuable information about a specific Fantasarian stronghold. Not to mention that stopping this Resistance may prove to be a significant blow to their tribe morale." He spoke with a conviction that demonstrated why he was Commanding Officer. "It's worth it. And we're doing it."

Mason took one final glance at the girl, then nodded.

Garen faced the girl once more. "And what do we call you?"

"My name is Sethera."

"I'm Garen." He inclined his head before turning to Mason. "That's Mason and—"

"Jenda," Sethera said. "Yeah."

"Yeah," Jenda repeated. "Just remember; if you're lying and my brother is, in fact dead, I *will* kill you."

They locked eyes. Jenda could see the fear there again, just under the surface. After a moment's hesitation, Sethera nodded in earnest and, if Jenda was not mistaken, respect.

THIRTEEN

REMAN

Reman woke, flat on his back, in the corner of a damp cellar. Unlike his first experience waking up unawares in Fantasarian territory, he sat bolt upright. There was nothing else in the room except a few meager torches sticking out of the wall. An unfamiliar-looking guard leaned against the far wall, the edges of which curved out of sight. A steady dripping echoed nearby. These must be the caves that Xettar had mentioned; secret tunnels behind the Assembly Hall that led under the nearby river and out of the village. No bars caged him in, but the air shimmered. A *Magical* barrier, no doubt.

Reman's right eye throbbed and stung. He lifted a hand to touch his face and discovered his arms weighed down by shackles clamped around his wrists. He sneered at them, but grazed his fingers over his cheekbone. Swollen, all right.

I should have known better.

"Reman, I am very sorry about this," Legren had said, "but you have to get in a cell."

He'd then launched into what sounded like a pre-rehearsed script, so rushed that the words blurred; something about an eldest princess arriving from the High Kingdom.

"So?" Reman had asked.

"She can't know you're a guest here. She doesn't know about the Resistance. None of the monarchy do, and—"

"You're doing this behind the back of your own government." The thought had crossed Reman's mind before. The Resistance was a great notion, but hardly strong enough to pitch to heads of state. In fact, it struck Reman as wise, to wait on going public until the movement was better organized and gained a substantial following...not just randomly-acquired passers-by.

"Fine," he said, "but why the cell? I'll just stay out of the way—"

"That's not enough."

"Why? She going to want a tour?"

Legren had exhaled sharply, showing a frustration that he was obviously trying to keep in check.

"Reman, I am begging you, just trust me."

"No."

"Oh, come on—"

"No," Reman crossed his arms and planted his foot solidly on the ground for emphasis. "Forget it."

That was when Legren sucker punched him.

Now, in the cellar, Reman shut his eyes. The right one throbbed a little, sending additional waves of pain through the rest of his head. Reman tried pinching the bridge of his nose out of habit, but that made it worse.

He stood up, attempting to compensate for the weight of the chains. He had never worn shackles before. Once, during Basic Training, he had been forced to wear double lock handcuffs in a prisoner-of-war simulation, but that had been a digital projection, far from the real slabs of Fantasarian metal, heavy and thick, encasing his wrists now. He didn't want to think about who else might have worn them. In spite of the freedom given to him since his arrival, Reman had actively looked for signs of incarceration or torture. At every turn, though, he found no more than an earnest homestead and a safe haven for refugees. If it was all well hidden, he presumed, then such affairs were probably so uncommon that it wasn't something for him to worry about. *You've been sleeping in a dead man's bed,* a voice chanted from the back of his mind.

Reman scowled at the shimmering, *Magical* field. When he'd woken up in the supply shed to the conversation between Legren and Bosa, this was how he'd expected to find himself; a detained prisoner. Nausea churned in his stomach as he considered that perhaps his initial instincts were right. Maybe there was no Resistance and whatever elaborate plan they were working on that involved him had gone awry and they needed to get him jailed and bound as soon as possible —

A creak of wood echoed through the room and blueish light flooded the walls around the corner from high above. Reman heard descending footsteps, along with the clang and smack of a large wooden door slamming shut from a great height. The guard didn't move as Legren rounded the corner. Someone followed him, but Reman just glared at Legren as he approached. Reman expected to see something in the Fantasarian's expression, but his face betrayed nothing except the briefest of warning looks. When he stepped aside, a stern-looking young woman drifted forward. She wore a haughty smile and a long gown of finer stuff than anything Reman had ever seen. She wasn't dripping in jewels, but her posture was tall and confident, angular shoulders pulled all the way back. She smiled at him, but said nothing. Neither did Legren. Finally, Reman shrugged at her.

"What?" he snapped.

Her eyes narrowed in what he could only assume was further judgmental analysis.

"We realize the hierarchy of the Mech culture is vastly different from our own, but we still assumed you would be bright enough to recognize Fantasarian Royalty."

"I'm sorry, am I supposed to be impressed?"

She chuckled. "You're right." She threw a look over at Legren. "Not very bright at all."

Legren just shook his head sadly.

"Pray, tell," the Princess said, and as she turned back to Reman, her demeanor shifted entirely. She now stared at him with wide open eyes, piercing and intense without any calm superiority at all. She stepped closer, looking as though she could kill him right then without the slightest qualm.

"What were you doing there?"

The question threw him. "Where?"

"The woods where you were caught, near that desecrated clearing. What brought you to Fantasarian territory...alone? Mechs always go out in numbers when crossing into our borders. Or any other territory, for that matter. So what makes you so special?" She punctuated every word, making clear she saw nothing exceptional in him, which suited Reman just fine.

"I don't know if you were aware," he said, allowing sarcasm into his voice, "but there was a blast out there—"

"You were well beyond that clearing when we found you. No. You had another purpose in being there. And you are going to tell us what it was."

Reman glanced past her at Legren, whose wary gaze, surprisingly, was fixed not on him, but the Princess. Reman floundered. He could try to lie — *my engines were failing and I needed to land* or *I had run out of food supplies and needed uncontaminated water.* He could repeat the truth — *I was looking for what caused the blast* — but knew neither one would convince her. Besides, now that she pointed it out, he had to admit that the circumstances were odd. How had he not noticed that before?

"We'll give you a hint." She leaned in even closer, her face mere inches away from the energy barrier, which flickered slightly, gauzy and semi-visible.

"Be careful, your Highness," Legren said, taking half a step forward himself, but she ignored him and spoke in an almost eager whisper.

"Does the term 'Resistance' mean anything to you?"

Reman blinked. Now he had to lie.

"Resistance to what?" he said, probably too innocently.

"You're part of them, are you not? The group of rebels who have turned against their tribes?"

He cleared his throat and tilted his head to the other direction.

"Who would want to join something like that?" He glanced back at Legren to see him shake his head, once, and curtly. Reman could only assume that it was too much and he should just shut up. It was probably the best course of action.

"You do not seek peace?" she said mockingly.

"With you?" Reman said before he could stop himself, old habits kicking in. At least it was believable. "Oh, yeah. I'm sure we'd be best friends."

"You may want to reconsider that." She spoke clearly and delicately now, savoring every syllable. Her demeanor, which had flipped again, was like that of one who had ownership of a secret and enjoyed dangling it over an ignorant second party. He couldn't fathom what she could be about to shock him with, but his anxiety increased a few clicks. He tried not to squirm.

"After all, they are the ones responsible for your being here."

Behind her, Legren closed his eyes in horror. With that one, single gesture, everything smashed into place. The Elves, Tali, Telena, and Sethera hadn't just stumbled onto Reman that snow-ridden afternoon. They'd been out there looking for him *per Legren's orders*. Reman hadn't just been lied to. He had been vastly manipulated. It was a more elaborate scheme than he had even guessed. Legren's own Princess had ratted him out without realizing it and now, Legren could only stand there in damning silence.

Reman scrounged for something — anything — else to say in case the realization showed openly on his face.

Then it struck him that her knowledge of his capture was awfully specific.

"How do you know anything about—"

"You did not seriously think that your precious, powerful ICORE would send you out into a blast site by yourself?" She mimicked his western accent on 'ICORE.' "Your Mech Representatives were furious when they called an emergency Council meeting. They demanded to know who had infiltrated their central base."

She glanced over her shoulder at Legren, who cleared his expression of guilt.

"Would you believe that, for once, we Fantasarians were not instantly accused the culprits?" she said. Legren raised an eyebrow.

"Is there another tribe to be blamed?" he asked innocently. Reman glared at him.

"No," she said and turned back to Reman. "Only some rebel group calling themselves 'the Resistance'."

Reman met her gaze, more angry now with Legren than he was afraid of her. Still, he couldn't see how admitting to his involvement with this 'rebel group' could benefit him; not even if he sold out Legren in the process.

He cleared his throat. "What has that got to do with—"

"You were never supposed to go out on your own. They arranged for your little excursion. It was either the intention of these rebels for you to be caught by us, or you are working with them."

Not too far off, either way. Reman tried to read Legren again, hoping he might give some sign that all of this was untrue, based in a supplanted falsehood, but Legren's face remained blank.

Without all the information, or knowing the extent of this lie, Reman swallowed his rising anger and gritted his teeth. "Why would I work with them?"

Her lips curved inward, turning into a hard, thin line.

Reman rambled on. "Why would I ever ally myself with you or anyone else in this backwards, rotten—"

Legren rushed forward. "You will NOT address the Princess in that manner."

Disgusted, Reman pivoted away, no longer interested in participating. He didn't trust himself not to spill truths just to afflict Legren. He moved back to where he'd been sitting before, but remained standing and crossed his arms as best as he was able with the shackles.

"My apologies, Highness," Legren said, "but you need not hear this traitor's thoughts."

"We are no longer sure if he is, in fact, a traitor. He hardly seems intelligent enough for subterfuge." She sighed. "Which is worse? A normal Mech or a Mech involved with anarchist radicals?"

"And this movement is real?" Legren asked in a hushed tone, so believable that Reman even thought for a half-second that he was actually worried.

"It is," the Princess said. "This setup with the Mechs was not their first act of rebellion, either. They've been in existence for almost a year now, and though they haven't done much, they've been exceptionally skilled in hiding their whereabouts and activity, which is why I don't believe this idiot is capable of being among them. And if he was, he is well out of their reach now."

Reman scoffed, both impressed and disgusted. Legren didn't just have a hidden agenda, he was evidently an expert in *subterfuge* as she called it.

Legren nodded. "I think you may be right."

"Come. We have much to discuss." She swept back, the way she came and the guard by the wall bowed as she passed. Legren followed her out, without looking back at Reman. The footsteps trailed away. Wood creaked above again, the the door thudded shut, and all was quiet once more.

"I don't suppose you can explain any of that, can you?" Reman asked the guard, who blinked twice, then disappeared around the corner, after Legren.

Reman nodded and sat back down.

"Yep. I should have known better."

FOURTEEN

REMAN

The guard reappeared a few hours later and led Reman out of the cave without saying a word. Hot, humid air washed over Reman as they stepped out into the night. The guard spun Reman around, removed the shackles, then stalked away.

The metal hadn't really done much damage. A faint smell of rust and sweat lingered and Reman rubbed his wrists as he meandered back to his room. The night was quiet and he met no one on the path, leaving the Princess' words to loop inside his head, accompanied by the embarrassed look on Legren's face.

When Reman reached his room, he crossed to his workbench and leaned closed fists on the tabletop, his knuckles bearing his whole weight. Shaking, eyes closed, he tried to sort out the mix of anger and humiliation flooding through him.

Long ago, he'd abandoned the suspicion that anyone here was a truly black-hearted villain. He'd even become accustomed to the general presence of *Magic*. At the end of the day, though, he was fundamentally the Fantasarians' diametric opposite. That day in the snow, Tali's arrow should have barely scratched him, let alone punctured his armor, but the Elven Steel knocked him unconscious. It left him with the flu-like hangover and feeble arm for days. While the wound didn't bother him much anymore, every now and then he would move just spryly enough to get a sharp reminder of the event. Contrary to his prior declaration, "I'll never be one of you," some tiny voice in his head chanted, tauntingly, that he had, in some small part, begun to feel like he belonged here. That being a Mech didn't necessarily define him, but, obviously, it did, consciously or not. More to the point, he was ultimately there as a tool in their Resistance plot.

A knock drummed on the door.

"It's open," Reman grunted.

Hinges creaked softly, the door clicked shut again, and Legren's voice was calm, even casual.

"How much have you pieced together?"

Reman didn't move. "Most of it, probably."

"Let's hear it."

Reman's anger spiked. "Yes, let's." He about-faced, but otherwise stood absolutely motionless. "I'm not going to jump through hoops on this one. I'm supposed to be part of the team, so don't stand there and observe me like you've been doing, 'cause I've got to tell you: I'm starting to get *real* sick of it."

"To be fair, you also tend to become irritated when told something you already know," Legren pointed out. "So I was attempting to avoid repeating myself."

"Fine. But unless you can tell me that you didn't set me up and that you haven't been lying to me this entire time—"

"I have not been lying to you this entire time."

"But you did set me up?"

"No."

"What then? Everything your precious princess said was a lie? I mean, forget the fact that you didn't bother to mention that this operation is in direct rebellion against your monarchy — I figured that much out on my own — did you or did you not arrange for me to be in that clearing?"

"I did not. I only knew someone would be there, but not who or why. That person, I knew, would be the key to starting—"

"How? How did you know that?"

"It's…complicated."

"Of course it is."

"What I can tell you is that, while we may be hiding this movement from the monarchy, there are others involved outside of this camp. Information that a Mech was being sent into our backyard was intercepted from ICORE and came to me from one of these sources."

"So I'm not the first after all…another lie…"

"You *are*," Legren insisted, "the first non-Fantasarian."

Reman snorted. "Technicality."

"It was not some diabolical plan, Reman. I was granted with intelligence, saw an opportunity and I took it."

"Why should I believe you?"

"Because you've done the same thing to your sister."

The words hit Reman like a whip. He opened his mouth to respond, so stunned and so outraged that he actually sputtered for a moment before any coherent words formed.

"I — It's not the same thing—"

"You've taken a leap of faith, put your trust in someone else to lead the proper people to you on a blind hope."

"And you couldn't have told me this before?"

"How would it have looked? The whole world thinks we stole the Oniyum and here we claim that we might be able to live without it. If the Royals found us out, they wouldn't merely squash us and keep it quiet or they would offer us up as a scapegoat; a way to escape our current persecution and regain Fantasarian reputation on Kabathan."

Like the night of chaos after the Nenjin attacked, Reman heard the words of the ICORE advert echo in the back of his mind: *whatever the cost.*

"I couldn't take the risk that you might not do the same," Legren added quietly.

"Ah, like Sethera warned you. I'm an evil outsider, looking for an opportunity to sell you out the first chance I get. Do I have that right?"

"You may have been. I needed to wait. It was always my intention to tell you eventually."

"When?"

Legren didn't answer.

Reman's rigid posture slackened. He folded his arms and slumped back against the bench. "Ever since I got here, you've been preaching tolerance, trust, equality, and I bought it. I told you about my friends and my sister and yet, all the while you're keeping secrets behind your teeth. How can I trust you? I mean, what else are you keeping secret?"

Reman knew his words were harsher than was fair, but the sting of betrayal was sharp and he couldn't shake it. He couldn't bring himself to accept that Legren had been acting out of caution, not mistrust.

"The wars have crippled us," Legren insisted through a tight jaw, his composed veneer slipping. "We *need* this movement—"

"Crippled *you?*" Reman shouted. His head swirled with old, longstanding prejudices and the new personal chagrin. "We've *all* suffered because of the wars! What makes you — *any* of you" — he gesticulated wildly about the room, indicating the whole of the camp's population — "so special?" He stepped back, shook his head, and took a deep breath to calm himself. "You know what? It doesn't matter. I won't stay in a place where I am still considered an outcast, still being lied to."

Legren didn't reply right away. In fact, he looked straight down, almost hanging his head. As irritating as this nothing response was, Reman waited, trying to steady his frenzied pulse. Legren took a deep breath of his own and reached into his cloak. He withdrew something small, fingers closing tightly around it. Reman felt a distinct shift in the room's energy. So much so, he wondered if there was *Magic* involved, but he didn't smell anything.

"Allow me to offer you an explanation." He extended his fist towards Reman, as though preparing to drop some sacred object before him. His face was no longer defensive or self-righteous, but tentative. Almost reluctant. "The truth behind the Resistance," he whispered.

Reman extended an open palm.

"Brace yourself," Legren added before he dropped an old, twisted piece of paper into Reman's hand.

The second it touched his skin, the room around them vanished. Something slammed into Reman, propelled him backwards, off his feet, and into a burst of all-encompassing light.

He is outside. The sun winks down through the trees. It is the perfect, late-summer color; a deep, rich gold, so potent a shade, you can almost touch it. You expect it to pile up in clumps the way it falls and lays over the leaves.

A beautiful day. Such a shame it will have to end in blood.

Shock and confusion warped Reman's senses. The scene around him trembled. He tried to stop moving, but couldn't. He only trudged ahead.

Moss softens the ground underfoot. Sweat prickles along his forehead. It's warm. He glances down at the plate armor covering his chest, mail and tunic beneath it. He is distracted by the leather bracers, however, branded with the King's Crest — the highest honor. He still feels a swell of pride from earning them, so many years ago.

Reman strained to comprehend the *Magic* at play here — what else could this be?

Were these Legren's memories? He was witnessing moments in real time… as Legren had lived them? Reman relaxed slightly, but still he struggled to maintain his own awareness in tandem with Legren's.

A full squad of Mercs. Close at hand and moving. All of them shall die. He and his warriors will see to that.

It's a quarter hour later, and the air is wrenched apart by gunshots. The sounds are alien and abhorrent. Legren can barely maintain concentration as he strides into the clearing and fights the Merc leader.

Shouts continue in his ears as he fights, sword flying.

There are deaths; the Mercs are all disposed of — or so he believes — but his own number has been diminished as well. Their party arrived with five. Only two leave; he and Marcus. Together, they stroll towards the tree line, without a second more to spare on sorrow. Neither of them speak as they retreat back towards their village.

A whistling echoes overhead, but it is not like the familiar melody of Xettar's Magic. *This is something else. Something unforgiving.*

He stops walking and looks up. Fire envelopes everything; the trees, the ground, Marcus and himself. All is noise and smoke and, finally, silence.

Lying on his back, he floats somewhere between awake and asleep…between alive and dead. Pain ravages his insides like nothing he has ever known, physical and mental. He chokes on sorrow. He pushes those thoughts away and new images swim before him and, out of the dancing cyclone, a specific one catches his focus: Sethera — no, her mother, Rewelle. Galvyn stands beside her. They turn to face each other, eyes frosted over with tenderness. Then they peer directly at Legren. And he understands. It's all for them, all for a future they might never see.

And he remembers.

He is back in the sitting room, telling them he has been chosen. Or, rather, wordlessly handing them the letter, unable to make a sound for his shock. Galvyn's face lights up so fast, Legren isn't sure he hasn't been beaming to begin with, that he didn't already know. He tosses the parchment into the air triumphantly and pulls Legren into a mighty embrace. A knight of the Royal Guard! he shouts.

Over Galvyn's shoulder, Legren can see Rewelle's eyes shining with a mother's pride.

Sethera is not nearly so happy for him.

You'll be going away, then?

He answers with a nod. Her face darkens, she bites down hard — almost a pout, but not quite — and flees from his company without saying anything else. As a child, she wanted to see the High Kingdom, but grew averse to the lights, false manners, and looming towers of stone. She couldn't bear the lifestyle at Court, but Legren had been entranced and his work has paid off. He has made an impression on the King and will no longer be sent to and fro on this mission and that. He will be stationed permanently at Court, as part of the Royal Guard. It is the highest honor he could have hoped for and as he watches Sethera's retreating back, he feels a surge of anger and disappointment in her for not seeing the same things as he. This is his chance to do good work, protect the realm at the topmost level. But that anger fades. She will see it, soon enough, and realize how important this is to him.

He knows, too, that she fears another truth that hits him suddenly and painfully. When will they meet again?

The four of them send hailstorms of letters back and forth over the passing year. Sethera is the first person he sees upon his return. He finds her in the pine grove, throwing daggers at a target. Her skills have improved, but she still holds the weapons awkwardly, almost reluctantly. She turns, looking at him blankly and they stand in silence until a smile pulls at her mouth. He takes a tentative step toward her and she suddenly bounds forward throwing her arms around him. He holds her tight, not realizing until this moment how much he has missed her or this place.

She wants to go with him this time, which he can't quite rationalize. He does not worry for her safety, only for her happiness. He explains the hardships and reasons why it is a less than favorable way of life. She turns those reasons back on him, asking why he accepts those awful terms, then. He can't answer her — can't find the words. It's just something I must do, he finally says, but that answer infuriates her. Deep within, he already knows she's right, but the luster of the High Kingdom's towers has not yet faded.

The battle is short, but nasty. He bleeds from several wounds. None are deadly, but he is severely weakened. He can only tell that the fight is over by the silence that's settling around the field.

Galvyn is gesticulating wildly. He is adamant about his cause. Behind him, Rewelle watches, utterly still. Legren interrupts the speech to ask what Sethera thinks. Galvyn stops talking and his hands drop. So, too, does Rewelle's gaze. Legren looks back and forth between them. Is this...shame? They confess they have not told their daughter the full extent of their plans. They wish to keep her safe. They've already received several threats and dodged one near-successful assassination attempt. You must tell her! He implores them. She has to know what they face. They circle back to the debate, to the Resistance, and ask, flat-out, for Legren's involvement again. He declines.

Sethera tosses a dagger at a target. She says she does not understand the wars, nor does she wish to. Legren admires her view, but cannot entirely agree. They are the result of a force of evil set loose, which is being combated on multiple fronts.

Galvyn and Rewelle will leave in the morning. Another journey to be made to finally put their plans in motion. Legren fears for them, despite their assurances. Surely, they are blinded by enthusiasm.

Legren finds Sethera by the fire that evening and suggests she come with him to the High Kingdom. He can teach her more skills there; but she still has little desire to be a warrior. Galvyn approaches, holding before Sethera an amulet of a bright green stone, carved into an Elvish rune, hanging from a string. He ties it around her neck and Legren recognizes the rune from one of Rewelle's rings. It is beautiful. Sethera beams at him. Galvyn tells her that this trinket is embedded with protective Magic for the days to come; she is to go with them. Not all the way, but enough so that she will not get left behind anymore. Watching, Legren is frozen between outrage and potential relief. Perhaps they will tell her the truth on their journey.

Mid-travel, Xettar surprises them all, arriving to take supper with them. He is an old family friend. He is still talking with them into the late hours of the evening when there is a knock on their Inn room door. A messenger greets Galvyn and hands him a small, crinkled piece of parchment. He reads it and beams at Rewelle. A look passes between them; an unspoken, mutual understanding of hope. An outward visage of shared excitement that all impossible dreams may yet come true. He hands the parchment to Xettar, who reads it and cheers. The paper falls to the ground as they exchange handshakes and hugs. Legren withdraws, not part of this joy, but this is a moment he should not break.

As he slips out, he scoops up the small piece of parchment from the ground. It's a token for the potential of this night. Whatever happens, it should be kept and saved.

Late afternoon brings rain. He hopes it has not delayed their travels, or the travels of others at their gathering.

A single sheet of paper changes hands.   Only a smattering of words are scribbled on it, but Legren's blood runs cold.   Those words amount to one meaning: assassination.

He strains, every force of will desperate to be there, to gain speed, go faster.   He prays that he is wrong, yearns for the chance to hang his head and laugh before the assembly for an overactive imagination.

Legren stumbles from his horse and throws himself up the porch towards Sethera, standing at the far end.   Have they left yet?   He asks in a rush, coming up beside her.   She stares at him, shocked almost to silence by his appearance.

She answers: first thing this morning.   He grasps the porch handle as horror sweeps over him.

Sethera does not wait.   She knows the way and they are running, flying.   It is far, but he feels no shortness of breath.   Not yet.   A stitch forms in his chest, but he does not slow down.   Thunder pounds the sky overhead.   A few pellets of rain smash against the stone road, the grass and the top of his head.   The drops increase until Legren's hair collects in thick ropes around his face, practically slapping him as he dashes forward.

I knew it, I knew it, I knew it.

They round the corner and she throws open the doors.   They pass no one as they tear through the halls.   They reach the conference room and everything stops.

There is an uproar at the long table.   People from every conceivable tribe yell and swing weapons, though no one fires.   He hardly notices though.   Galvyn already lies dead on the floor.   Rewelle moves towards him and is, in turn, struck, by what or whom Legren does not know.   A slash appears across her back and even at this distance, Legren can feel her life force leaving her.   She buckles, not dead, but mortally wounded.   She lurches toward Sethera, hand stretched out.   Sethera screams, then screams again, a wretched sound she has never before made, nor did he know she could make.   She lunges forward.   Before he knows what he is doing, he lurches forward too, holding her back, but barely containing her.   She fights, straining to get to them, but as the light leaves Rewelle's eyes, the struggle ceases.   Good thing too, as the weight of it all slams into Legren, watching her fall back, alongside her husband. Sethera drops, unable to stand, and he pulls her into an embrace, as much for her comfort as his own. She hangs, frail, in his arms and his senses finally kick in. He backs up hastily, scanning the room. No one sees them — or they don't care — nor do they approach the two dead on the floor. None but Xettar, who kneels down, next to his friends. Silent tears stream down his face. He stands again, towering over the table of hollering enemies, it seems over the whole room, says nothing, and vanishes in wisps of gray smoke.

Legren is reeling, wanting to crawl out of his skin or vanish himself, or sink into the earth and never move again. But he can't. He drags Sethera away from the war room as she weeps into his shoulder. Her sobs rack through his whole body. Each one somehow expresses his own sorrow and he manages to get them back to safety. They flee now, back to their own territory. Alone. She holds onto him the entire way.

Six months pass. Galvyn and Rewelle are known around the globe. Some call them martyrs, a few call them heroes, but most call them anarchists. Terrorists. All sorts of hateful things. Sethera doesn't speak anymore. She sobbed nonstop in the days immediately after, then went silent. Legren doesn't speak much either. What is there to say? And of that, how does it even begin to be said?

He can stand it no longer. Legren escapes in the middle of the night like a bandit out of prison. He makes for the sea. He needs to get away; out of the woods. He has never known life beyond the trees, but it feels like the place he needs to be. He finds work on a merchant ship. He finds new friends, too. The ache goes away. Somewhat. More than he had hoped for, anyway. He loses track of time. He knows, though, that he cannot hide away forever. When he begins to miss Sethera more than fear the empty spaces he left behind, he knows he must return.

She stands in the sun-drenched woods holding her father's knife. He barely recognizes her. Was this what it was like for her when she watched him leave for the High Kingdom? Did she fear for him? For who he was becoming? Did she fear for his soul? He can think of no words to speak. They are strangers.

A sliver of pain rips across her face and her eyes fill. He teeters forward, reaching for her, but she pulls back. They stare at one another, so close, yet so distant. A tear rolls down his face, but he remains rooted to the spot. After what has passed, all that has changed between them, they can never repair the damage, never return to their lost lives.

Everything blurs, ricochets, as he's pulled forward, back to the clearing, now engulfed in smoke. Severed pieces of ash and bark drift, weightless, through the haze. He can no longer see the sun, but somewhere above the dust cloud, it must still shine. Regret lingers in the back of his head. His face burns. His left eye throbs. He reaches for it and his fingers meet torn skin, slashed and slick. He opens his mouth and screams...

Reman careened backward until he hit the wall, hard. The paper slipped from his fingers and floated down to the floor, all spark gone out of it. He slid into the corner, back in his own, shaking skin. The torch in the opposite corner still burned. The flame popped and crackled, but the room was otherwise quiet. His ears rang from whatever *Magical* thing had just overtaken him, like the aftermath of a bomb's explosion.

Though the memories faded, and though they were not his own, his throat strained to hold back sobs. He knew this pain. *He knew this pain...*

"I'm sorry you had to see that."

Judging by where the voice came from, Legren had to be standing against the far wall. He may have been speaking to himself, as well as Reman; sorry that anyone had to see it, sorry that it happened, *so, so sorry...*

Reman raked both hands through his hair, forced several shaking breaths, and looked up at Legren. His eyes were bloodshot with dark circles underneath, but dry, unlike Reman's.

"I hope it gives you a different perspective," Legren added, his voice steady.

"Her parents," Reman croaked. His throat was like sandpaper. "They started this? They—" He couldn't bring himself to say the rest.

"Killed before they could see their ideas through," Legren finished. "Died trying to make a change. Their ideas...extinguished."

You're doing this for them. And for her. Reman recognized this sentiment in himself. It was why he joined ICORE. He'd wanted to do what was right, and hadn't known what that was, so he followed Jenda's lead. He'd hoped it would help unite them after their own loss. It hadn't.

The isolation, mixed with consuming loss, and the inability to reach for the one person who mattered most, to clutch at the only semblance of family left…they all understood it. So much of Sethera's behavior slid into focus. They were forced to be reminded, each and every day of her parents. Galvyn and Rewelle's words were now theirs. Their mission was only being kept alive by whether or not Legren's efforts succeeded.

"I have to believe that the Sethera I used to know…she's still in there somewhere. This tragedy shut her down, closed her off. She's become jaded and cynical. She lost and she's hurt, and I'm worried about her."

He'd always been worried about her, though. His memories told that much. It only hurt more now.

"I've tried so many times—" Legren cut himself off, but not before there was a catch in his voice. "Any secrets I've kept from you, this is why."

Because it hurts. It's personal. And it hasn't just been his to share.

"It is not the mentality here that you are inferior or unequal," Legren continued. "It was never my intention for you to feel that way."

Reman wanted nothing more than to believe it was all still a lie, but he couldn't.

Legren clasped his hands together and leaned forward. "This Resistance has to happen. The violence and corruption that have infiltrated our world do nothing but create tragedies like this and so many others that go unseen. And for what? A way of life? A system of government? The world is changing. And so we must change with it. Else nothing will be left but confusion and misery."

"I get it." Reman's voice shook in spite of his every effort to hold it steady. Legren may have told the truth at long last, but it was having a stronger impact than he probably intended. All Reman could do, all he could manage in that moment, was a single condition.

"I'm still in this. I'll still be a part of it, but only *if* I am part of it. Don't leave me in the dark, or set me up, or lie to me again. All right?"

Legren's head bobbed. "Very well."

It wasn't enough. Reman pushed against the wall to sit up straighter. "Can I hold you to that?"

"You have my word."

Reman still wasn't sure if he bought it, but his resolve withered. He sank back against the wall and pressed the heels of his hands against his closed eyelids. Legren's boots scuffed against the floor, retreating, until the door opened, closed, and silence fell again.

Whatever *Magic* had occupied that piece of parchment had wreaked havoc on his nervous system, just like Tali's arrow. The otherworldly sensation receded, but is throat and chest were still tight. His hands trembled and his stomach churned. Legren's memories were so like his own. The day his parents died, he and Jenda hadn't been together when the bomb detonated. He would never know what or how she'd experienced that moment, and she would never tell him. Whenever he'd reflected on it, or tried to imagine what had happened on her end, he pictured her looking the way he had felt — devastated and inconsolable, as Sethera had been — but when he found Jenda surrounded by a sea of rubble, theirs and so many other homes blasted to scraps and sawdust, she was *fine*. She handled her anguish — no fuss — but had to pull away and sever their bond. Just like Sethera and Legren.

What makes you so special?

It was the phrase of the day. First the princess used it, then Reman turned it on Legren, and now it ricocheted back through Reman's mind. What made any of them special? *Nothing.* The simple truth was that they were not so different.

Isn't that the point to all this?

Another knock tapped against the door, but Telena didn't wait for his answer before stepping inside. She approached Reman, still huddled on the floor, and extended her hand, offering him a tiny bottle. "To calm your nerves."

"My nerves are fine," he grumbled.

Her expression softened. "They may not be, later."

He considered it a useless, though friendly gesture, so he took the bottle and she left.

Later that night, however, after the third stretch of nightmares — a disarray of his own memories, blending and mismatched with Legren's — Reman clamored from his bed, desperate. He fumbled for it in the dark, snatched it off the bedside table, uncorked it, and chugged the liquid inside.

It didn't make the dreams subside, but he was able to sleep through them.

When Reman woke the next morning, earlier than usual, he felt groggy, but not sick and overtired. Through the restless night, something became clear. As he did not wake with dread or uncertainty clawing at his insides, he would continue onwards as though nothing had changed. He would wait until he and Jenda came face to face and stand, ready.

He stumbled outside about an hour before daybreak, still half asleep and pulling on his left boot. When the door clicked shut behind him, a chill ran up his spine. The previous night had gone out hot and humid, but just now the air was crisp and cool. A mist hovered over the village, cold and slow-moving. The whole place felt austere and unfriendly and it bothered him. He'd felt at ease here from the first night. The only outward sign of dislike or unpleasantness had come from the people, not the material surroundings. He wondered, attempting to shake off the chill, if it was a delayed reaction on his part; dormant Mech instincts finally catching up with him.

Only a few other civilians were out and about at this early hour, checking crops and setting up for the day. He chalked up his fleeting unease to the unpredictability of Fantasarian geography and his still being an outsider. He'd run a quick, manual scan, then go back to bed.

Bleary-eyed, he roamed to the edge of the village and looked down at the scanner in his hand, seeing a perfectly clean display of the area. All appeared calm and safe. Reman shut off the device and pocketed it. The exercise might have been unnecessary, but the walk felt good. Refreshing.

He had nearly rounded the entire perimeter; up ahead, the front entrance appeared through the thinning mist. Reman rubbed his eyes, dismissing the last trace of his earlier unease.

Then movement quavered in the corner of his eye.

A woman stood a few feet away, her back to him. Reman skidded to a halt. Though he didn't personally know every individual who lived in the camp, something about this person seemed...abnormal. Maybe it was the stillness with which she stood there, facing nothing, doing nothing. Reman hedged towards her with slow, ginger steps, but his boots crunched twigs and dry leaves. She didn't move.

"Excuse me..." He stretched out a hand. "Are you all right?"

The second his hand touched her shoulder, she whirled around. He was just able to see the white of her eyes before she threw him backwards with unexpected force, knocking the wind out of him. On the ground, dizzy and barely able to take a breath, he attempted to reorient himself before the woman — a pale-faced, skin-rotting zombie — reached for his face with one hand, her long, grotesque fingers outstretched. They wrestled as she snarled and clawed the air in front of his face. He grabbed her wrist with one hand and, with the other, punched into her gut. She stumbled back, grip loosening, and he slipped from the creature's grasp entirely. Half-kicking, half twisting, he drew his pistol and fired frenzied shots at its head until it burst.

In the ringing silence, he stared at the dead thing, thunderstruck. The sight of it, lying there, did not compute. A zombie? Here?

Another, undead-like screech echoed behind him. He spun around. Through the gate and between the houses, Reman saw several more zombies stalking into the camp.

To his relief, a siren roared to life. *Xettar's Mech-Fantasarian hybrid alarm.* Now, the whole camp was alerted, even if the zombies had a head start with their attack. It would not be a repeat of the Nenjin invasion. It couldn't.

Reman reset his pistol and charged back towards the entrance.

FIFTEEN

SETHERA

Sethera didn't worry — or even pay attention, really — until the sparks started to fly out of the console. The pod dipped and swerved and a burning smell filled all of the tiny space. Sethera's eyes watered as Mason loosed a string of profanities, Garen yelled techno-babble over him — they'd hit some sort of problem with the navigational controls — and Jenda dove between the men to adjust levers and switches on the dash.

"Just land the damn thing!" she shouted.

They plummeted. Sethera clutched the metal rod above her head as the sight of the field below sped closer. She expected the pod to sprout legs to catch them, but it remain unchanged: a steel ball, headed for an open field. *I sincerely hope this isn't how it ends*, she thought.

The initial THUMP onto the ground was impressive and gave them all a good lurch forward, but, once landed, it continued to slide, eventually coasting to a stop. No one spoke and a loud hissing noise filled the cockpit. The two men sprang up, reaching for the tiny metal doors, while Jenda climbed backwards, past Sethera. Smoke followed, huge clouds of it, smelling like rancid seafood and manure. Jenda threw open the side hatch and climbed out, Sethera close behind, coughing, eyes running.

"Don't wander off or anything," Jenda advised, hand on holster.

"Wouldn't dream of it," Sethera replied. It wasn't like she could get away; they'd left the blinking manacles strapped around her wrists. Jenda smiled, but her hand didn't stray from its perch on her weapon.

Looking around, mist hung thick in every direction. Sethera planted herself on the edge of the hatch, legs swinging. She'd felt a little motion sick even before the crash, stuck in a greasy little corner behind the pilot's seat, but the fresh air chased away both her nausea and the smoke's odor.

The men bickered at the front of the vehicle, where dark smoke billowed out from under the raised hood. Not a good sign.

Sethera speculated that they might manage the rest of the way on foot. She actually recognized the area, even in the hazy, overcast light. She looked back at the Mech trio. Jenda grimaced at the smoke, absently jiggling her left foot and twisting the fingers not hovering near her pistol. Anxious.

Sethera wondered if Reman had any idea how much this quest meant to her; how much he, himself, meant to her. Unlikely. He would have said so.

Fools.

If not for her reaction when Sethera first dropped Reman's name — tensing up, the lift of hopeful eyebrows — Sethera would never have believed that this woman was Reman's sister. To start with, they looked nothing alike. His hair was sandy brown, while hers was almost black. Then, unlike Reman, Jenda clearly knew how to deceive. Reman wasn't a total pushover, but he didn't seem to have the natural "kill-or-be-killed" instinct. This woman was *tough.* From her posture and how she held her gun, Sethera recognized the confidence in one's weapon, earned from experience. In that, Sethera wondered if she was more like Jenda than her own brother.

How ironic. And while Sethera might predict how Jenda would react in a given situation, understanding her so well also came with a level of respect. Jenda's absolute commitment to finding her brother was downright admirable.

That wasn't exactly a pleasant thought.

"Can you work any faster?" she called.

"You think your voice helps?" Mason grumbled back. A cool, damp wind picked up. Sethera looked skyward to find low-hanging clouds, thick and voluminous.

"You're all aware that rain is on its way, yes?"

"Oh, will you melt?" Mason asked cheerfully.

"No, but your precious engine might," she said in a sickly-sweet tone.

"Just keep working," Jenda advised him. "Rain or no rain, the sooner we get moving, the better."

"Agreed," Sethera muttered.

Jenda scoffed.

"What? You still don't believe me?" Sethera said.

"I still think you're hiding something."

"Aren't we all?" Sethera said sagely, but her amusement evaporated on the spot as she caught a flick of movement behind Jenda's arm.

Sethera dropped to the ground, palm flat against hard-packed dirt. She stared at that spot, no more than a displaced curl of fog, but every instinct told Sethera something was wrong.

"What is it?" Garen moved closer, behind Jenda. Mason leaned around the side of the hood.

"We're not alone." She was about to tell them to trust her, to wait, when the smell hit her. It was just a fleeting whiff, but that was all she needed.

"*Zombies.*" She popped up to see above the hood, into the field behind her, the line of trees hidden by the fog. A lump of anxiety formed in her throat. If they were surrounded, and she had the chilling suspicion they were, then they were trapped inside a frosted bowl without any means of escape except to fight their way out —

She jumped as Mason's rifle squealed, charging up. She turned to find them all taking up their arms completely.

"You're sure?" Garen asked, striding closer to her.

"Yes."

"How do you—"

"Can't you smell it?"

Another flicker of movement stirred, off to the right. Her head pivoted to try and catch it and, this time, she wasn't alone. The Mech trio all looked in that direction as well. Jenda and Mason raised their guns, while Garen drew his own.

"How many?" Garen said.

"I'm not sure, but probably…several."

"All right, then." Mason took a few steps away from the vehicle. He assumed what Sethera could only presume was a much practiced battle stance; feet planted firmly apart, weapon aimed straight ahead. "I could use a good zombie-killin'."

"Keep your voice down," Sethera hissed, keeping her eyes pinned on the last spot of movement, but still no sign of anything more.

"Why?" Mason growled, cocking the gun — loudly. "If there *are* zombies out there, then they already know we're here, don't they?" He looked over his shoulder at her. "So why be quaint?" he whispered — also loudly — sounding, momentarily, like rocks scraping against glass.

Almost in answer, in the distance, a sound unlike any she'd ever heard echoed over the field. All of them looked eastward.

"Mech signature," Garen said.

"Reman," Jenda whispered, probably inadvertently. Even under the circumstances, Sethera rolled her eyes.

"I *told* you," she said, "we've nearly reached the camp, and if they're under attack—"

Something encircled her neck and yanked her off her feet. Choking, she tried to fight back, but her wrists strained against the Mech-shackles. Fighting panic, she used both hands to claw, desperately at rotting, rubbery skin clamped around her neck. How could the undead be so unbelievably strong?

She heard a single, distant click before the creature's head exploded in a shower of thick, slimy skin, bone and dried blood.

Sethera dropped in an unbalanced heap. She dug fingers digging into the damp ground as cool air surged back into her lungs. When she looked up, steam billowed from the barrel of Mason's massive rifle.

He grinned. "Now we're talking."

Zombies poured out of the mist in torrents. From all sides, walking, staggering, some even flat-out ran towards them. Sethera blinked away spots on the edge of her vision, while the three Mechs sprang into action. They took cover against the pod and raised their weapons, not in unison, but in a well-established pattern. Within seconds, the clearing was full of flying laser blasts and corpses dropping.

"Release me," Sethera tried to shout, but her throat strained and barely any sound came out. With what little strength she could muster, she pushed herself up into a stance just as Garen spun and fired over her right shoulder. A corpse fell against her shoulder as it collapsed. The touch sent a shudder ripping through her. She leapt forward, onto the vehicle itself and, even with her wrists strung together, she climbed up the side and onto the roof. The horde surged through the mists below, but the stream seemed to thin at the tree line. Even so, Sethera needed her hands back, she needed to fight —

Something moved, isolated, higher in the trees. A woman, woven among the branches like a snake, watched the zombies scramble below, her eyes wide and all-seeing.

If there's one…

Sethera's eyes flicked around the rest of the clearing and she spotted them: three more hooded faces, all watching the animated bodies with the same wide, hungry eyes.

"Necromancers!" Sethera yelled. "Four of them!"

She fumbled with the folds of her shirt, searching for her amulet. It pulsed with the dull beat of one, maybe two spells within. Not remotely enough for combat.

Only the first Necromancer noticed Sethera. As their eyes met, even over distance, an unearthly chill ran down Sethera's spine.

Her shoulder popped with a sickening crunch as a hand yanked on her elbow. Zombies sprawled along the side of the vehicle, clambering up towards her. She dug her heel against the flat metal underfoot and threw her full weight against the creature's grip. Its fingers slipped and her limb snapped free, disorienting them both. It soared away, while she stumbled and fell onto one of the pod's rails. Balance back, Sethera gripped the steel with both hands and propelled herself forward. She swung out in a tight arc, scattering two more zombies behind the first. As she landed on the edge of the vehicle, opposite of where she crouched a moment ago, something grabbed her around the neck again. This time, she tightened her elbows together and threw them into the gut of the creature that held her. It buckled instantly and she twisted, shoving it sideways, off the roof.

"Let me out of these!" she shouted again, voice stronger now. She crossed the roof to look back down at the three Mechs — but found only Garen and Jenda below. A deep BOOM resonated some feet ahead. She glanced forward and spotted Mason, clearly enjoying himself, firing in every possible direction with the more average sized gun. The zombies gave him a wide berth, but kept coming, nonetheless.

"Like we have that kind of time!" Jenda hollered back as she fired rapidly in varying directions.

"Take them off!" Sethera repeated, throwing a quick glance over her shoulder. The first Necromancer had vanished. Sethera looked desperately back at Jenda, only to find that she and Garen were nearly overwhelmed by the creatures. The Mechs stood back to back, firing into the fray with careful precision, laced with an edge of panic.

"And give me back my knife!" Sethera whipped around to look down at Jenda, who is in the middle of reloading, looking down.

"Let me fight!" Sethera yelled, even louder over the snarling increasing around them. "Take the shackles—"

"They're not shackles—"

"Whatever they are!" Sethera screamed. "Get them off of me! We'll all die here if you don't!"

"No, you'll just run off!"

"I won't."

Her voice must have conveyed her honesty — which, if true, would have been a first — because Jenda stopped firing and looked up at Sethera, every trace of uncertainty blatant in her eyes. Her head even twitches slightly, involuntarily, to one side, unconvinced. The sound around them seemed to die away.

"I won't run." Sethera took even herself by surprise with the quiet sincerity in her voice. She thrust her wrists and the manacles forward, not even trying to hide her own desperation and vulnerability. Though she wanted her freedom back, she didn't want to escape or give away her game by doing so. She wanted them to free her. She wanted their acceptance.

I want what? she demanded back at herself. *I want* what*?!*

The confused look on Jenda's face was completely warranted as she watched these thoughts play out on Sethera's face. Still, Sethera continued to stand there, shocked by this revelation. She didn't want to lie to them, or keep playing them, and not because of Legren's intentions or because resuming the play would be too much work...she genuinely didn't want to keep misleading them or betray the trust that she'd evidently gotten.

That might make our return to camp a bit awkward —

"Jenda!" Garen shouted.

Zombies pushed past him and Jenda raised her gun to loose several shots into the surrounding group. Sethera gritted her teeth and glanced toward Garen — perhaps he would release her? — but then Jenda reached up, pressed a single, hidden button, and the shackles fell away, lifeless.

"Catch!" Jenda called, even as she continued to fight.

Sethera heard the hum of her knife soaring through the air. Like a magnet, the handle landed in her outstretched hand.

She jumped down and joined the brawl, blade flashing amongst the shower of laser blasts. Her knife whipped through the corpses and bodies soared away in tatters.

She fell into rhythm with the Mechs' attack and, slowly, the numbers thinned. Once the nearest zombies had been cleared, Sethera scanned the trees again. Only one Necromancer still perched there, like an oversized vulture. Her face contorted with rage.

"Mason!" Sethera shouted. His head spun and she pointed into the woods at the figure. "There!"

He shifted the gun, but before he could fire, she sent another chilling glance at Sethera, raised her arms and vanished. Mason fired anyway, severing branch from trunk.

Around them, the zombies collectively stopped snarling and withdrew. They scampered back towards the woods the way they came, like troops ordered to retreat. Only Mason gave chase, and not for long.

For a few, terse seconds, the air was completely still. They held their breath, waiting for any sight or sense of movement from the metaphorical graveyard around them. What if they had just missed one? What if there was unusually smart, unusually bold one that was playing defeated, waiting to catch them off guard?

Slowly, their heads turned in one another's direction, looking from face to face for validation that the danger had passed. They took turns nodding until their postures relaxed in earnest. Sethera searched the tree line for any sign of Necromancers, but they had all fled.

"Why did they attack us?" she asked aloud. A few weeks ago, the thought never would have crossed her mind. She would have abandoned the Mechs, the mission, and gone after them, just like Mason, desiring answers and retaliation.

Just how much influence has Legren had over me?

"They're zombies," Jenda snapped. "Isn't that just what they do?"

Sethera shook her head. "They were being controlled."

"Who cares?" Mason holstered his pistol and swiped grime off his rifle before he joined Garen at the front of the pod. The sides were dented, scratched, and the whole frame tilted to one side.

"What's the damage?" Mason leaned over Garen, who knelt by the panel, and Jenda pulled out a scanner from a side pocket.

Garen lifted the torn wires, most of them shredded nearly to confetti. "Considerable."

He heaved himself up from the ground and shook his head at his companions. Jenda scowled but lowered the scanner.

Sethera scanned the trees again. "They were after us…"

"Why?" Mason barked.

"I don't know, but Necromancers use dead bodies as puppets. Dark *Magic* in all its glory."

The Mechs started blankly back at her. Hailing from the far side of Kabathan, they had probably never even seen a Necromancer up close, let alone know the full background of one's power.

"So we're stranded?" Mason's voice interrupted Sethera's thoughts. Turning to look back at the Mech trio, she saw that, rather than answering, Garen looked to Sethera.

"We're not far," she told him.

"Which means…?" Jenda prompted.

Sethera opened her mouth to respond, but stopped when the sound of a distant, blaring alarm met her ears. Her head pivoted towards the sound and she listened, hard. The alarm continued, interspersed with more laser blasts.

"What?" Jenda took half a step forward. Sethera swallowed, grasping that only she, with Elfin hearing, had heard. She opened her mouth again, when the noise of several screeching zombies reverberated around the clearing.

Not a retreat, Sethera realized. A relocation.

Our village.

She plunged headlong into the underbrush. In the midst of her sprint, Sethera realized that the Mechs had fallen behind her, but not because they were unable to keep up. They were following her, trusting her, and she was glad. Not in the smug way she may have done even a few hours ago, but, to her chagrin, in a swell of emotion she could only recognize as gratitude.

Blast! She trusted them right back. More than that, too, she felt a pang of guilt, knowing the truth they ran towards and how she contributed to misleading them.

Even at a run, she laughed.

Well played, Legren, she thought. *Well played.*

Sixteen

Reman

Sprinting towards the village square, he could see it was already overrun; a frantic siege compared to the eloquence of the Nenjin. Zombies tore open doors, smashed windows, and grasped at helpless citizens. One zombie charged out of a building, dragging a young girl into the square. It threw her to the ground and reared over her, its rotting teeth bared. Reman fired at it and the laser blast knocked the zombie sideways, off its feet. The girl scurried backwards, too shaken to even scream. Reman ran to her, offering his hand. She jumped and pulled away from him. Chagrin and ostracism loomed, but when she recognized him, relief swept over her face and she grabbed his hand.

"Get to the caves," he urged her. "Hurry!"

He repeated the same shout to the other frightened civilians running by.

Another pair of zombies stalked toward Reman. He fired and missed, but one pelted sideways as an arrow took it in the head. Reman spun. On the far side of the square, high in the tree branches, bows drawn, Tali and Telena sent arrows flying, each one landing on target.

More zombies clustered a few feet away. They turned simultaneously towards him, but then, for no apparent reason, they paused mid-step. In one motion, they turned and left Reman standing alone. Dazed, he followed their trajectory. Six meters away, Legren and Brock entered the fray, swords flying.

Off to the right, Xettar fought under the trees, casting spells and swinging his staff. Reman, however, was completely safe; all of the zombies' attention focused on the others. *What was going on?*

Movement on his left lugged his attention sideways. Almost obscured from view, a pale-faced female figure, draped in a long, black cloak hovered in the shadows of a building, watching the fight, her light blue eyes bright and sharp on the leaders across the square. Another pale-faced woman leered around another building, fully engrossed on the fight.

A screech tore across the square. Reman spun in time to see Brock grab a zombie and twist the head sideways. The body stopped moving and fell, lifeless, as he released it. Reman heard him growl, "I hate zombies," before charging back into the melee.

The women's smiles flickered. Reman stared at them, looking from one to the other then back to the fight. As he turned to look at them a third time, one set of eyes slid over and met his. Even across the square, his breath caught and a chill spread through him. Her gaze, otherworldly and somehow hollow, held him. His mind went sluggish and foggy, slowing the world around him to an incoherent blur. He felt no pain, but his limbs grew so heavy that each movement required enormous effort. By the time he managed to turn his head, the tips of decaying fingers brushed his face. Jarred out of his trance, Reman lunged backwards and fired almost aimlessly. Instead of producing blasts, however, the gun sputtered and moaned. The few lights on the side of it dimmed and sputtered out. He backpedaled as the zombie — and three more — came at him, picking up speed as he retreated. He shook the gun, smacked it, swore at it, but it remained useless.

The main zombie pounced. Reman caught it by the wrists but it snarled at him, slipped his grip, and seized his shoulder. It wasn't an especially forceful strike, but it tweaked the remnants of his old wound and pain seared through him. His strength slackened for just a moment and the zombie forced him down. Now sprawled on the ground, Reman wrestled with it, just as he had with the first. With no gun to reach for and his shoulder burning, sweat broke out across his face. His arms began to shake from waning strength. The additional three stalked closer. Adrenaline surged and he got a free hand of his own. He felt, frantically, around his belt searching for something, anything and his fingers found a small pocket knife. He flicked it open and stabbed, burying it in the creature's neck.

It screamed once and collapsed sideways, on top of his weakened shoulder. He struggled under the corpse's weight as the other three closed in above him. Reman pushed against the ground with his heels, sliding backwards, brandishing the little knife — hardly enough to hold off three at once. He prepared to roll sideways, bracing himself for whatever more pain might kick up in his shoulder, but a spray of laser blasts struck the creatures from behind.

As each one dropped, Reman searched for his savior. Jenda, gun still raised, stood not two feet away, staring down at the three zombies. Reman's heart leapt. Relief flooded through him, yet the sight of her shocked him into motionlessness.

She ran forward. "What's the first thing they teach you in Basic?" Her voice was calm, collected, practical, just like he remembered it. She kicked the creature off of him, then threw out her hand. He grabbed it and she pulled him up. He toppled a bit, trying to regain balance while staring, open-mouthed at her. She unholstered her second pistol and thrust it at him.

"Never go anywhere without your gun," she finished.

It was like nothing had happened; as though they were on the training grounds at ICORE's Southern Central Base and he'd lost a few points for failure to prepare. Reman wrapped his fingers around the handle of the pistol. In those few seconds, he considered protesting — he *had* taken his gun with him — but the look in her eyes was not sincere reproach. It was relief, which he knew she probably didn't want him to see, but it was there, a small fraction of what she was feeling, just from seeing him. Alive. He released a breath he had been holding since first mentioning Jenda's name. A matching knot of worry in his stomach loosened.

They had made it, unharmed.

She's here.

Realization seized him. On some level, he never actually thought she would come.

He had wished, had spoken of her as a possible ally in the same way he used to tell himself he might see her during holidays or when they were on leave. Possible? Yes. But when those visits had grown shorter and shorter, he began to fear that the distance between them stretched too wide, too deep. She no longer cared about him.

So why would she follow some Fantasarian girl who dropped his name? Better, yet, why would she be out searching the wilderness for him at all?

But she's here. She came.

Renewed hope sparked inside his chest.

Something blasted behind him, shattering their silent exchange. He looked over his shoulder. Zombies were still closing in and the combat still raged, Mason and Garen among the fighters. Reman smiled, even more relieved at the sight of his friends.

He turned back to Jenda, powering up his new gun and, without another word, they both pivoted, raised their pistols and ran back into the fray.

They eventually moved, but stayed side by side, fighting together. Reman never saw Sethera, but figured she had to be there somewhere. He thought he caught a flash of silver at one point, her ever-prominent dagger, flying through the air, but it could have been his imagination.

Several hours passed before the fight ended. Zombie remains lay, scattered, across every corner of the camp grounds, punctuated by a smattering of fallen Fantasarians. Reman shuddered. It would take ages to erase these images from his memory.

The Nenjin attack had been loud, full of screams and cries in the night, followed by shouts, fires, and buzzing insects. It was nothing like the unearthly silence that surrounded the village now. Even the bugs were quiet. While the noise had implied action, this lack thereof bore a new weight of helplessness.

The remaining, living warriors were bruised and tired, but already moving, carrying bodies out of the square. Others gathered deserted weapons and helped the more severely wounded. On the far side of the square, Tali and Telena were reclaiming arrows.

Reman still had his pistol raised and only lowered it when he heard the click of Jenda re-holstering her gun. If she thought it was safe, it probably was. He turned to face her. Explanations rose up in his throat immediately, all fighting to spill out of him first, but before he could say a single word, Jenda pulled him into a tight embrace.

He was, for the second time, struck speechless. He knew she was glad to see him, but Reman could never have predicted such an action from her. Even as kids, she'd had a detached nature. And yet, here she clung to him as though for dear life. The shock ebbing away, along with the soreness in his shoulder, he settled an arm around her just as she drew back. She looked over his shoulder as Garen and Mason appeared. Both covered in muck, but smiling, they clapped Reman on the back and, in spite of his surprise, Reman beamed back.

"This raid's left everybody confused and exhausted," Jenda said. "We should go. Now."

"They'll probably notice if we just stroll through the main gate, though," Garen said.

Mason consulted his portable scanner. "There's a breach in the *Magical* perimeter on the north end of the camp. We can sneak out there."

"Any zombies lingering?" Garen asked.

"No, we're clear for fifty meters in every direction."

Jenda nodded. "Let's go."

She grabbed Reman's good arm, pulling him towards her again as they made to leave.

"Actually..." He leaned back, out of her grasp. "I'm not going anywhere and neither are you."

Jenda's gaze was already wary, but Garen took a deep breath, as though expecting this. "Reman, trust us. Don't believe their lies. Sethera told us about this Resistance and she's right. It's a suicide mission."

"So we're getting you out, whether you like it or not." Jenda tugged his arm again, but he resisted.

"No." Reman was proud of how confident he sounded saying it, but it tasted bittersweet. It was the first time he had ever stood up to her. He could see the uncertainty register on her face; her eyes slightly narrowed, brows bunched together. Reman glanced at Garen, who looked cautiously from brother to sister.

"Come to think of it," Mason's voice cut in, breaking the suddenly uncomfortable silence, "you don't seem all that surprised to see us."

"That's because I knew you were coming."

"Excuse me?" Jenda said.

Reman took a deep breath. "It wasn't supposed to go like this."

"No?" Mason said, crossing his arms.

"Well…it's complicated…"

"So, explain," Garen said, still the calmest of them all, but even his tone contained an underlying impatience. Reman surveyed each of them, landing lastly on Jenda.

You've done the same thing…to your sister.

Reman clenched his jaw. He had not lied to them and he would prove it.

SEVENTEEN

LEGREN

*N*ow what?

Legren studied what was left of the camp. Rotting, dismembered corpses lay everywhere. Smoke drifted off the ground from dying embers. Not only was everything filthy, but the day had grown sticky and damp, somehow making it all more uncomfortable.

Legren looked skyward. The clouds hung low, dense, and seemed ready to burst. Distant thunder had rumbled off and on through the day, but no drops had fallen. He wished the skies would just crash open and release a storm to scrub away the stench of death and fighting.

I'm willing to risk all that I have.

He didn't want to look down again. He feared that, were he to look too closely at the dead faces, he would see Galvyn and Rewelle among them.

Lives are at stake.

None of his reasoning seemed to matter in that moment. It was his fault; they'd been far too careless and it had led them to this unforgiving conclusion. Over the deafening stillness around him, he caught the timbre of Telena's voice. She and Tali collected arrows and fallen weapons on the far side of the square. Even at a distance, Legren recognized the worry on their faces. He speculated that their words were not even the common tongue, but their hallowed dialect of centuries past, which they never used except in times of great strife.

The knot in his gut tightened.

Was that another roll of thunder he heard in the distance? *How appropriately dramatic,* said a small voice in his head that sounded very much like Sethera. Legren searched the square for her, but the sight of four Mechs gathered in a tight cluster at the far edge of the camp distracted him. For all the arm-waving Reman was doing and the reddening faces, they were clearly deep in argument. Another pang of guilt struck Legren. One more piece of the plan gone awry.

All for naught. He felt like his old self again, trembling with old anger, old resentment for the futility of their situation and an underlying fear that nothing would or could ever change.

On the other side of the square, Xettar had joined the Elves. Legren searched the area for Sethera once more. Still not seeing her, he drew a deep breath and he, too, started forward.

"What happened?" Legren asked as he met them. His manner was blunt, towards any of them who could answer. He didn't see the point in being delicate on the subject, not anymore.

"Necromancers, but it's like they weren't even here," Xettar said. "They left no *Magical* trace whatsoever. I couldn't even tell you how many zombies there were, let alone how they got in." Xettar shook his head. "I apologize."

"For what?" Legren said.

"My *Magical* traps failed a second time—"

"You've been distracted," Legren said shortly.

"Perhaps, but—"

"What *do* you know?"

"Only that it was — from what I could tell — three Necromancers who had Animated the corpses to come after us, the leaders. I haven't reasoned out why yet."

"Do you suppose they're in league with another tribe, like the Nenjin?" Tali proposed.

"I doubt it."

"In any event, we are no longer safe here." Legren faced Tali directly. "Evacuate the citizens through the tunnels and see them to the main Northeastern Encampment. Take with you however many warriors you think necessary."

She nodded once and hastened away.

"Those too wounded to travel are being taken to the Assembly Hall as a makeshift hospital," Legren continued to Telena. "Oversee that operation and keep me informed of the progress. And for that reason," Legren added, turning to Xettar, "we still need protective cover. Do anything, whatever you have to, to make that happen."

"Anything?" the Mage said quietly.

"*Anything.*"

Telena and Xettar exchanged a quick, nervous look.

"But what about the—" she said.

"The Resistance will have to wait. We are compromised."

They did not press him and he was glad. He wasn't sure he could answer them properly if they did. In their silence, however, the question hovered between them, unasked. *Wait for how long?*

His fingers had gone cold. He closed them into tight fists, nails digging into his skin.

"We need to start tending to the wounded right away, then," Telena instructed Xettar. "Anyone showing signs of infection should be brought to me immediately…"

As she continued, Legren ran through practical precautions they could take and Brock would be best to —

Fresh worry fluttered through his chest.

"Wait," he interrupted Telena, "where's Brock?"

And then Legren saw him. Scowling, shoulders back, short sword down but drawn, he pounded across the grounds, headed straight for Reman's turned back.

In an instant, Legren knew exactly what was about to happen. He dove forward, but did not reach the group before Brock grabbed Reman's shoulder, shoved and forced him around so that they were face-to-face. Though surprised, the Mechs instantly formed a line around Reman and whipped out their guns, though only one of the soldiers — the biggest of the three — actually aimed at Brock.

"And what have you got to say, eh?" Brock demanded.

"About what?" Reman retorted, barely fazed.

"Brock!" Legren called, still running towards them.

"You got all these Mech gizmos everywhere and yet not one of 'em picked up on a zombie attack?" Brock continued.

"I don't know what happened, I was—"

Brock's dagger snapped up, pointed at Reman's chest. The two remaining Mech guns swung up, all three barrels now aimed at Brock's head. He was outnumbered, but it didn't stop him from leaning closer to Reman.

"What's the point of your being here if your toys don't work?"

Legren finally reached them and pulled Brock back, forcing his hand and blade down.

"They *have!*" Reman insisted. "They detected the Nenjin, didn't they? And the alarm Xettar and I installed clearly functioned as intended." He looked past Brock, to Xettar, who had joined them as well. "I'm glad you got to it before I did."

Instead of nodding or making a witty reply, however, Xettar shook his head. "I...didn't."

Reman blinked, confused. "Then...who did?"

He and Xettar looked around at the group, but no one spoke.

"A lot of good it did for the injured folks in the Assembly Hall," Brock said, pushing forward again, but Legren stepped between the two groups. The guns stayed raised, two following Brock, one now fixed on Legren.

Reman spread his arms, hands waving on either side. "Stand down."

Slowly, the weapons lowered.

Legren swiveled to address each group evenly. "Our defenses have been breached threefold; twice *Magically* and now through Reman's technology."

"We didn't pick up any activity on our scanners, either," one of the Mech soldiers agreed, holstering his gun. The silver pin clipped to his chest indicated him as the leader, Garen. Everyone turned to look at him, but he continued, unaffected. "The only thing that clued us in was that alarm. We didn't know what it was, but it got us here."

"Our enemies continue to get smarter," Legren said. "The last thing we will do is assist them by creating discord within our own ranks. Everyone here is to be trusted and believed." He looked pointedly at Brock. "No exceptions."

Brock jutted his chin at the three new Mechs. "And them?"

Reman gestured to them respectively. "My friends, Garen and Mason. And my sister, Jenda."

Legren nodded to them, then faced Brock and Xettar.

"As I said, our safety here is paramount. Brock, collect a group to stand guard around the perimeter. With *Magic* and Mech both failing, I want to utilize every possible option. We have work to do."

Brock threw a last, nasty look at Reman, then stalked away, followed by Xettar. Legren waited until they were both gone, then turned to face Jenda, Garen, and Mason fully.

"My apologies for the rather unconventional welcome. And my thanks for your assistance in this battle. I am Legren, head of this Fantasarian settlement."

He bowed slightly. Garen nodded, Mason re-holstered his gun, and Jenda just stared.

Reman shuffled his feet. "This way." He gestured away from the square. Slowly, the trio backed away from Legren. Reman tugged on Jenda's arm and Legren half expected them to start bickering, but she just shrugged out of his grip and followed, silently.

Once alone again, Legren heaved a sigh. He felt relieved that it hadn't gone worse, but downtrodden that a fight had nearly broken out between them at all. Just then, he noticed Sethera crossing the adjacent field. She was just slipping her dagger back into its sheath when her head came up and she met his gaze. He nodded to her, once, and she copied him before resuming her walk, back towards the Assembly Hall.

Legren didn't yet have the energy to assign her new orders as he was sure she was likely to come asking of him before long. But he also wanted to know the details of her mission. What conversation had gone on between her and the Mechs? What was the likelihood that they would join the Resistance? Did she overhear any details of the goings-on on the Western Continent?

One of the larger fire pits roared to life nearby. Two soldiers lifted zombie corpse and threw it into the blaze.

Legren couldn't watch. Though disgusting, soulless creatures, they were also puppets, devoid of free will, pulled from their resting places for another's purposes. Whatever the purpose in sending zombies here, it was still a loss on all sides. It would take any Necromancer several weeks to amass a force that big again. Like with the Nenjin, though, they were after something... but what? In spite of all he had going on, Legren considered reaching out to the Royal Guard for more support; to inform them that something had caused interest here. They'd be hearing about this event anyway —

No. He'd have to hide not just one Mech now, but four.

Legren buried his face in his hands, the enormity of his goals, the Resistance at large, suddenly stretched out before him like a desert, unbeatable and endless.

Sharp and shrill, his heart cried out for the Oniyum, and, in that moment, Legren felt that all he wanted in the world was to see it again.

Eighteen

Reman

All Reman could think about was his last full conversation with Jenda. Shortly after their parents died, he found her bustling around in a well-practiced ritual of preparation, perfecting her appearance with all her pins and sashes for ICORE's afternoon swearing in ceremonies.

"What's with you?" she'd asked, searching through a case of badges. He'd muttered an incomprehensible reply.

"If you're going to make me dig it out of you, then let's do it later; I'm gonna be late as it is—"

"I've enlisted."

She laughed, genuinely amused, as she bent over to tie up the laces of her boot. "Right, okay."

"It's not a joke," he insisted, though gently. She laughed again, but this time there was definitely a chiding note mixed with the amusement. He wondered if the *Reman doesn't lie* mantra had rung in the back of her mind.

"Please," she said. "You, join the military? Take up arms? Go out onto a battlefield and kill?"

"Why shouldn't I?"

She hadn't been able to come up with a reply. Silence planted itself between them and took a sort of permanent residence. That had also been the moment that he realized he'd grown taller than her.

When did that happen?

"What?"

Garen's voice, and distant. Reman spun around. The three others had stopped a few yards back from him, huddled together. They'd followed when Reman had walked away from Legren, around the nearest corner, and already a massive gap had formed between them. Mason grumbled something, fingers twitching towards the pistol at his hip. Garen returned a raised eyebrow. Jenda's mouth was a hard, thin line.

Questions flitted through Reman's head, closing in on panic level fast. Should he run back across the divide, launch back into the story? The plans, The Resistance itself? Or would it come off as desperate? One question, though, clanged louder than the rest: *Will they just leave?*

Garen rubbed his chin, then marched forward. Jenda and Mason followed tentatively, exchanging an uncertain glance.

When the four of them stood in a huddle again, Garen considered both siblings. "Why don't you...take a moment?"

Jenda's eyes flicked back towards Reman. He shrugged one shoulder. She inhaled sharply and rubbed her forehead once, hard. Nodding furiously at the ground, she grumbled, "Yeah. Sure."

Reman could practically feel her vibrating with pent up energy. Any private conversation between them might have been necessary, but not likely to go well.

Garen managed a half-smile while Mason rocked back on his heels, arms folded. Already bored, awaiting orders.

There wasn't time to explain the set up with the tents or when the communal meal would be. *I can't just let them wander around, though.*

So, Reman pointed over his shoulder, in his previous, intended direction. "About ten meters that way, you'll come to a grey stone building. That's where I...where I've been staying. There's a lock on the door; nothing fancy, but you'll need to punch in the code. It's 620."

Jenda chuckled dryly, clearly recognizing their mother's birthday.

Garen nodded once, clapped Reman on the shoulder and proceeded with Mason down the indicated route.

Reman turned back to Jenda. Better get this over with.

She followed him across the grounds to the Assembly Hall. Neither of them spoke as they stepped inside, met with a minor uproar of moans, shouts, and coughing. Practically every Fantasarian head twisted to stare at them as they walked and he couldn't fight unbidden memories of the night after the Nenjin invaded. He shuddered. The looks on their faces then were eerily similar to the ones that gazed up at him now; he thought he'd never have to see those looks of doubt and mistrust again.

How naïve.

As swiftly as possible, Reman moved past the chaos, deeper into the building than he normally went, searching for a quiet, empty space. He repeatedly glanced over his shoulder, checking to make sure he hadn't lost Jenda, but she was always there.

Again, he felt that momentary leap of joy. *She's here.* He still wanted her approval, wanted to make her proud. More and more, the amount of time they'd spent apart sank into him. In spite of everything that had happened between them — or hadn't happened, hadn't been shared — he still craved her approval. But between the murmur of the townsfolk and the walls, buzzing with *Magic,* her eyes darted around uncomfortably, her nose wrinkled and shoulders hunched.

They passed one of the main meeting rooms where a deer roasted on a spit, nearly picked clean. *When did someone manage to find the time to go hunting?* In a smaller, side room, soldiers Reman didn't know clustered around a table, heads bent over maps.

Finally, Reman and Jenda reached an alcove at the end of the hall where, in spite of the open doorway out onto the grounds, he knew they wouldn't be bothered — or bother — anyone else.

As soon as she crossed the threshold, she erupted. "I didn't even think you were *capable* of this level of deception."

"That's not fair," he countered, beginning to pace back and forth.

"You lied to us, Reman. You've never done that before!"

"I did not *lie*—"

"Oh, okay, right. You provided Sethera with the information and means to lie for you. You're right, that's in no way the same thing."

"What would you have done?"

"I wouldn't have allied myself with these freaks in the first place!" Both of their voices rose so rapidly, he knew they'd soon be screaming at each other. With very strong effort, he resisted the instinct to match her volume.

"Look, the point was to get you guys here. We had a whole system laid out, but the zombie attack threw everything off."

"So the ends justify the means, huh?"

Despite her condescension, he again refrained from yelling, struggling to disentangle the dozens of explanations overlapping in his head.

"Where do you get off acting all incensed anyway? Isn't lying part of your normal routine?"

She shook her head, ignoring him. "We need to get back to Base. Pretend none of this ever happened."

"I'm not going anywhere."

"Reman, snap out of it! This is lunacy! You're gonna get yourself killed."

"As opposed to fighting in the Corps, back home?"

"At least there I trust the people you're fighting next to; you wear armor and you carry guns!"

Reman pivoted to close the gap between them and looked her square in the eye. The only way to reach her was to be entirely up front.

"I hate these wars, Jenda. I *hate* them. And you know perfectly well why."

He was prepared to spell it out if necessary — *they took our parents and drove you away* — but then her head drew back. Her gaze dropped. He recognized that move. Years dropped away from her, as did her conviction. The bomb was bursting somewhere behind her eyes. He had prepared for this moment. He knew what to say, but as that single second stretched on, he hesitated. Would she finally open up to him?

No. Her eyes snapped back up to meet his and the moment had passed.

"I thought joining ICORE would be a step to bringing an end to the wars, not just skewing the options. But what we're doing here is—"

"What you're 'doing here' has probably been put on hold after the events of today, Reman, come on."

"How do you know? You won't even let me explain what the Resistance really is, what we're actually doing here."

"So, what? The Fantasarians want peace? They're the ones that took the Oniyum to begin with!"

"Says who? Where's the proof?"

"It disappeared in their territory during their rule."

"And a very beneficial move it was for them, too," he said sarcastically. "Do you realize that they have the highest death toll of all the tribes?"

He watched the information sink in; the first trace of doubt entering her mind. Her eyes flicked to the side, then back to him, considering, as he had done so many weeks ago.

"Is that so?"

"Double our own."

She didn't respond to that. He leaned back against the wall and sucked in a deep breath.

"Look, I know that this is a gamble, okay? But these are good people, Jenda and I trust them. You would too, if you'd give them a chance."

"Does this Legren plan to invite the zombies to join his Resistance? Or how about the Vampians or the Necromancers?"

"Oh, come on! It's a process. One which we'd love to explain to you if you'd just give it the time of day."

Jenda crossed her arms again. Any consideration from the moment before evaporated.

"What do Garen and Mason think of all this?" he asked to fill the silence.

"Mason wants to lay siege to the whole of this camp—"

"Not surprising," he scoffed.

"—and Garen isn't sure. He wanted me to talk to you first."

"And what are you going to tell him?"

"That the problem is bigger than we expected and we can't just drag you back home like we'd originally planned."

"You think that would've worked?" he said, laughing.

"Yeah, there's three of us and one of you."

"And when we got back home, you think all of this would just be forgotten?"

For the first time in their entire exchange, the corners of her mouth tilted up. "Nice to hear you still call it home."

Reman almost muttered something disdainful about 'old habits,' but couldn't quite bring himself to do it. That would make *him* the one spoiling for a fight.

"Just give this a chance," he pleaded. "Give these *people* a chance. You three are here as guests, not prisoners. So long as you don't interfere with the things going on—"

"Does that go for you, too?"

"I'm not a threat to the peace and safety of these people. You three could be."

"What did they expect, holding a Mech captive—"

"I am NOT a captive!"

His volume surprised him, but he didn't care. If his shout carried all the way to the main room, if he had scared any nearby livestock, then so be it.

She raised her hand to her eyes, pinching the bridge of her nose. The familiarity of the gesture forced him to look away.

"We're not getting anywhere here," she said. He didn't respond. The conversation was over. He could feel it.

"Is there someplace I can clean up?" she snapped at his turned back.

"There's a washroom down the hall." He flung his arm towards the doorway, and she was gone.

Now alone, Reman stared out the window on his other side. Darkness had fallen completely, blanketing the grounds. He could see nothing but his own, warped reflection in the glass. Where had the day gone?

Reman ran a hand through his hair and let out a long breath. He'd done it. He'd stood up to her; stood *against* her. She hadn't looked at him the way he'd feared — or hoped. She acted the soldier, thinking only as far as her orders. He had anticipated initial friction, of course, but had ultimately expected some sign of progress, however minuscule. Now, he doubted if there would be any shift at all and fear prickled across the back of his neck.

In the past, he had almost always taken her side, no matter the issue. He joined ICORE because of Jenda's influence. Replaying their argument in his head, he suspected that she had been waiting for him to cave, as usual.

But I won't.

Reman didn't smile. He didn't hold his chin high in triumph. His conviction only reverberated through his mind in a resigned, heartsick whisper. His previously fuzzy, hopeful vision of the future pulled into sharp focus. Rather than reconnection or reconcile, he saw only Jenda's retreating back, leaving him alone in the dark.

PART THREE
RESISTANCE

NINETEEN

LEGREN

*S*now.
    A lone figure.
    A faceless Mech solider.

Sethera, her face twisted in agony, wet from rain and tears.

A pirate woman smirking at him through long lashes and thick, blonde waves.
    No, not a smirk, a smile. A private look, just for him.

A knight, his own Fantasarian kin, pouncing on Sethera, then vanishing into thin air.

Blood dripping down his arm. Unfamiliar-looking woods. Falling down, into a well-hidden foxhole, stray leaves fluttering. A girl, no older than sixteen, rail-thin, eyes bright. He does not recognize her, but knows that she is in immeasurable in danger. He must help her.

The clearing. Lifeless Mercs scattered in every direction. The bright sky above he and Marcus, standing a few feet away. Regret, then agony. Fire enveloping everything and the side of his face being ripped apart...

Legren sat up fast, gulping down air, his heart thrashing. Phantom pain shot through his body, summoned from memory. Thick, steady rain pounded the roof above while dense thunder rolled. He'd seen this tumbling mess of imagery before. Many of his nights were haunted by them, but never in the same order. Some were old now, but others still felt fresh. He knew it was the Oniyum, somehow alive and stirring inside his mind. So many weeks after his two near death experiences, vestiges of whatever had saved and scarred him still lurked under his skin. He'd wondered, irrationally, if the Oniyum was present nearby — he recalled Dorojin's words — but whether that or only a sharp echo of the real thing, he didn't care. It was great and it was terrible and it haunted him.

He was trembling. So, too, was the room. Shadows quaked over the walls and floor. He glanced up and saw a single candle, still lit, its flame whipping back and forth in some breeze. Legren stood, aching with each slight movement, leaned over and doused it, plunging the room into darkness in the hope to attain some real rest at last.

Unfortunately, his sleep was not peaceful after he finally managed to drift back off. The dreams faded, but his head pounded with the multitude of concerns waiting at his door, not least of which was the imminent return of the Royalty. He prided himself on his friendship with the Princess, Catherine, but even his good humor would not deter her for long. Of course, he had not even the slightest idea of when she'd return. He dreamed of her riding into the camp on horseback, a fleet of armed Knights with her, breaking down doors, searching for the Mechs. Thankfully, his mind did not conjure up some nightmare of anyone else being slaughtered or executed. In fact, despite the previous day's horrors, his dreams were absent of zombies, Necromancers, or the lost and injured victims.

When he woke the following morning, Legren dressed quickly, intent to get to the Assembly Hall and see how the hospital was progressing. He dreaded knowing if there was yet a death toll, and how high it might be, but he had no choice.

The moment he stepped outside, he met cold mist that had enveloped the grounds and apart from the sound of water rushing from the cottage roofs and gutters, all was still and silent. Chilling, in every sense of the word.

The Assembly Hall had completely transformed; curtains hung in every direction, through rooms and halls, sectioning off otherwise massive, open spaces. Legren recognized every face, but did not greet or speak to anyone. The hour was early and most still slept, but those awake recoiled slightly at the sight of him. *Not me*, he realized, *these hateful scars.* They would try to refocus and smile at him, almost apologetically. *As though they have anything to be sorry for.* At a loss for words, he only returned as much of a smile as he was able before proceeding past them, cursing silently. He berated himself as he walked for his haste, for forgetting his bandanna, and for the weeks he'd spent putting any of these people at risk. They had lost so much and in his attempt to help, he had only made it worse.

In one of the smaller, side rooms, Legren found Xettar tending a boy with a broken arm. The damaged limb hung in a sling but Xettar held it steady with his free hand, applying some sort of healing spell with the other. Brock watched over the Mage's shoulder, absently twisting the edge of coarse bandage wrapped around his wrist. Neither of them regarded Legren as he entered the room. In the opposite corner, Telena applied ointment under a patient's head bandage. She caught Legren's eye, and murmured something to her patient. She slipped through the half-curtains, to make her way through the room.

"All seems to be well here," Legren said as she approached.

"Some recoveries are happening more quickly than others, but there appear to be no fatal wounds. My biggest fear was long-term illness, transmitted from the more severe bites, but there doesn't appear to be any permanent infections."

"How soon do you think they can all travel?" Legren asked.

She gave pause and looked down, considering, but also uncomfortable.

"That remains to be seen." Her eyes swung back and forth between his. She didn't wince at his scar, only seemed to gauge his reaction before he actually gave one.

"Have you an estimate?" he said.

She shrugged. "A few days for the more recovered. As to the rest…" her voice faded as she tilted her head and shrugged.

"Right," Legren mumbled.

She bit her lip and retreated back into the corner, passing Xettar and Brock, who strode forward to take Telena's place.

"All the artifacts have been re-positioned along the boundary," he said.

"How far does this set us back?"

"What are you hoping to hear? It was going to be a huge amount of work anyway, regardless of what we'd already started."

Legren closed his eyes against the beginnings of a headache. His old self agreed with Brock and was bursting to say so, while his newer, re-formed perspective heaved in protest at the notion that they might have to give up, even if temporarily. *It might mean forever and you cannot not let that happen,* bellowed a voice inside him, so forcefully, nausea rolled through his stomach. He opened his eyes quickly, anchoring himself once again in reality.

Brock didn't seem to notice. In fact, he spoke quickly, his tone eager. "Xettar seems to think there might be another way to create the barrier, if we—"

"His attention needs to be focused on our security here, not on our plans for the Resistance," Legren interrupted.

"For how long?" Brock challenged. "Once the wounded can travel, we're escorting them to the High Kingdom, yeah? And once they're gone, we pick up where we left off?"

"Your point?" Pained as he was, Legren would neither deny or commit to such a plan.

"We can't just put everything off. We—"

"I will not put these people in danger again," Legren insisted. There was a faint waver in his voice. He couldn't tell if Brock heard it. Or had it happened at all? Had he only felt, in the back of his throat, a ripple of fear that it was all falling apart?

Either way, Brock leaned in closer and spoke in a deep, calculated whisper. "The Royals are going to hear about this, Legren. The entire population of your camp shows up, and you're not there, nor are your soldiers? Come on. Don't you think they're going to find it at all strange?"

"Let me worry about that." He thought Brock might force the matter, but instead, he raised his hands in a gesture of surrender and slinked away, towards the door and passed Tali over the threshold.

"How did it go?" Legren asked her.

"Successfully. His Majesty offered to send further assistance, but I declined. I implied that our numbers here were too small to warrant any additional help."

"Good; the last thing we need is for them to come here and discover our newest guests."

Tali nodded, then rapidly scanned the room, as though making sure no one was watching or listening. Like Brock, she dropped her voice to a whisper. "It is my understanding, however, that reports were sent immediately to the High Kingdom."

"As was to be expected," Legren muttered, then forced a smile. "Well done. Truly. And my thanks. Take some time now to rest."

She bowed and silently withdrew.

Legren surveyed the room. Xettar was no longer performing any *Magic* and the boy next to him flexed his fingers gingerly, experimentally.

"Your arm will be sore for a few days, but you should be back to normal after that," Xettar told him. "Just be careful, eh?"

The boy's head bobbed emphatically and Xettar patted him lightly on the back. Xettar headed for the door, not looking at Legren.

"This was my fault," Legren blurted out.

Xettar stopped and gave Legren a weak, but sincere smile. "What good does that do, really? Laying blame anywhere? Best we just keep moving forward, don't you think?"

Legren stared at the injured around them and whispered, "At what cost?"

TWENTY

SETHERA

Residual rain cascaded from the stable roof and dripped pleasantly into numerous puddles that had collected around the stable's surrounding paddocks. The sounds of dripping were interrupted only by distant birds' chirping.

Sethera leaned on the gate of one of the horse stalls before her snowy white mare. She slowly stroked the horse's neck and hummed, low and soft, harmonizing with the animal's gentle breathing. A welcome, all too seldom moment of peace.

Approaching footfalls met her ears, but she tried to ignore them. The mare, however, reared and retreated into the stall just as Reman stomped into the stable. Focused on a device in his hand, his head was tilted down, but when it swiveled up, he saw her scowling at him and he stopped in his tracks.

"Sorry, I just—" he started, but she ignored him, reaching forward into the stall in attempt to coax the mare back to her. No luck.

"Thank you."

She wasn't sure she heard him right, but she refused to look at him. "For what?"

"Getting my sister and friends here safely. I mean, I know you weren't thrilled about having to bring them here to begin with," he rambled, "especially after some of the things I said before you left, but I've been more worried about them then I realized and…"

She heard shifting gravel behind her. Glancing over her shoulder, she caught him pawing the ground with his boots. *He's apologizing? Or trying to?*

She frowned at the top of his head and pushed away from the stall. "Save your breath, Mech."

She strode towards the doorway.

"So that's how it's going to be?"

She froze, right next to him. She didn't want to give him the satisfaction of gauging a reaction from her, but the righteous tone of indignation could not be left unchecked. "You expected something different?"

"I'm still here, aren't I? I didn't sell you out or contact anyone, and even you know I didn't let those zombies in."

He may not have been wrong, but in that moment, the idea of trying to convey to him the scope of what else remained unaltered between them seemed beyond her ability. As his voice ascended into a whine, she started to walk away again.

Until she felt his hand close around her shoulder. And he pulled. "Just listen to me for one second—"

She spun and pinned him against the nearest post, blade drawn. She pressed it sideways against his throat, mimicking its angle from their first meeting. However, Reman did not tense under her grip as he had then, nor did he fight back, and she didn't see his pulse quicken or jump in his throat.

"Nothing has changed," she hissed. "Do you know why you're still alive to thank me at all? Because Legren ordered it that way. If it hadn't been for him, I would have left you dead in the snow the day we met."

Sethera leaned back and sheathed the dagger. She wouldn't actually harm him, of course — not here, not now — but she had to make the point. *Don't test me.* She took one step back, when he grabbed her wrist. His grip was stronger than expected. Reman meant business, with every intent of being heard this time. Sethera could free herself in a single motion, but the fact that he had done it at all took her by surprise. How much had he changed since she'd been gone?

"Would you have?" he asked softly, in great contrast to the force of his grip. "This isn't who you really are, is it?"

He struck a nerve. No, she was not an outright killer, but she had mastered the will to survive — to do whatever was necessary. Her life as a warrior may have been fairly new, but he didn't know that, did he?

She wrenched her wrist free. "You don't know anything about me."

He didn't argue. Instead, he closed his eyes. "Maybe you'll never stop hating me, but, for what it's worth…" His eyes opened again. "I'm sorry."

"For what?" she said again.

His brows arched upwards. It gave him the look of an innocent, doe-eyed child. He leaned forward a little. "I lost mine, too."

It actually took her a few seconds to register what he was saying. When she did, she held her face very, very still. "He told you?"

"He showed me." He didn't sound especially happy about it.

It had always been part of the plan; to disclose the whole truth to Reman. He had to know, but her hands curled into fists. For him to just blindside her like this —

"Sethera…"

She rounded on him. "Stay away from me."

Fighting every instinct to hit him, she stormed away. Out of the stable, she climbed the path around the horse paddocks. *Retreating from Reman again.* She doubted that he would heed her last statement. Persistence definitely ran strong in their family. He wasn't going anywhere, Legren had been right about that, but what was he playing at? What did telling her accomplish?

He knew. So what? Did he expect them to have a good cry together? Sethera hadn't shed tears since those first days after they died and she intended to keep it that way.

The hill behind the Assembly Hall was unusually slippery. The rain had left behind thick piles of mud and churned up grass. The front of the Hall was also unusually vacant, void of any soldiers, let alone civilians, yet it didn't feel empty. The rain had dispelled the heavy heat, replaced with stillness — but not emptiness. In spite of everything lost in the past two days, a buzz of energy hummed over the village and it somehow felt more alive than ever.

The Hall itself glowed around the windows and smoke billowed from the chimneys. Sethera knew Telena and Xettar were within the hospital, hard at work, but doubted she would find Legren there.

Sethera entered the cabin without hesitation, but when she stood before the entrance to his study, obscured by a single, thick drape, she paused, collecting her sudden nerves. They hadn't properly spoken since she'd been back. Sethera drummed her fingers on the wooden frame and he called, "come in." She pulled back the cloth and found him seated at his desk, as he had been countless times before, sorting through letters. She could see the green spiral inked onto a number of the sheets; an insignia inspired by the pendant hanging from her neck. Legren had confessed to drawing it next to his signatures when he first got started, but he fiercely denied urging others to do so. According to him, it just caught on. He'd called it a sign.

Sethera realized that she was tracing the pendant through her collar. She dropped her hand and cleared her throat. When Legren finally looked up, everything about him seemed...wrong. He had always been lean, due to a naturally lanky frame, but up close, he was thinner than she had ever seen. Dark circles pooled under his soft brown eyes. The blue scars around his left socket stood out even more than usual. Not that she was used to it. She didn't know if she would ever be able to look at him and not be reminded of the cause. *Mercenary invaders.* The marks left behind were a small price to pay for his survival, but they also made it impossible to forget.

"You don't look well," she observed. He shrugged, but didn't answer. She cleared her throat again. "You told him, then?"

"Her Highness paid us a visit while you were gone. It pushed things ahead of schedule."

"How so?"

"She tried to mislead him; make him think the Resistance manipulated getting him here. But it was time for him to know. You agreed," he added quickly, "back at the beginning, you said—"

"I remember," she assured him. "What did you show him, exactly?"

"What I remember. Bits from my knighthood, and up to when I...when I came back."

She remembered that day all too well. He'd looked such a mess. She hadn't recognized him at first. His beard had grown long, but he'd cut his hair short, and his clothes were little more than scraps and rags. Those things hardly mattered, though. He was different, somehow. Transformed. *Happy.* His face, suntanned and weather-beaten, had seemed blithe and carefree. From the way he'd looked at her, though, the way the light dissipated from his face, she must have seemed just as unrecognizable to him. *Good.*

Legren had moved towards her, but she pulled away. In that moment, he was a stranger.

Nothing had been the same since.

Though her insides burned at the thought of those awful days — both before and after he went galavanting with sailors and pirates — she shrugged.

"Fine. He knows the truth, now. I can live with that. But it stops here."

She held out her hand. He sighed, reached into his pocket and withdrew an old, coiled piece of parchment. The summons. The thing that beckoned her parents' fate. Legren dropped it into her open palm. She was glad, albeit surprised, that he didn't argue.

Her fingers closed into a fist around the parchment and immediately jammed both hands into her pockets. "My family is off limits from here on out. That goes for everyone. Especially the Mech. He just tried to have a heart-to-heart with me about it."

"And you'll have none of that," he said, sounding a bit like Xettar, but she could tell he was fishing.

"None." She smiled, but it was no joke.

"Understood."

She noticed again the dark circles under his eyes, his ashen complexion, and the slump of his bony shoulders.

"Are you all right?" she asked. "Really?"

"Are you?" he countered, sending her concern right back.

She tried to answer while holding eye contact, but couldn't manage it. "I've already told you — several times, now — that I'm fine."

"As am I."

"I don't believe you," she said before she could stop herself.

"That makes two of us, then." He hadn't moved, and neither had she, but she could feel him reaching out to her. For half a second, she was tempted to lean in, reach back, but recoiled immediately. It had taken her too long to piece herself back together. Her outward shell was solid, but brittle. If he touched her, she might shatter, and then what?

He looked back down at the desk. "Thank you for bringing the Mechs here safely."

Whatever gesture she thought he'd been extending, had been withdrawn. With nothing else to say, she withdrew herself, and backed away, out of the room.

TWENTY-ONE

REMAN

Just after nightfall, Tali knocked on his door. "We are gathering in the square in a quarter hour."

After taking a few minutes to consider his options, Reman headed for the square, but stopped by Jenda's tent on the way. She wasn't there. Neither were Garen or Mason in their tent. It made him wary, not knowing their whereabouts, but he'd have to seek them out later.

The fire pit was blazing by the time he arrived. The flames billowed high enough that the shapes clustered around it were indistinct silhouettes. As he joined the group, Reman distinguished their profiles; Tali and Telena on the far left, Legren, Xettar, and Brock seated on an iron bench. Standing closest to Reman, though, farthest from the fire, were his fellow Mechs. In all their black and grey battle-ready gear, they looked like part of the darkness, hiding themselves both figuratively and literally. Jenda even had her thermal jacket on, the collar turned up. He stifled a laugh as he neared them. He would never say so, but it didn't look that different from many of the high-collared cloaks he'd seen on the Fantasarians. She would hate that.

"What?" she said, seeing his grin. He shook his head and tried to stop smiling.

On her other side, Garen leaned towards Reman. "You do this sort of thing often? Casual fireside meetings?" His tone was condescending, but genuinely curious. Gathering intel. Reman shrugged.

Beyond them, Legren and Xettar huddled close together in quiet conversation, while Brock, seated on Xettar's right, scowled up at Reman. Reman tensed, but Brock didn't reach for his dagger, only continued to glare. *One step forward, two steps back.* Jenda saw the exchange and stepped forward protectively, throwing Brock her own dirty look. She gripped Reman's shoulder just like she would have done back in their school days to a bully picking on him.

"Don't." He shrugged her hand away, trying not to sound embarrassed. Brock, however, missed all of it, having looked away already. Reman scanned the rest of the group, making sure no one else saw — and only then did he spot Sethera. Farthest away, even more so than the Mechs, she knelt on the ground, staring absently at the fire. Reman wasn't sure what he'd do if he caught her eye, but she remained focused on the flames. Not even as Legren began speaking, did she look up.

The first point of order was the state of their wounded.

"Most everyone is healed," Telena reported. "Most should be able to travel within a day, but there are a few that need more rest. Medicinally, we've done all we can. No strain of travel can be asked of them for, at minimum, another five days."

"And you're sure?" Legren said.

"Quite."

"All right." He stood up. "We will begin an evacuation in six days time. Will we be safe for that long?" He directed the last to Xettar.

"Protected for the most part, yes."

"The surrounding tribes are holding steady for the moment. Another invasion is unlikely," Brock added.

"And if any of them do, we'll know soon enough to get everyone out," Reman chimed in.

"You're sure?" Brock snapped.

Reman expected Jenda to tense next to him and she did, but so did Garen, on his other side. Reman tried to ignore it. "Yes."

"I'm holding you to that."

"Go right ahead."

"Moving on," Legren said loudly, continuing.

Jenda's head fell forward. "That's it? That's all he's going to do?"

"It's fine."

"Why are you sticking your neck out for these people again?"

"Would you pay attention?"

Though it wasn't an amiable back-and-forth by any means, it wasn't anywhere near the fervor of their last argument. This was more like the bickering they used to do. As frustrating as she was being, the familiarity of it was a relief.

"Once the evacuation is complete, only those of us willing to stay involved with the Resistance will stay behind," Legren said.

"In-*sane*," Jenda half-sang.

"Yeah," Reman hissed, "you've made your opinion abundantly clear on that, now I'm trying to listen—" He cut himself off, realizing that Xettar had just said something about them becoming outlaws and vagabonds. "Wait, what?"

"We cannot operate from inside the High Kingdom," Legren explained, "and the Assembly is only a few weeks away. When we do not travel there with the rest of the civilians, our colors will be made clear."

"Why? Can't you just make something up?" Reman asked.

"Perhaps, but it would most likely get seen through," Xettar explained.

"And I will draft a false report and send it ahead with a messenger," Legren added. "It may buy us some time, but they will know the truth before long."

"Doesn't make much of a difference to me. I'm already a fugitive," Reman said with a shrug.

"This will be different," Legren insisted. "I just want to be clear on what you are all volunteering to do..."

Reman was just starting to think that this was becoming repetitive when Sethera stood up.

"We are," she said, drawing everyone's eye. It was the first thing she'd said all evening. "Is there anything else?"

Legren had barely shaken his head, no, before she stalked away.

There didn't seem to be anything left to say. Legren mumbled one of his "very well"s, nodded, and the group dispersed. The Mechs started to retreat, except Reman.

Jenda pulled on his arm. "Come on."

He shook her off and didn't look at her. She gave up and followed Garen and Mason, leaving him alone by the still-roaring fire. Reman meandered over to the bench where Legren and Xettar had been seated. As he bent to sit down, something chirped at his wrist. According to his scanner, one of his sensors had picked up a heat signature in the stable, besides the horses. He swiped through the other readings and everything else was quiet. It was probably nothing; someone cleaning the stalls, returning something to the supply shed, or perhaps one of the scouts had returned from a journey. However, Reman had learned the chore schedule and the stables were clean when it was still light. The scouts were all on duty…but wasn't this how the Nenjin snuck in last time? And the zombies hadn't shown up at all. He couldn't ignore it, but considering he wasn't picking up anything else unusual, he made his way to the stable alone.

He didn't hear or see anything abnormal as he moved along the side wall. A few of the torches still burned, casting a warm glow, as well as harsh shadows. He consulted his scanner. The signal hadn't moved. He gripped his pistol and slid over gravel as he rounded the corner. So much for surprising an intruder.

It wasn't an intruder, though. It was Sethera, standing with her back to him, in front of an empty stall. Reman sighed, relieved — the barest sound — but enough to make Sethera whip around.

Damn.

He lowered the weapon so hastily he almost dropped it. "Sorry," he stammered.

"What part of 'stay away from me' do you not understand?" Her voice was tired and slightly strained; not at all up to its usual bite.

"No, you tripped a sensor, I—"

He stopped, observing in her slouched posture and, though difficult to tell in the orange light, red eyes. She clung to her green pendant with both hands. Something about it made him think of his family photo and how he so similarly gripped it.

"Are you all right?"

"None of your business." She turned her back on him again. Feeling suddenly desperate to be anywhere else, he holstered his gun and knelt by the nearest beam to re-calibrate the sensor. It beeped twice. Sethera didn't turn back around. Reman shuffled towards the entrance, but couldn't bring himself to cross the threshold. Their earlier conversation rolled through the back of his mind. It was like dried paste on his hands; sticky, unresolved, and unpleasant.

"I'm sorry for what I said," he blurted out before he could stop himself. "Earlier today. How I acted. It wasn't right."

She didn't move. Her shoulders didn't even tense. *You should leave, you're just gonna make it worse,* he warned himself, but the words were already tumbling out of his mouth. "I know you want nothing to do with me. You haven't exactly been my favorite person, either. I didn't understand before, but now... I know what it feels like. You can't go back, but you can't move forward. You're just...stuck. You don't really trust anyone — except, of course, you do because it would hurt too much otherwise, so it's just what you say to people. Because you've turned into someone else. Someone you never thought you'd be."

You get used to the new voids in your life — but you still hate being alone.

Her head turned, and he braced himself for a comeback, dismissive or combative. He thought she might draw her knife again and he wouldn't have blamed her. Two weeks after the bombing, he'd shoved one of his squad members against the wall for making a quip about just "needing time." But Sethera didn't draw her knife. She was looking at him over her shoulder and to his astonishment, her eyes shone with tears. She wasn't smirking or grimacing, but listening.

"It all...converges inside you," he continued, easier now. "It's not fair. Why me? Why them? You're so driven by hate that you end up taking it out on everyone around you and crippling yourself in the process."

You take up running because you're never at peace sitting still anymore. If you stop moving, reality crashes back in and you can't bear it.

"It's not the same, of course, but I know that it hurts. And it drives you away from the people you care about most. The people you need most. Anyway." He gave himself a shake and let out a quick breath. "I won't bother you again. Don't worry about the sensor when you leave."

As he turned to go, her voice rang out. "I wasn't there when it happened."

His footsteps halted.

"But then," she chuckled softly, "I guess you know that."

He twisted back around in time to see her shake her head. "I promised myself that I would never forgive them."

"Who?"

"The ones responsible."

"I thought—"

"I never knew the specific person or party, but I didn't care." Her head swung up suddenly, as though she were hearing the words for the first time; had never before said them out loud. "I...didn't care. Everyone was to blame..." She looked down at her pendant. *"What have I been doing?"*

He wasn't sure she meant to say that last aloud. It sounded profound, though, half-whispered into her palm, nearly drowned out by the torches, crackling and popping.

So it startled him when she let out a howl from between a clenched jaw and hurled a kick at the wall. Her boot didn't leave that big of a mark. It was more muddy than dented — nothing that couldn't be mended — but she stood, staring at it, hard. Tiny globs of dirt slid down the white paint. He wondered if she would kick it again; release her anger on the stall, kick it again and again until it was sawdust. Or maybe she'd run at Reman and smash his head against the post like she'd nearly done earlier that day.

Instead, she deflated. She leaned against the wall and sank down to the ground. "I'm so tired."

Reman drifted closer, hesitated, then crouched beside her. "Holding a grudge means getting all the poison that comes with it."

"I had to stay strong."

"By going it alone," Reman translated. "Legren and the others — they need you."

She scoffed.

"They *do*," he insisted, "but not the heartless person you're trying to be. You'll lose them and cripple yourself in the process."

"That's how you see me," she whispered. "Just a weak Sarian."

His eyebrows shot up. *She cares about my opinion of her?* Nearly laughing, he shook his head. "No one thinks you're weak, Sethera. Least of all me."

She swallowed hard.

"There's a power in truth," Reman said, "stronger than any forced refusal of grief. Took me awhile, but the only way I was ever able to get past the pain was to embrace it. There's no shame in that."

She swallowed again and then asked, "What did you do? When it happened?"

"Pretty much the same as you."

She squinted at him, but as he hung his head sheepishly and said, "I enlisted," her mouth curled in a glimpse of her more usual, impish side.

"Everything went downhill so fast. There was nothing left but to join as a soldier." He laughed. "You should have seen the look on Jenda's face when I convinced her I'd enlisted. She was *furious*."

"I'll bet," Sethera said, then looked off, past him. "*I* wanted to find out who was responsible. I still do. No matter what it takes. That's why Legren's plans interested me. I planned to play along until I found out who killed my parents. And I'd make them pay. I never gave the Resistance another thought."

"It's still your parents' Resistance, though, isn't it? Seeing their mission through and finishing their work would mean that they didn't die in vain. That you, Legren, all of us will be finishing what they started. I mean…" He gestured to the pendant in her hand. She looked down at it for a long time before her fingers closed around it. She shut her eyes closed and the tears she'd been holding back finally fell.

Reman considered reaching out to grip her shoulder, but didn't. More tears streamed down her cheeks. This was her moment and he would not interrupt it.

When she opened her eyes again, she peered down at her fist through wet lashes. "You're right." She unfurled her fingers again and the pendant seemed to dance in the firelight, like a living thing. In a way, Reman supposed, it was.

"Who'd have thought?" she said, still quiet, sharing the moment with him.

"Does this mean I don't have to worry about you killing me anymore?"

She laughed — a bright, impulsive sound — and, for the first time in his presence, cracked a genuine smile. Her guard had come down. She and Reman were not likely become close friends anytime soon, but one thing had shifted: the disdain between them was gone, chased away by her laughter. It was the most at peace he had known in a long time.

Too bad it couldn't last.

A shrill alarm blared from his wrist, making them both jump. It wasn't the same tone as the one that brought him here, to the stable. This was a more severe alert. He knew, just from the sound of it, that Garen, Mason, and Jenda's devices had to be lighting up, too. He tugged back his sleeve, brought up a holographic display for a better view, and his mouth fell open. So did Sethera's. An enormous cluster of shapes headed straight for the camp's left edge.

Their eyes met through the grid and locked for a few, shocked seconds before they scrambled up and out of the stable.

TWENTY-TWO

KEXINA

They had no idea she was there. They hadn't even guessed. Kexina had lingered on the fringes of their little community ever since she and the raiding party had broken in and set the place on fire. But she was the only one. In fact, she had travelled some distance with the party before she stopped and something drew her back. Dorojin called her a fool, but Kexina insisted that there was more she needed to know.

They'd attacked Legren's camp for answers, for a new trail on the Oniyum, and found nothing…except for the mysterious plans Kexina uncovered in Legren's study. They amounted to little more than a string of future dates and a mess of locations and names — sprouted from all over Kabathan. Kexina had found no pattern, no code, but knew that it was valuable information. Did Legren still operate under Royal orders? Or had he gone rogue? Equally dangerous outcomes, but knowing which one would decide how to combat them.

Truthfully, though, Kexina would have returned to spy on Legren's camp even without having laid eyes on his plans. There was a Mech there, and he didn't appear to be a prisoner. Kexina had never met a Mech before, let alone fought one, but he certainly hadn't behaved like a Fantasarian, nor had he denied her accusation. When she'd called him 'Mech', she'd expected the ruse — if it was one — to slip. Any Fantasarian would have objected openly, considering it the highest insult. He hadn't even flinched.

She'd told no one about any of this — not even Dorojin — and she would keep silent until she had acquired answers.

She'd backtracked and spent her days in the woods and shadows, watching the place recover and trying not to let guilt seep too far into her consciousness. No one was supposed to have died that night. Dorojin had gotten carried away; they all had. She'd watched the Mech boy specifically. He dressed off and on in the grey and black of his tribe, wandering around, planting his strange devices. She'd watched the tide turn in his favor; the harsh glares in his direction and hurried quicksteps away from him dissolved into uncertainty and, of late, mild acceptance. He was becoming one of them.

When the zombies came, she'd avoided the fray, steered clear of the Necromancers, but didn't abandon her post. She'd sounded the alarm. While watching the boy install it some weeks earlier, she'd determined how it worked — well enough to get it to make noise. She didn't really know why, other than she most likely wanted a clear conscience.

When they started talking about leaving, she suspected it was time she do the same.

That night, she left her post outside Legren's village to finally report all that she'd uncovered to her own tribe. Would she actually tell Dorojin that Legren still lived, though? She could not determine why, but she thought she might hang on to that information a while longer. Of course, Dorojin would be furious if he found out that she'd kept it from him. Then again, the King's Favorite had survived — again. Dorojin would be outraged either way.

She walked on foot, her bare feet sifting through fallen leaves and pine needles, when she heard the first rumble. The ground itself trembled, ever so slightly. She climbed the nearest tree and waited. Three minutes later, she saw them: automobiles, approaching from the north. It had actually taken a good deal of effort to spot them. At a distance, they looked like large, squat snakes, oozing through the layer of green that surrounded Legren's camp. Dark and sleek they were, or must have been before the mob of stray twigs and flyaway rocks had left dents and grooves, white trails cut deep into the black paint.

As they grew nearer, beneath her, Kexina realized how massive they were. She could only guess at how many people each one held. They weren't silent, but neither were they loud.

The tires slowed, coming to a stop some feet ahead of Kexina's tree. It seemed as random a spot as any other. She watched, curiously, as the doors opened and they poured out.

Mobsters.

Dozens of them swarmed around the vehicles in a blur of gray, white, and black, all suits and suspenders. Most of their faces hid beneath wide-brimmed hats. The first few men circled around to the back of the car and opened the cavernous trunks. The rest — all men, save two women, by Kexina's count — lined up as those first few began handing out pistols and other such weapons. Kexina grimaced. Most firearms didn't bother her, though she could recognize them fairly easily. There was something inherently cruel about the sound of the *Thompsons* — as she'd heard them called once. Once every pair of hands held a pistol or two or three, a last man emerged from the front seat of the lead car. The tallest man there, he moved with ease and refined dexterity, a gun already at home in his grip; a longer rifle with a circular drum below the barrel. This had to be their leader, confirmed a half second later when he raised his free arm and signaled to the whole group. They marched in an adjacent direction from the one in which their cars had been driving. Kexina followed, crawling through the branches to stay with them. They didn't notice as they crunched ahead not speaking, save for an indistinct murmur between a pair of them. Their voices drifted with a casual indifference she had only heard among the Mobsters. They were a crew, but not a team; it was a group of individual fighters, not a collective unit. They walked, determined but with a certain swagger, until, abruptly, they stopped in unison at the top of the hill that sloped down into the valley that led to Legren's village. They hid in places around the larger trees, squatting down and waiting. A set up. Kexina doubted it was anyone from Legren's camp that they were hunting, given that they were still a safe distance from the actual settlement, but Kexina knew of no other movement nearby. The recent zombie attack had been unexpected, even to her.

She waited with the Mobsters for about ten minutes — slightly more anxious than she probably should have been — until she detected movement roughly thirty feet ahead. Three figures in shades of Royal Blue materialized out of the green. Two Fantasarian knights followed a short, stocky figure in a long grey robe and black hood. He carried a staff adorned with specific lacing and charms, which Kexina knew made him more than a Mage; he was a Wizard. Kexina tensed. Wizards were true masters of *Magic*, even the elemental *qì*. They were rare across all of Kabathan, even in Fantasarian culture. She respected and revered them, but they had become something akin to collectors items in the High Kingdom. These were not faces she had seen in Legren's village. The Fantasarian Monarchy kept Wizards close to their capital, deeply entrenched in politics, which clouded even the purest of minds.

Like the council. And the rest of the planet. The global mindset was murky as a whole and thereby dangerous from lack of clear thinking and understanding.

The knights, however, were a different matter. Their armor and clothing signified high rank, but one wore plate armor, his face completely hidden beneath a Spangenhelm, the helmet of battlefront knights. He clutched a traditional Fantasarian broadsword; the crossguard blunt and straight. The other knight was some form of high-Elf, her face exposed completely, showing off large, pointed ears, slightly webbed. She wore no other armor and Kexina wondered if she was a *Magic* user as well, but of a much lower class. Her sword was curved and lean, almost like a Nenjin blade. Kexina had never before seen its match. She scoffed slightly, not loud enough to even make a noise. *No wonder these Fantasarians have not yet been beaten. They continued to advance their culture, even under these world-war circumstances, rather than move backwards.*

Of course, she countered herself, *the Oniyum would help with that.*

The lead Mobster lifted his hand slightly and the others collectively shifted, tensing with readiness.

The Elf stopped. Her head jerked to the right, exactly where the Mobsters were hiding. Her fellow knight and the Wizard also stopped and turned in that direction. The swords raised slightly along with the staff.

Two Mobsters stepped out from behind the trees; the leader and another fellow in one of the sleeker white hats. No words passed between Mobsters and Fantasarians, but the Wizard along with his knights, faced their foes. Kexina hadn't the slightest doubt that all three of them were perfectly aware of the rest of the Mobsters, even though they were hidden from view.

"Evening," the one in the white hat said. "Bit far from your High Kingdom, ain't you?" His voice was soft and charming. "You's lookin' lost. How's about you come with us?"

Ah, Kexina thought. *The Mobsters probably think this is a transport of some kind, maybe even the Oniyum itself and hope to snatch it, mid-route.*

The Fantasarians, however, said nothing, only poised their weapons to strike.

"Please," White Hat said, his voice still smooth and friendly, "this could get ugly. We'd prefer to—"

"On your way, Sir," the Wizard interrupted, directly at the leader. His voice was a deep rumble, an audible expression of the power he undoubtedly possessed — an unseen force not to be reckoned with.

White Hat glanced, sidelong at the leader, who considered, then sighed. "More's the pity."

He leaned his massive gun against his shoulder, freeing his right hand to snap his fingers. On command, the rest of the Mobsters stepped forth, around their trees, looking outright gleeful at the chance to do so. The one nearest the leader even cocked the rifle he held in his arms.

The Wizard never took his eyes off the leader, who stood completely still as his men flowed ahead of him. As the Mobsters advanced, the two knights exchanged a quick glance, then began easing backwards. The Wizard didn't move.

The Mobsters splintered. The bulk of the group stayed fixed on their path toward the Wizard, while a few veered in opposite directions, following the knights. Kexina leaned forward slightly, expectantly, certain that something entertaining was like to happen.

Sure enough, the lack of a display of fear from the Wizard — or the knights, really — seemed to frustrate the Mobsters. Their pace quickened. They rushed him.

Before they could reach him, however, the Wizard raised his staff straight up, then slammed it back into the ground, where a blinding flash exploded out of it. Mobsters soared backwards, off their feet and even Kexina had to cover her eyes. By the time she looked back, the Wizard and the knights were bounding away from the fallen Mobsters. Several lay unconscious, but a few sprung up and, guns raised, gave chase to the Fantasarians. Shots cracked through the otherwise silent air. For city dwellers — all of them, even the Fantasarians — Kexina had to hand it to them; they weaved through the trees exceptionally well, as though vastly familiar with the terrain. Their movements, too, somehow obscured their number. From above, Kexina had lost count of how many there were. She remembered, of course, but at a glance, it was impossible to tell. She lost track, too, of the helmeted knight. He had vanished entirely; or possibly moved beyond her vantage point. She could still see the Elf, who turned and threw spells over her shoulder every few feet.

The Mobster leader leaned over to kick and shake his fallen men, eventually grabbing the back of their collars and forcing them to their feet.

"They got *Magic*, Lou!" one complained.

"Of course they do, genius!" the leader, Lou, shouted back, rounding on the protestor to smack the back of his head. "They're Royal 'Sarians! We got a job to do — now GET!"

The group managed to collect themselves and press forward. Lou brought up the rear, shaking his head and scowling. Kexina waited until he had moved far enough ahead that she could drop to the ground. She landed smoothly, but kept low to the forest floor and crawled forward; carefully, but fast enough to keep Lou's hat in sight.

The fight had definitely travelled ahead, but the echo of fired shots bounced all throughout the space, coupled with unearthly quakes through the ground. More *Magic*, no doubt. Lou descended the hill, dipping out of sight and, instead of following, Kexina scurried up another tree to peer down at the scene.

She heard it before any of the rest of them did, but not by much: the unmistakable sound of a mechanical charge. Following it, something blue and electric streaked past the Fantasarians and collided with one of the Mobsters, killing him. The Wizard and his knights whipped around to look across the valley and saw Legren and his six warriors darting up the hill, weapons drawn. Behind them, bedecked in black and silver armor, sprinted the four Mechs, their laser guns radiating blue orbs in the twilight.

The mismatched group fanned out through the trees and the Mobsters hesitated. Some stared at the inconceivable combination of Mech and Fantasarian. Others spun around, shouting confused obscenities at Lou, who flicked back the tip of his hat for a better view of the oncoming group. Kexina heard him mutter, "Well, I'll be...the rumors are true..."

"What the hell is this?" one of the Mobsters shouted.

"Just more targets!" Lou answered, jamming his hat back down his head. "Keep shootin'!"

He raised his gun and pulled the trigger. The drum spun and the battle resumed.

The initial three Fantasarians continued the attack, while Legren's group joined the fray, dodging bullets and lobbing spells, multicolored laser blasts, and flaming arrows at the Mobsters. Kexina wondered, at first, if the Fantasarians would be any challenge for the Mobsters' guns, but the Mech firearms were proving to be quite advantageous.

Off the right, White Hat drew back and circled around to the side. He seemed to have targeted Legren and was setting his sights there. He lined himself up around the side of a particular barren tree trunk. The shot was perfect. It would take Legren's life.

Should I intervene?

This was the Fantasarian who had survived a Merc missile strike and Dorojin's blade, within three weeks of each other. It wouldn't be long before he was metaphorically placed on a pedestal and hailed as some sort of...other. The only folk able to escape death were Jallorian Knights, and not even they had stories in which they were struck dead and then lived again. They were simply never struck in the first place. What about a Mobster's bullet, though? What if that was the unexpected culprit to claim the otherwise in-destructible Fantasarian?

But if Legren dies here, what becomes of his secrets?

White Hat cocked his gun.

Kexina leapt forward.

She grabbed his shoulder and shoved his wrist down just as he pulled the trigger. The shot fired and ricocheted, but she did not watch its path. She knew she'd disrupted it enough to miss the target. Only once White Hat had fallen — hat itself slipping from his head — did she look up. Legren was still fighting, still running, completely unaware of her act, but someone else watched her. The Mech boy — Reman. He crouched by a tree six meters away and, hands clamped around his gun, she expected him to raise it, take aim, and attempt to shoot her as he did in their last encounter...but he remained still. He blinked in recognition and gaped at her, seemingly unable to make sense of her presence.

He saw me. He saw me save Legren's life.

He leaned away from the tree — even stepped towards her, but he lowered the gun, instead of raising it. Did he expect them to converse in this mayhem?

As if on cue, an energy bolt erupted close to her left, heat brushing her face. Her head whipped to the side. Lou was on his knees, bleeding from the chest. His gun fell, followed by his hat, then his whole body, tumbling into a lifeless heap in the dirt.

The firing decreased on all sides. Using the distraction, Kexina took soundless flight, back up the hill.

"Jig's up! Let's go!" A Mobster's voice echoed behind her. She swerved, running in the opposite direction of where she remembered their vehicles were parked; they'd soon be following her. She reached for a tree branch in her path ahead, gripped it, and spun around the trunk, the balls of her feet scraping against the bark as she heaved herself up. Once high enough, she allowed herself to catch her breath. The Mobsters streaked by underneath her, a scant remainder of the strapping force they'd been on arrival. Some limped, but none crawled, and all were still fast. They clambered back into their big vehicles, the engines coughing to life. Debris sprayed in every direction as the gigantic tires spun and the cars surged forward, back the way they came.

It was one of the strangest battles she'd ever seen. Not only had it involved the unusual team of Mechs and Fantasarians, but she'd personally changed the outcome without fully understanding the context or repercussions. She still recalled the initial unpleasantness of seeing Legren fall from Dorojin's strike. At the time, Legren had been a normal threat; a former, but still powerful Fantasarian leader who could be cut down. A statement to Fantasaria's Monarchy. Whether Legren lived or died in the end was irrelevant to her personally, yet she had never felt right with Dorojin towering over Legren as he bled out. In her own fight with the Mech, Reman, on that night, she had not intended to kill him unless he forced it, and he hadn't. He and Legren were alike. They did not abide death and aggression. Dorojin did and always had. When she'd first camped outside of Legren's township, Kexina had intended only to observe, not raise a hand to aid Legren or whatever mission he was on. But she'd helped him twice: first with the alarm and now with a possible third escape from death. Was she trying to make up for Dorojin's actions? Perhaps Legren would have brushed off a bullet to the heart as he had done a strike from a katana. She had not witnessed either of his other moments of survival. Was someone else protecting Legren? Was it the Oniyum after all? And if so, why?

She considered going back to listen in on whatever conversation was to take place now that the Mobsters were gone; to hear the new Fantasarians' reactions to the sight of Mechs fighting aside their kin.

She climbed down the tree slowly, still weighing her options. If she returned to the village or retreated back to her own camp, she had no doubt that her path would cross Legren's — and Reman's — again. Her feet eased onto the ground. She considered her paths. To her right, her own people; to the left, Legren and his mystery. All was still silent, but she knew, without a doubt, that the quiet would soon be broken. Probably slowly, with barely more than a mumble or a murmur, it would grow, until all of the woods rang with their voices.

TWENTY-THREE

REMAN

None of the Mobsters looked back, except a young woman with long, blonde hair. She stopped and clutched a tree while her fellow Mobsters raced up the hill and vanished through the trees. She gawked at the mix of tribes, probably trying to make sense of it, until the last of the Mobsters ran past. She pushed away from the tree and followed, into the dark.

The last traces of wingtips and loafers scrambling over fallen leaves resounded through the clearing. The fight was over, but nobody moved. Not even when a crack and rumble of gasoline-powered engines roared to life and tires screeched in the distance.

The forest descended into an uncomfortable tranquility, almost entirely silent, save for the shifting of fabric and clicking of weapons. Reman's mind rewound to first stepping out of his mech pod into soundless, snow-covered woods.

He scanned the trees where he'd last seen the Nenjin woman, but she had vanished, too. Reman wasn't really surprised, but the mystery of her showing up at all stuck in his brain like an insistent computer error. She'd fixed him with the same heavy-lidded stare as before, all cool composure…but only after *helping* them. Wasn't this was the same woman who had watched, remorseless, as her partner loomed over a murdered Legren? What changed?

Jenda appeared at Reman's elbow. She holstered her gun, but her eyes flicked back and forth between the three strangers.

She'd joined the fight...but why? Just basic soldier instinct or had she changed her mind?

A scrape of metal drew Reman's attention back to Legren, who sheathed his sword and faced the Wizard.

"Cyntrenn," Legren muttered, addressing the Wizard with a stiff bow.

The old man pushed back his dark hood, unveiling close-cropped, silver hair that shone as he inclined his head.

"Legren," he said in a rumbling baritone.

The rest of the group circled around them, including Reman.

"I trust you have a reason for being here?" Legren asked. "And bringing this fracas with you?"

Cyntrenn chuckled and looked over at the four Mechs. "These must be your first recruits."

Garen and Mason swapped wary looks while the Fantasarians — and Jenda — all held perfectly still.

"Indeed," Legren confirmed, "and there will be more."

"His Majesty seems to think so, too. And his daughters." Cyntrenn's smile disappeared as he leaned closer to Legren. "They know about you, my boy. And they are coming for you."

"Your concern is appreciated, but unnecessary," Legren said. "Her Highness was here recently, and I have successfully—"

"More intelligence has reached them since then. They now know that the Resistance formed within our realm and they have begun discussing it with the Council."

Legren nodded. "She told me that. I am not concerned that they will figure out it is me—"

"You should be." Cyntrenn rattled the staff in his hand. "They know more than you think. For three straight days I overheard nothing but reports that indicated you and your friends here. And in the days since I left, they will have put it all together."

"And if they did, what difference would it make?" Legren rushed the words, waving an impatient hand.

"It is only a matter of time before they arrive. They will detain all of you, kill the Mechs, and burn your cause to the ground."

Reman waited for Legren's next stubborn dismissal, but it didn't come. Instead, Legren's head fell forward. In the silence that stretched between them, Reman considered Cyntrenn more closely. He had mentioned the Resistance, but with a curiosity, rather than disapproval. *But if he's not actually Resistance, then…*

"How did you know Legren was behind all this before the rest of them did?" Reman asked.

Legren ignored the question and rocked forward to stand directly before Cyntrenn.

"Are you certain of this?" he asked very quietly.

Cyntrenn raised an eyebrow. "Aren't *you?*" His voice was gentle, but Legren winced. Reman squinted at the two of them, totally lost. They must have crossed into some sort of personal reference or history…but then a memory rattled in the back of Reman's mind.

I knew someone would be in the clearing…it's complicated.

Could Legren see the future? If so, it must not have been a refined or favored skill.

"You always knew this was a possibility," Cyntrenn said. "If you are as committed to this as you claim to be, then you must act. Now."

Well, he's certainly not against *the Resistance.*

Jenda gave Reman a confused look. He could only shrug back. Even if he could find the words, he had no idea if he was right about any of it.

"Take your men and go," Cyntrenn advised, and gestured to the two knights that stood behind him. "We will stay and care for the wounded."

Go? Go, where? By the sound of it, the whole of the Fantasarian Army would arrive any minute. Fantasarians were the most hated group on the planet; if these members of the King's Court weren't safe in their own territory, then—

Legren stepped back and drew himself up, calling out to their whole group. "Back to the village. We leave at dawn."

Brock, who had been monitoring the two knights, snapped his head in Legren's direction. "Wait, what?"

He wasn't the only one to look thunderstruck, either. Both Xettar and Sethera's eyes widened.

"We evacuate and carry on," Legren announced. "We won't be coming back."

He marched past them, back down the hill the way they came. Though he spoke clearly, Reman had the impression that each word physically hurt him.

Reman could see it because he felt it too. The entire plan was forfeit. Without any alternative, they must leave, headed into an unknown and dangerous future with targets painted on each of their backs. It all rang a pretty familiar note. Reman recalled the last time he had wound up in the woods faced with the prospect of abandoning Legren's village. But Reman was not alone among this group anymore, even without his fellow Mechs beside him. He couldn't imagine what any of this meant, or where they'd be headed, but returning to ICORE was out of the question. He would have to face the unknown and that prospect no longer scared him.

Jenda scoffed next to him, snapping Reman back to reality. Around them, the Elves whispered to one another, while Sethera and Xettar swapped nervous glances. Brock trudged after Legren and, one at a time, the rest of them followed.

Jenda gave Reman another, *are you serious?* sort of look, to which he responded with another shrug and began walking back with the rest of them.

"And we're just going to believe him?" Jenda called from behind him. "Just like that?"

Before he could tell her to *just come on*, Xettar passed in front of her and smirked.

"Do you have a better idea?" he asked.

It was a far better response than Reman could have come up with. Jenda shrugged and fell into step beside Xettar while Cyntrenn and his group brought up the rear.

As they walked, Reman replayed the battle in his mind, lingering on the Nenjin woman. *Does she know about the Resistance? Is that why she saved Legren?* Why else would she go out of her way to save someone she'd helped kill less than two weeks earlier?

It could have been a strange fluke, of course. Or perhaps Nenjin would be next to join the Resistance. *Or at least* she *will, whoever she is.*

If the Resistance survived. Legren still lived, but something about his heavy footfalls, the stoop in his shoulders and the finality in his voice earlier made Reman question their future in a whole new light.

And, if the Resistance ended, what would he do then?

TWENTY-FOUR

XETTAR

About the only positive result from the miserable turn of events was that they had not separated by tribe. The Mechs had even split up. Jenda had stayed in step beside Xettar for the length of the trek. Garen and Mason stayed side-by-side, but walked between Brock and Sethera while Reman hovered near Telena and Tali. Silver lining.

Of course, they all drew back together after shuffling back into the village. Brock and Tali delivered the news to the citizens and refugees, while the Mechs huddled together. Reman touched Jenda's arm, but she didn't look at him. He surveyed each of them in turn, but no one met his gaze. Reman rubbed his forehead and walked off on his own.

Xettar didn't linger, either. He returned to his own room and boxed up the trinkets, amulets, bottles, and books that he had not already packed away after the zombie raid. He wrapped each item with care, in cloth and twine, buried deep into a rectangular trunk. Just as quickly, he turned back out into the square to make his way to Legren's study. Along his route, Xettar spotted citizens extinguishing torches and individual campfires as usual. Meanwhile, others assisted wounded parties away from the Assembly Hall, presumably to their homes. Xettar felt pummeled by a mix of comfort and remorse.

"We'll make for the southern camps first," Legren said, pulling the last of his maps off the wall of his study. He rolled up the parchment and tossed it into an unsealed crate with several other wrapped and tied sheets.

"The Resistance does have a few supporters down there," Xettar said. He leaned against one of the bare walls, trying to work out how this room managed to look so much more lifeless than his own.

Legren scooped up a small, green spice bottle from his desk, but didn't pack it away. He turned it over in his hands, running his fingers over the faded paint and tiny seahorse etched on the side.

"Or should we leave Fantasaria entirely?" he asked quiety.

Xettar recognized the bottle. Legren had never spoken of it outright, but it had only appeared after he'd returned from his sea voyage.

"I think we'd have better luck out west," Xettar said.

"The Clockworks?"

"No, that's too close; less than two days ride from the High Kingdom. We should press all the way to the coast."

"Pirate Islands?"

Xettar nodded. "They're no fan of the High Kingdom's politics — or anyone's — and they were receptive to our early scouts." He nodded at the bottle. "Heard anything from your Pirate Captain?"

Legren bit his lip. "Two days ago," he said to the floor.

"And? Would we be welcome?"

Legren nodded.

"Marvelous!" Xettar threw up his hands in delight. "Why didn't you say—"

"It was a long time ago that I sailed with her, " Legren said. "How can I repay her by bringing such undeserved trouble to her door?"

"She offered, didn't she?"

"Yes, but…"

Xettar chuckled. "My friend, we'd best take whatever open invitation we can find right now. Any port in the storm and all that."

Legren wrapped his hand around the bottle, hiding the seahorse completely, and nodded.

"And we'll need protective charms for all of us on the road, of course," Xettar pressed on.

"We won't be able to stay anywhere for long. We'll have to be on the move almost continuously," Legren said.

"Nomadic lifestyle doesn't bother most of us," Xettar said. "The Mechs may find it difficult, but the Elves and I are more than used to it."

"We won't be able to come back here. Ever."

"No, but—"

"We'll have no guaranteed place of safety. I did not exaggerate earlier. We are fugitives now and we'll be on the run—"

"Yes, we're all aware of that. We all knew that it could — and most likely would — always come to this. We never really loved the idea of going completely rogue, but that was why everyone was so reluctant to join in the first place."

Legren blinked and looked away. He strode over to his window, gripped the sill, and gazed out at the grounds. "Is it worth it, then?"

Xettar's mouth fell open. "How can you ask that?"

"Because I've forced us out of the one place we call home."

"This is what it takes, Legren. Radical movements always make things worse before they get better. I...thought you knew that."

"I failed them," he whispered.

Over Legren's shoulder, the tips of the refugees' tents rippled and swayed in the breeze.

"How can I lead a Resistance if I couldn't even protect a town of innocent civilians and refugees?" Legren glanced back at Xettar. "They had nothing to do with the Resistance, which now has to stop, the Assembly is on hold, possibly forever—"

"No, no, no, you can't back down now." Xettar crossed to the window and whipped Legren around, clasping both of his shoulders. "You survived *twice* in order to do this. You believed when no one else did; so much, you made all of us believe, too. You've had visions which we've seen transpire. So, for all of our sakes — Galvyn and Rewelle's included — you *must* keep it together." He glanced out the window, towards the tents. "*They'll* be fine. They're in good hands with Cyntrenn here and our leaving is probably the best thing we can do to keep everyone safe. The less they know, the better. The Royals won't waste their time with them."

He offered a smile, but Legren only frowned back.

Xettar sighed. "We've taken a loss — many losses — and we must run, but all that means is finding a new place to settle for awhile. Maybe permanently. Who knows, this might lead us to the perfect new home. The Assembly will still happen, I promise. The *Magic* is so close. I just need a little more time and a place to work. No matter what, though, we can't stay here. The secret is out. But that's good."

"Oh, you think so?"

"Yes. You — and all of us — can now concentrate fully on the Assembly without distraction."

Legren scowled. "That what Sethera said when Reman left."

"Except he didn't, did he? He came back, which set this whole thing moving faster. His fellow Mechs arrived safely, they're all still here, Sethera hasn't left, and neither has anyone else, come to that. All the more reason to give up the stupid pretense. Our Resistance is out in the open. So much the better." Xettar clapped Legren's left shoulder lightly and released him. "No more hiding."

Legren winced again. "Hiding our intentions, anyway."

"It's natural to have doubts. I'm surprised it took this long. If you don't believe in yourself right now, that's okay. We'll believe it for you. But, remember: the Oniyum spared *you*. And only you."

Legren traced the scars around his eye. Xettar could practically hear him thinking, remembering.

"I will write a letter to Rhea — Captain Nephele — and send it forward with Tali and Telena," Legren finally said after a stretch of silence.

Xettar shook his head. "I'll reach out through *Magic*."

Legren nodded and Xettar turned to go.

"Did they have doubts?" Legren asked hastily, in such a voice that Xettar wondered if Legren had been yearning to ask the question for some time.

"*They* had a daughter," Xettar answered. "And no one behind them, save for me. They would not have gone forward on their own for fear of losing all they had. I would not let them feel that they were alone and I'll do the same here. Never give up. Not even when we must run. We've got four Mechs in our party now, plus a Nenjin on our trail."

"You've seen her again?"

"Not since yesterday, but we'll know soon enough. I imagine she'll join us before long."

Legren forced a smile. His scars crinkled, but his eyes did not. "We'll see."

The faintest chirp of birds met Xettar as he stepped back out into the square. Morning was only a few hours away. The knights stood before the Assembly Hall doors, calm as you please. Cyntrenn was not with them and Xettar was glad. He had no idea what he would say to the court Wizard. He respected and resented the man simultaneously. At one time, Xettar had hoped to attain such stature, but those aspirations had long since faded. He owed that change to Galvyn, a memory not easily forgotten.

A flickering light made him turn, distracted. The central fire still burned, vibrant. With a pang of reluctance, he knew it must, like the rest of the torches, be extinguished. Nearby, a villager doused the wick of a lamp post. Xettar paused. This was one of the men whose wounds he had tended after the zombie raid.

"You're looking well," Xettar called out to the man.

He turned and nodded. "Thanks be to you."

Xettar smiled, then gestured towards the fire. "I trust you're going to see to that?"

The man looked over his shoulder at the blazing fire. He swallowed hard. "It should be last, shouldn't it? It seems so…"

"Final," Xettar finished. "It certainly feels that way. But it's just the end of one day before the start of another."

The villager nodded again, but his shoulders sagged.

"You *will* see to it?" Xettar asked again.

"Yes, sir."

"Good man," Xettar said and turned away, trying to forget the melancholy, dispirited look on the villager's face.

Brock closed the lid on a trunk, deep in conversation with Tali. Xettar hovered in the open doorway, listening.

"Bounty hunters most likely," Brock was saying. "It's the most efficient."

"For so many of us?" Tali said.

"They'll want to test the situation before they risk diverting the main forces."

Tali turned to face Xettar then, unsurprised by his appearance. "A public announcement makes more sense, does it not?"

Xettar stepped further into the room. "Does it matter? We'll have the crown after us. As to how they give chase…" He shrugged.

"It *matters* because that determines how we move on from here," Brock countered. "What are we even doing? Do we have a plan?"

"We'll head west, to the coast. Captain Nephele has offered us sanctuary aboard her vessel."

"Pirates," Tali mumbled. "Lovely."

"But why?" Brock persisted. "To hide out? Just wait for the storm to pass?"

Xettar snorted. "Hardly. Once we're out of immediate danger, we'll pick up where we left off; continue to gather allies and plan the Assembly. That hasn't changed."

"We've outgrown this place anyway," Tali said. "And we were already planning to move on in a week."

"Legren is preparing a response to the Captain, which I will send by *Magic*. We leave tomorrow, as he said, bound for the seashore," Xettar explained.

"I'll inform the others—" Tali started.

"Wait, shouldn't we scatter?" Brock said. "Some of us depart tonight?"

Xettar shook his head. "No, we stay together. If we must separate later, then so be it, but, for now…" He reached out and squeezed their shoulders. "We're all each other has."

TWENTY-FIVE

SETHERA

We leave at dawn.

Sethera sat on the edge of her bed, twisting the pendant between her fingers. A single drawstring bag lay on the floor by her feet and she'd swapped her usual shirt for a more travel-worthy tunic. Legren hadn't said it aloud, but they all knew to pack light. A hard journey lay before them, likely across rough terrain, probably without horses. There weren't enough to spare and the villagers would need steeds for farming.

They were on the run now, just as Legren said they would be. Was it only hours before? They would be hunted, even in their home kingdom.

It made no difference. She would keep seeking answers until she met her quarry and finally took her revenge —

Her thoughts stumbled and she winced, like she'd accidentally bitten her tongue. Reman's words echoed back to her.

Holding a grudge means getting all the poison that comes with it.

She looked down at the pendant in her hands. Reman had been more right than he realized. She'd felt betrayed by Legren. Abandoned. So, she learned to adjust without him — even pushed him away once he did return. It gave her cause to withdraw from him, from the world, to lash out, and that break of connection had scarred her. It had made her numb. If she did lose them, not just Legren, but Xettar, Tali, Telena, and even Brock, then she would be truly alone.

It won't bring them back.

She'd told herself this before and Reman's words repeated it. Like him, she'd settled on a "search and destroy" mission, with little else to do or quench the thirst of sorrow. What other option did she have?

Finish what they started.

Sethera always known it, deep down, but she hadn't been ready to see it clearly. Tainted by the fear of inaction, she speculated letting their killer go free would be an even worse crime than the murder itself. And Sethera wanted justice more than anything.

But that wasn't true...not anymore. She really wanted, more than anything, to keep them close and the best way to do that meant honoring their lives, not their deaths.

The new mission.

Outside, a warbling flute drifted into the room from the town square.

Music? At this hour?

The melody grew louder; somber, until a sprightly harp joined in, followed by the bang of a drum. Before long, a bittersweet and joyous tune seeped through the walls.

Sethera slipped the pendant back around her neck and hurried outside.

In the square, the fire was not only still lit, but roaring. A trio of minstrels clustered on one side, while a few healed citizens gathered on the other.

Sethera drifted towards the circle along with the others. She stood next to the minstrels, soaking in the warmth of the music and the flames.

Tears stung her eyes. *Our last night here, ending in song.*

The notes plucked memories out of her past; days when she would sing along with the music, finding her voice in harmony with her mother's. Sethera opened her mouth and drew a deep breath to sing, but her throat tightened. Happiness and heartache welled in her chest and, for the first time in a long time, she did not berate herself for such sentiment.

The gathered citizens began to dance. They spun around the fire, changing partners and catching one another's hands. Sethera stepped back, not wishing to participate, and slipped her hands into her pockets. In the left one, her fingers met paper. Puzzled, she withdrew a familiar-looking piece of parchment. The summons, still old and still curled, but no less intact. *The thing that beckoned their fate.*

"Fancy that," she muttered to herself.

She'd meant to stash it somewhere safe. She'd wanted to keep it as a totem, as a reminder of what she was fighting for.

It's still your parents' Resistance, though, isn't it? All of us will be finishing what they started.

With her free, right hand, Sethera touched the pendant resting over her heart.

Two totems. Two options.

Vengeance or revolution?

You can't go back, but you can't move forward. You're just…stuck.

The memories of her parents' last moments broke over her. The scene played out in her mind's eye, unrestrained. Her mother's face, her outstretched fingers, the crease of surprise between her eyes before she fell…

But as the scene finished, Sethera's mind swept back further, over other warmer memories. Her father's voice. Their arms around her, their home, their lives together…

Tears spilled down Sethera's cheeks, but she didn't wipe them away. Her throat burned and her breath caught on sobs. Shame clawed up, through the grief, demanding she suppress this display. She'd exerted so much effort hiding any sign of weakness and now, she would weep openly in the square?

Yes.

She embraced the pain; let the wave crash around her, until the voices faded, the images blurred, and Sethera was once again, back in the square. She opened her eyes, blinking fast to clear her vision. Her right hand wrapped tighter around the spiral pendant, while her grip loosened on the parchment. It slid through her fingers, caught a passing updraft, and soared into the fire. The flames popped and shot sparks of green and indigo. Those embers sprung up, radiant against the dark sky, climbing higher and higher until they blended in with the stars. Gone.

"It's over," Sethera whispered, hardly believing it. Her voice, though steady, faded into the music and laughter and crackling flames.

A hand brushed her shoulder. She knew it was Legren without having to look. Her eyes filled again, but she did not shatter. With the summons gone, something had healed inside Sethera. She was whole.

She faced Legren and smiled. His eyes twinkled back at her like they used to, even through his scars.

"I'm proud of you," he said. "And so, too, would your parents be. I see their strength and their compassion in you. I always have."

Sethera drew a deep breath, honored and humbled by such a comparison.

"This won't be easy," he added. "It only gets more difficult from here."

She thought he spoke more to himself than to her. For once, he needed reassurance, and she could offer it.

"I'm ready," she promised him in earnest.

He squeezed her shoulder. "I don't know what the future holds for us, but I promise you: I will not let their vision be forgotten. Nor their deaths go unavenged."

A lopsided grin slid across his face; a hallmark of his younger, ambitious, troublemaking self. Sethera reached up and clapped her hand over his, on her shoulder. Time and history would not be erased, nor would they forget all that had transpired. Some distance still needed closing, but whatever had broken — that *snap* of separation — was mended. They had found their way back to each other.

"Miss?"

Sethera looked down. A young, blond-haired boy stood before her, apart from the crowd of twirling dancers.

"Would you like to dance?"

TWENTY-SIX

REMAN

From the edge of the square, Reman watched the dancers, captivated, until he spotted Jenda. She leaned against the iron bench next to the fire pit. Dread squirmed in his stomach. She'd taken her hair down, half-hiding her face, and she still wore her black jacket. Mason hovered behind her, deadpan, his hands clasped behind his back. The merriment didn't seem to touch him, but he looked bored, rather than dour. At least his hands weren't anywhere near his gun. Garen didn't seem to be there at all.

Despite fighting the Mobsters together, Reman and Jenda said nothing the whole walk back to the village. In fact, they had exchanged no more words since their earlier bickering here, by the fire and their estrangement gnawed at his insides even worse than before. Back home, they never saw one another, but now she was *here*, but seemed somehow even further away.

Reman studied his sister's profile. Contrary to his expectations, she watched the musicians play without a frown. Her arms were folded across her chest, but her expression was soft.

Between the firelight and the music, newfound courage sparked inside Reman's chest.

One more try.

He strode toward the bench. All former defensiveness dispelled with each step. As he edged next to Jenda, she glanced at him, unmoved.

I miss you, he wanted desperately to say. *Won't you stay?*

"I…just want us on the same side," he stammered.

Jenda's eyebrows pulled together, dubious, but he kept going.

"Us, fighting the good fight. Together." He gently nudged her shoulder. "You know?"

Her mouth stretched, trying to suppress her own smile. "Yeah, yeah, all right. Easy on the gushing." She turned back towards the fire pit and waved a hand at the dancers. "Maybe you should join in."

"Thought about it," Reman admitted, "but I don't know the steps."

"You'd figure it out. Go on." And she pushed him — harder than he expected. He staggered forward; not by much, but close enough to the fray that one of the passing dancers grabbed his hand. Too fast for Reman to protest, she pulled him into the horde, and Jenda's laugh fell away behind him.

After a few stumbles, he found his feet, took outstretched hands, and spun with the rest. He just started to find the rhythm, to anticipate the steps and feel like he knew what he was doing — like he even sort of belonged — until the next change of partners. He careened around and threw out his arms, only to find himself face-to-face with Sethera.

They both skidded to a stop. The delight on her face disappeared. So did his. Their arms fell, slowly, back to their sides and her eyes dropped, down, around, anywhere but at Reman. Flustered, he twisted on the spot, hoping to just back away, but the other dancers already swirled around them. Trapped.

In front of him, Sethera stared at the ground with pinched lips. Her hands twisted at her sides and she tapped her foot, out of sync with the drum beat. What happened? The camaraderie they'd shared in the stable…had it all been a fluke? Or was she just embarrassed by her moment of candor? Maybe they were supposed to keep up appearances and pretend like it never happened. Or perhaps they had not made such a tremendous breakthrough as he thought. Back to square one?

All the fighting, all the bloodshed and mistrust that's spread across Kabathan, how could we possibly return to life as it was?

For the first time, the whole picture snapped into place. This is what it meant. He and Sethera, two stationary figures, faced each other in the very center of the village, dancers flowing around on all sides. One moment created a microscopic but tangible representation of the giant impasse fracturing the whole world.

Trembling slightly, Reman extended his right hand.

Can we start over?

The very same question of the Resistance.

Can we forgive each other and begin again?

Sethera stared at his open palm. He swallowed hard and waited, hand held steady. It didn't matter if she refused the offer, smacked his hand or shoved him away, but still he braced himself for rejection.

She shot wary, narrowed eyes back up at him. As her mouth curved up into a sly grin, his stomach lurched, hopeful. She grabbed his extended hand and the one at his side. She pulled him forward, nearly knocking him over, and they spun back into the dance.

Reman's brain and limbs staggered to catch up, but eventually, he found the rhythm again. Though Reman still didn't know the steps, he danced anyway. He trusted Sethera and followed her lead, and they swayed around the fire with everyone else. As another partner change separated them, he glanced back over his shoulder. She met his gaze without guard or malice, open and public for everyone to see. *Friends.*

From the center of the square, flyaway embers and rollicking music vaulted into the dark sky. The night eased towards morning in a swirl of color and music and light. As Reman spun around the fire in different intervals, he thought he saw Garen sit next to Jenda and put his arm around her; Xettar and Legren clap each other on the back; Brock and Mason shake hands.

In this tiny Fantasarian town, Reman could sense the very earth moving underfoot.

This is where it begins. This is how we change the world.

Legren had asked Reman if he was willing to risk it all to find a new source of Light.

Yes.

None of them knew what would happen the next day — or any of the days after — but they would cross the threshold of a new future without looking back. No matter what perils lay ahead, they would keep working, keep fighting. Reman had never seen the ocean before, not up close or outside of a ship, but already he could smell the salty air.

They would meet those challenges and conquer them. Together.

They would dance anyway.

EPILOGUE

"Jean?"

She jumped, startled, out of her doze. She collapsed into the high-backed leather chair immediately upon returning to the warmth and safety of the house. She had never been fond of that particular chair, but she'd returned bone-tired from fighting Drones with her bare hands. As she stirred, so did the throbbing pain across her knuckles and up her calves. Her joints ached, too. It had been a long night.

"Jean."

Andy was seated, as ever, at his writing desk on the opposite side of the room. The surface of it was invisible beneath a sea of dissected relics, glass bottles, screwdrivers, and a gigantic magnifying glass holding down a towering stack of paper; pages from books, scrolls refusing to unfurl and Oniyum knew what else. The oil lamp burned beside his left elbow, but between the pile of paperwork and the little golden box over which he was currently poring, he was mostly obscured in self-afflicted shadow. He sat up with his right hand extended towards her. He was not looking at her, but peering down into the box.

She shoved her brass goggles down, around her neck.

"What?"

Andy gestured frantically again. "Come 'ere."

"Why?"

"There's a broadcast comin' in."

"So?"

"Just…!"

The necessity in his voice, not of an unfamiliar note, convinced her to shove herself back up out of the chair and stomp over to the desk. She dropped a few of her weapons onto the carpet as she went, unconcerned about the mess just now. She leaned over Andy's shoulder, and he moved aside to let her gaze down, into the box, at the rounded glass screen bolted into the desk's surface. She'd never been sure how he managed to make this stuff work, but she didn't especially care. It was as good as *Magic*, no matter how he rationalized it.

The screen itself blinked and shuddered with static for a few seconds, then a full image popped into view. It was a camera feed; one of those high-tech types from across the sea, which attached directly into combat armour. But the picture was fuzzy and continued to flicker with interference, but still viewable. Definitely a sunny day in the woods. No sound accompanied it, which Jean decided very quickly was for the best. Whoever wore this device was angled towards a girl, standing some significant distance away, but the image swayed, then toppled backward and sideways. The picture went still and then the girl approached at a calm, steady pace, materializing out of the watercolor-like background into focus. She was a Fantasarian, judging by her garb, pointed ears and long, dark hair. Her elfin face was blank, but confident. She lifted her hand, showing the viewer a curved dagger in her grip. It glinted briefly in the sunlight before she plunged it forward, just beneath the camera, which shuddered and jerked, even after she drew the blade back in a curt swipe. She stared into the lens for another few seconds, then turned and walked away just as calmly. The camera stopped jerking and slid smoothly sideways until it ceased to move altogether. An added splash of static flashed, indicating a punch of impact as the person or camera or both collided with the ground.

In her peripheral vision, Jean saw Andy's head swivel up at her. "What does this mean? Bloody impossible, innit?"

She looked down at him. She was probably imagining the emotions dancing on his face; a fraction of uncertainty, tinged with fear and strangled, long-buried hope. Still hurt, though, real or not. She took a deep breath and squared her shoulders. They wanted for practicality and reason, now more than ever.

"Just what you think," she answered calmly, even though she believed neither her words or the images before her. "It means that Sethera is still alive."

Acknowledgements

*M*ost *humble and sincere thanks.*

To my friends and family who encouraged me to stay the course, even when I wanted to give up.

To H.L. Shepler, I am so grateful for wisdom of language, the time you spent reading so many pieces of this book, and your unwavering belief in me.

To Neville Emmanuel, for encouraging me to stand up for myself so many years ago. Also for an amazing map of Kabathan.

To the Beta-Readers: Sarah Thomas, Brian Pennington, Benjamin Cairns, and Jennifer Haines. Thank you for the generosity of your time and perspective.

To Barbara Brutt, for taking on this project with so much enthusiasm and for your tough love.

To my Mom and Dad, thank you for support through every phase of my life. You have been my emotional rock through this and every project.

To Annamarie C. Mickey for your spectacular cover art.
To K.B. and Chris Pennington for your lovely illustrations.

To the *Genre Wars* cast and crew, for your participation and friendship.

To Ron, for the spark, the push, and the blessing.

And to Justin, for inviting me on the journey.